Come Walk With Me

Also by Joan Medlicott

JOAN MEDLICOTT

Come Walk With Me

**Doubleday Large Print
Home Library Edition**

POCKET BOOKS

NEW YORK   LONDON   TORONTO   SYDNEY

Pocket Books
A Division of Simon & Schuster, Inc.
1230 Avenue of the Americas
New York, NY 10020

Copyright © 2007 by Joan Medlicott

First Pocket Books trade paperback edition
December 2007

POCKET and colophon are registered trademarks of Simon & Schuster, Inc.

Manufactured in the United States of America

ISBN-13: 978-0-7394-9064-8

**This Large Print Book carries the
Seal of Approval of N.A.V.H.**

**To women friends,
both yours and mine.**

1

The Retreat

A man walked with long strides over the crest of the hill, and Claire Bennett gasped. He was solidly built and tall, and something—the way his long arms swung by his sides or his close-cropped salt-and-pepper hair?—reminded her of her husband, Phillip, gone these last eighteen months. Claire's heart hammered.

"Sir," she called, rising from the stone bench. "Wait a moment, please."

He turned his head toward her, his face inscrutable, then moved quickly away, crunching autumn leaves beneath his boots. His seeming rejection of her stung like a slap across her face, and she brought her hand to her cheek.

The monastery bell rang, its peals rising over the thick stone walls of the cloistered garden, the rich and vibrant sound sweeping across the open lawn. In years past, this bell had called monks to prayer. Now it summoned her and the others to dinner.

Claire started across the grass to the arched gateway. Inside the garden, brick pathways formed a complex pattern of flower beds. Those who came on retreat were welcome to silently assist with the raking of leaves, weeding, or planting, depending on the time of year. The leaves of young maple trees along the walls held the promise of rich fall color. Clouds had dominated the sky earlier, then raced away to the east and now the sun slipped into the horizon.

Claire's pace accelerated. She was late for the evening meal again. Dinner was probably another vegetarian's delight: a nondescript vegetable casserole, brown bread, unsalted butter, and fruit of the season. She eased the heavy wooden door open and slipped into the wood-paneled dining room. No one looked up or acknowledged her arrival; no one beckoned her with a hand or a look. Self-conscious and feeling a fool for calling to the stranger, Claire took a seat at the end of the table, far from where he sat. His head down, intent on consuming every last bean on his plate, the stranger who reminded her of Phillip ignored her.

Each time the swinging doors opened, the smell of fresh-baked bread wafted from the kitchen. A water pitcher traveled the length of the table and back. Claire cleared her throat. A woman alongside her did the same. Farther down the table, a man coughed. Others coughed. Occasionally someone smiled at someone else, though not at her.

This food is awful, it needs seasoning, Claire thought. Yet several people served themselves to second helpings.

The gray-white walls of the cubicle assigned to her oppressed Claire. On her arrival she had removed the crucifix hanging above the narrow bed and replaced it with a Connecticut Scenic Highways calendar, thrown into her suitcase at the last minute. Were the former occupants of this cell midgets? The tiny mirror was hung so low that at five feet six inches, she stooped to put on her makeup.

Why had her therapist, Dr. Mary Delanny, suggested this place? It wasn't silence she needed. Having spent her adult life cultivating the art of conversation, a cruise, with its glamour, activity, and gregarious strangers, would have been preferable. She languished here, her vivacity stifled among drab folk who strolled the grounds with their heads down, hands locked behind their backs, or sat and stared into space. Three days of it were enough.

"Were you ever content?" Dr. Delanny had asked at their previous session.

A ridiculous question! Of course she had been content, what with going to business every day, exercising at the gym twice a week, her weekly bridge game at the club, and volunteer work raising funds for the local library. Working behind the scenes, she had been the steel in Phillip's backbone, the drive behind his rise to prominence in the community, his success in their business, Antiques Unlimited, an international purchasing service for select customers.

On her initial visit, Dr. Delanny had asked, "How did you feel about working behind the scenes?"

Claire laughed. "Powerful. I thrived on it."

Now, Claire shifted in the hard, narrow bed and thought of her son, Paul, a naval officer. What had he been thinking, running off and enlisting in the navy directly after high school? Perhaps it was time to discuss her relationship—or the lack of it—with her children. She had avoided it so far; their discussions so often felt like a game of chess, with her dodging those calculated, clever questions from the therapist.

She kept going due to sheer, utter loneliness, loneliness so deep and bitter that many nights she cried herself to sleep. She had wrapped her personal life completely around Phillip, and with him gone she desperately needed someone to talk to.

Claire finally drifted off to sleep, and dreamed that she was in a shipwreck. As she struggled to tread water, Phillip, her daughter, Amanda, and Paul stood unconcerned on a rock-strewn coast. A rowboat appeared. Ignoring her, her family climbed into it, and though she called to them for help, they rowed away and vanished in the mist. Claire jerked awake, her heart pounding, perspiration coating her face. The dream, so clearly about abandonment and betrayal, terrified her.

It's this place—this creepy place. Hastening to the tiny bathroom, she splashed water on her face and neck, then read a romance novel until dawn arrived.

2

Back Home

Behind a tall wrought-iron gate, the Bennetts' English Tudor home in the village of East Hampton, New York, sat two blocks from the ocean. From the attic window, the long, thin line of the horizon was visible. When he was a boy, Paul practically lived at that window with his telescope. The sea and ships had fascinated him. After high school, he had rejected the higher education his parents valued and joined the navy. It nearly broke Phillip's heart. And hers, too.

Where was Paul now? He had come home when his father left eighteen months ago, and had been as cool and distant toward her as he had been since he was twelve. Since . . . No! She would not think about that. Three days later, when Paul departed, they had not exchanged a meaningful word.

When Claire returned from St. Dunstan's retreat, she immediately climbed the stairs to the attic. Coated with dust, Paul's telescope lay on a small table near the window. Claire wiped its length, cleaned its lens with her shirttail, and lifted it to her eye. Ships in full sail, part of the regatta she had helped organize as a fund-raiser for the library, crowded the horizon. It was the second weekend of October and cold out on that water.

Would Phillip's yacht, the *Crescendo,* which she had sold to his friend Charlie Millikin, win this year without Phillip at the helm? Her eyes misted. No one sailed with the adroitness of her husband.

Claire returned the telescope to its place on the table. To her left, a square brown box sat on top of an old trunk. As she lifted its dusty lid, the scent of cedar rose to greet her. Inside lay Terrance's sneaker, a bag of marbles, and a photo of his smiling seven-year-old face. Pain, as stunningly sharp as the day it happened, pierced her heart, and Claire slammed the box shut. He had been seven, only seven, her precious child, her pet, her favorite. The hit-and-run driver who slammed into Terrance's bike had flung him twenty feet into the air, a ferocious and fatal blow. Claire dropped the box and hurried down the stairs.

On a tray in her den, her housekeeper had placed a letter. She recognized her daughter's handwriting on the lavender envelope. Claire set it aside and checked her phone messages. Could they count on her for a fourth at bridge next Friday? *Why not?* She absolutely must come to the award dinner for the Friends of the Library this Saturday evening. *Certainly!* Would she chair a fund-raiser for the YWCA? *No.* Her Volvo was ready to be picked up. *Thank goodness.* Claire carried Amanda's letter to her desk and slid the fine point of her letter opener along the top.

Mother
    Tom and I have moved to Tom's hometown, Weaverville, just north of Asheville in North Carolina. Tom is converting his dad's old barn into a house for us. No, we're not living with cows or anything like that. The area is gorgeous, with hills, valleys, and waterfalls.

**We plan to be married in the spring.
Will you come? Tom's dad says you're
welcome to stay in his farmhouse. It's
a real farmhouse with a wraparound
porch, Mother, or if you prefer a motel,
there's one about fifteen minutes away.
Call me. Our number is 828-646-2601.**
    Mandy

Claire hated it that her daughter preferred
Mandy, such a common name, to Amanda.
And now Amanda was going to marry a
farmer's son. Maybe she would go to the
wedding or maybe not.

The phone rang. "Hello, Mrs. Bennett. This
is Louann, Dr. Delanny's secretary. Doctor
asks if you can come in this afternoon instead of tomorrow? She's had a death in her
family and is leaving tonight for Arizona."

"This afternoon?" The immediacy of it
jarred Claire. She needed time, time
for . . . what? To reply to her messages and
have her hair done? But she needed to tell
her therapist what she thought of St.
Dunstan's retreat center. She needed to talk
to someone. "I'll be there," Claire replied.
"What time?"

"Four o'clock, Mrs. Bennett."

Claire hung up and dialed the beauty parlor. "Angie, can I get an appointment with Tonio before three this afternoon?"

There was a pause while Angie checked. "I'm sorry, Mrs. Bennett, but Tonio's booked solid. Marty's available and Tonio recommends him highly."

Claire sighed. She'd have to take what she could get. "Marty will be fine. Thanks."

Mary Delanny sat behind her desk, her chestnut hair secured in a tight bun at the nape of her neck. She looked at Claire through oversized round glasses that framed her dark eyes. "Please come in, Claire."

Claire settled into one of the mauve wing chairs that faced each other before the rosewood desk. Photographs of children were displayed on a bookcase behind the desk, and on cream-colored walls hung a series of photographs of shiny red-, cinnamon-, ochre-, and rust-colored stones, clearly visible beneath placid shallow water. Sometimes, to collect her thoughts, Claire focused on these stones. Something about them soothed her, gave her breathing space, and a moment to delay answering whatever Dr. Delanny had asked.

"You left St. Dunstan's early?"

"Yes, I did. I hated it."

"What about it did you hate?"

"Everything."

"Can you be more specific, Claire?"

"My room was dreadful, small and musty."

"And?"

"The food was absolutely awful."

"You didn't go there for the food or the accommodations, did you?" Mary Delanny asked.

"Well, no . . ."

The therapist leaned forward. "Can you speak a little louder, Claire? I can hardly hear you. So you left early."

Claire's eyes sought the stones, then she said, "The silence. I simply had to get out of there."

"The silence bothered you?"

"It certainly did. That's not what I needed."

"If you felt that you didn't need or want silence, why did you go to a silent retreat?"

"*You* wanted me to go."

"You went because you thought *I* wanted you to go? I recall listing it among a series of places."

"So, I made a mistake. Is there any reason why I can't prefer conversation to silence?

I'm alone in my big house. No one understands what I've gone through since Phillip left."

Mary Delanny's mouth tightened. "Phillip did not leave, Claire. Leaving is an act of volition. Phillip became ill and died. We've talked about this for several months now."

Her words impacted Claire like a hammer striking an anvil, and she flinched. Tears formed in her eyes and she dabbed them with a tissue from a box Mary extended to her. "We always worked together, Phillip and I. I was so happy. Now God's punished me for being too happy. You can't be too happy or love someone too much, or you'll lose him." The dusty box in the attic rose before her. Terrance, her baby, and now Phillip.

"Why do you think that?" Dr. Delanny asked.

"My grandmother always said so. If I heard it once, I heard it a hundred times. And it's true. I've been thinking about my son Paul—about how much I miss him."

"You haven't said much about Paul. Tell me about him."

"He was a beautiful boy, with curly brown hair and blue eyes like his father. He loved

the ocean like Phillip did, and when he was
ten Phillip taught him to sail. I worried so
each time they went out to sea. We were
so close, Paul and I. And then, just like
that"— she snapped her fingers—"everything changed when he was twelve." *When
Terrance died.*

"How did it change?"

Claire shrugged. "We were close, and then
we weren't."

"Why? Did something happen?"

*Why does she always have to pry? I'll tell
her what I want when I'm good and ready,
and not before.* Claire felt herself closing
down. *She keeps asking about my own
childhood, too, and it's just too painful to
go there. To remember my mother, how
sick she was, how crazy she was, how
she messed with our heads, shredded my
father's heart . . .*

They sat in silence for a time. Mary
Delanny did that, let them sit there without
saying anything. Is this what she was paying
the woman for?

Claire studied the photos of stones. That's
how her heart felt—hard and cold, like a
stone. "Paul and I laughed a lot, we had our
own secret little jokes."

"You had a closeness with your son that was special, and it ended just like that, in a snap?"

"That's right. Overnight. No more jokes, no more special times. He closed down and nothing I said or did reached him."

Grief probably, but I'm not ready to talk about that.

There was another long silence in which Mary jotted things in her small blue notebook. "Claire, would you do a bit of homework?"

Claire blew her nose and nodded. She wanted to weep, to have this woman hold and comfort her, but that wasn't what therapy was about.

"I'd like you to draw two lines down a sheet of paper, making three columns. In the first column, list the things you've really wanted. Start way back when you were a child, go through high school and your college years, and up to the present. In the second column, indicate if you got it or not. For each no, note in the third column if it was taken from you and how. I think you'll find the results surprising. Sometimes it helps to see things in writing."

"I can do that," Claire said.

"I'll be gone for a week. Louann will make an appointment for you the first day I'm back."

Claire stood. "I'm sorry about your loss."

"Thank you. My grandfather was a hundred years old. He had a good life."

"Phillip was just fifty-nine when he left. I'm only fifty-five. I'm still attractive, aren't I? I'm much too young to be alone. Why did he leave me?"

"Phillip died, Claire." She placed a hand on Claire's arm. "And we aren't finished talking about your experience at the retreat."

"I figured as much." Clutching her handbag, Claire walked from the office thinking about lists. It seemed she was never finished with lists: grocery lists, to-do lists, the lists of over-the-counter medications Phillip insisted on bringing when they traveled, and so on. She must stop and get a yellow pad on the way home.

3

The Award

Women in bright, fashionable cocktail dresses floated like flowers in a sea of black tuxedos. Laughter rose and fell. Crystal glasses clinked. Claire mingled, smiled, and chatted about the weather and the regatta, which had been won by Thomas Franco, a newcomer.

Margaret Verey, a local self-styled matron of the arts, sidled up to her. "We've missed you at bridge, darling. You've been away?"

"To a spa. It was marvelous." Claire turned her attention to Jane Thick, a former customer of Phillip's. They leaned toward one another and kissed the air alongside each other's cheeks. *Jane looks like an elephant in that gray dress, despite the designer label.* "You look wonderful," Claire said.

"Thank you, it's one of a kind. Lucille Kiplet is *the* designer these days. Darling, we've missed you at the club," Jane said. "Where *have* you been?"

Just then, Jerry Turner, president of the library board, took Claire's arm and guided her toward a seat at the head table between Olden Riverdale, the president of the Friends of the Library and president of the most prestigious bank in town, and the librarian, Rhonda Saunders.

Years ago, on her first day in the village of East Hampton, Olden had stepped out of the bank onto New Town Lane, waved down their car, poked his head inside to greet Phillip, and welcomed Phillip's bride with a quick kiss on the lips. Then he'd dashed away and vanished behind the imposing, carved wooden doors of his bank.

"I do prefer Cornish hens and wild rice stuffing to plain roasted chicken," Olden said, indicating the plates being set before them.

Claire nodded her agreement.

"You had a good rest?" he asked. "You needed a little time away. Where did you go?"

"It *was* good to get away. A much-needed rest." She diverted the talk to his daughter, Francine, and two grandsons who were staying with him. "How are the little fellows?"

Pride filled his voice and it softened. "They're scamps, those boys. We wouldn't want it any other way, though, would we now?" He laughed and spoke of the latest escapade involving a water hose and a neighbor's dog.

Claire smiled. "Boys will be boys."

Once dessert had been placed before them, Olden pushed back his chair and went to the podium. He adjusted the microphone down to a comfortable height and began to speak in a deep voice that seemed incongruous from this slender, balding man with glasses.

"Never judge a book by its cover," Phillip used to say when she poked fun at Olden's early baldness or his five-foot-eight-inch height. "He's a powerhouse in banking on Long Island."

"Ladies and gentlemen, tonight we honor

our volunteer of the year." Olden turned and beamed at her. "Claire Bennett. Her untiring efforts have raised over two hundred and fifty thousand dollars for the new children's wing of our library, for who among our business community can resist her charm and persistence? It is with great pleasure that we honor Claire and name the new wing of our library the Claire and Phillip Bennett Children's Library," Olden boomed.

As everyone clapped, Olden offered Claire his hand and conducted her to the podium, where he presented her with an engraved silver plaque.

Claire smiled. "On behalf of Phillip and myself, I thank you. We are deeply honored. The library is very dear to our hearts, and I pledge that we shall continue to work on its behalf."

A soft murmur rose from the audience, and Claire bit her lip, embarrassed. She had done exactly what Dr. Delanny insisted she must not do, speak of Phillip as if he were merely out of town, and everyone here was laughing at her.

"You're denying reality," Mary Delanny had said again and again.

Now, standing before her so-called friends

and business associates, she felt a perfect fool. Her eyes found Margaret Verey's. They were rivals at the bridge table, and those steely blue eyes mocked her. Claire reminded herself that *she* was the benefactor of the library, and that it was she and not Margaret Verey who had received recognition tonight.

Claire had little regard for most of the women she played bridge with. She only continued to do so for the social contact. Few of them had ever worked, not even in their homes, and she found them especially contemptible when they whined about their husbands. Did she complain? Never! Her life, her marriage, had its flaws. Whose life didn't?

But she and Phillip had been a team, she dreaming big dreams, Phillip implementing the dreams. They had enjoyed traveling and working together. It was much, much harder on her to lose Phillip than it would be for any of those empty-headed women to lose their husbands.

Later that night, in the quiet of home, Claire picked up the yellow pad and settled into an armchair. She drew uneven vertical lines creating three columns, then her teeth fastened on the end of the pencil and sank into the soft wood. What had she really wanted? At first she couldn't remember; then she recalled wanting a car when she was sixteen. She noted "car" in the first column, and moved to the second column where she wrote "yes." It had been an old but reliable vehicle and had served her well through high school. Her senior prom! Yes, she had desperately wanted a new and expensive dress for the prom, and she'd gotten that, too. She bit into the pencil. She'd looked gorgeous that evening, her long dark hair trailing across her shoulders, her dark eyes gleaming under the seldom-used mascara. She had danced all night with Hugh Tupperfeld, the handsomest boy in high school. They'd gone steady for a while and she'd worn his school ring, but they hadn't had a thing in common, and in time they had drifted apart. Did that count as something lost? No. When their relationship ended, they parted as friends.

She had attended the college of her choice, where she aced a major in art history, and seduced every boy she wanted. Maybe Granny had been wrong. After all, she had wanted and gotten Phillip Bennett—but now she had lost him. Tears came, marring the lines when she rubbed them with the ball of her hand.

With a degree in art history, an interest in interior design, and butterflies fluttering in her stomach, she had talked Alfred Thomas into hiring her at his antiques store not far down the coast from home. Phillip Bennett, tall with curly brown hair and blue eyes, one of the young buyers who frequented the store, attracted her immediately. Phillip recognized and loved antiques; what he lacked was vision and drive. Claire possessed enough ambition for them both, and Phillip, emboldened by her faith in him and her encouragement, had been successful beyond his wildest expectations.

Her list went halfway down the page now, with no indication that she had lost anything she had desired and obtained. Until Terrance, of course. And now Phillip. Then Claire remembered her puppy, Claudius, named for the Emperor Claudius of ancient Rome. She had treasured that little dog, slept with him, shared her secret thoughts with him, and taken him everywhere. Then one day, he disappeared. She had shed copious tears, scoured the neighborhood, slapped posters on electric poles and taped them to storefronts, but Claudius was never found. She'd believed someone had stolen him, and even now, so many years later, the memory caused her pain.

"Claudius," she wrote on the left side of the page. Hesitantly, with trembling hands, Claire then wrote "Terrance" under Claudius. Tears brimmed and spilled from her eyes. *Terrance.* Claire pressed the pencil hard against the paper. "Terrance. Terrance. Terrance," filling line after line to the bottom of the page. Then she wrote "lost, lost, lost" down to the bottom of the page, thinking how one loss built on another and how the pain never completely left one's heart. *Claudius. Terrance. Phillip.* Many pains; one enormous ache; like a snowball growing with every turn.

For weeks after Claudius vanished, Claire had hardly eaten. She had phoned her older sister, Marian, and sobbed long distance. She wept on the shoulder of anyone who would stand still long enough.

"Why are you going on and on like this about a dog?" her younger sister, Marjorie, asked.

"Because I loved him!"

Remembering, Claire hunched in her chair and rocked, wishing she could grow a callus, hard and tough, over each scar to stop the pain.

The following morning, Claire pulled herself from bed and dragged her heart up from her toes. She showered and dressed, plastered the obligatory smile on her lips, and drove to the club to play bridge. She couldn't concentrate, though, and bid carelessly and ruined her partner's game.

Susan Pelitzer, the only woman she considered a real friend, asked, "What's the matter with you, Claire? You're not yourself."

In a fit of pique, Claire laid her cards face up on the table. Shocked, the others stared at her. "I don't feel well," she said. "I have to leave."

Claire drove to the beach, where she stripped off her shoes and stockings and walked along the firm, damp sand. Lacy fringes of foam lapped the shoreline, and driftwood, disgorged from the sea, lay scattered on the sand. The wind tousled her hair and slapped her skirt against her legs.

Out on the foreboding gray ocean, freighters

steamed past. A navy vessel, perhaps a cruiser, overtook and outdistanced a smaller ship. Claire stood on a rocky outcropping and waved at a freighter, closer to land than the others. She thought she saw a hand raised in greeting.

Gradually her mind stilled, and the heaviness that burdened her heart eased. Would it be easier if she believed in God? In her sane periods, her mother vowed disbelief in God, yet in the throes of her illness she could be heard muttering, arguing with God. Her father was an atheist.

Most of the people at the retreat had believed in God, judging by their reverent manner and frequent visits to the church. She had been left alone, the outsider once again.

The receding tide deposited small, shallow pools between the rocks, and a round, red stone, clearly visible beneath the still water, attracted Claire's attention. It reminded her of the stones in the photographs at Dr. Delanny's office, and she dipped her hand into the pool to pick it up. It felt good in her hand, cool and smooth, hard yet soft. She slipped it into her pocket, then started back down the beach.

Dr. Delanny had suggested that Claire was in a state of transition. "Fear and possibilities lie at the heart of every transition," the therapist had said. "Understand that and go easy on yourself."

4

Longing

When Claire awakened the next morning, soft light spread like melted butter along the horizon. Pillows lay helter-skelter on the bed and floor, the sheets tangled her legs, and sweat moistened her face and the valley between her breasts. Exhausted, she marveled at the intensity of her dream, and for a moment she felt again the faceless, heaving body above her, the passion that had elevated her to bliss. Why had she had such a dream? Why now, and why had it never been like that with Phillip?

That was the torment of it. With all his virtues, Phillip lacked sexual passion and had failed to match her fierce intensity in bed. This had been the millstone privately weighing down their marriage, the issue around which most of their arguments centered. Yet she had been faithful to him. Tempted, yes, but unyielding and virtuous. Her hand stretched across the big empty bed. She would still choose a lackluster Phillip over this crushing loneliness.

Claire shoved a pillow under her head and stared at the ceiling, contemplating her life. Her shapely figure and the combination of her dark chestnut hair and blue eyes still turned heads when she entered a room. So why had no one, no friend or associate, introduced her to another man? Why had none of the dissatisfied spouses at the country club, men who had flirted with her when Phillip was alive, approached her? Not that she would have anything to do with them, but the flattery would be welcome.

Phillip used to say, "You're so beautiful. If you were a showgirl, you'd be a showstopper."

Claire imagined herself onstage: minimally covered, high kicks exposing well-shaped legs, the smooth long line of her neck as she tossed her head, and the thundering applause following her performance.

When Claire was a teenager, her grandmother had warned, "With your imagination and your good looks, you'll get yourself in trouble one day."

Grandma had worried a lot. But then, if *she* had had a daughter like Grandma's, whose behavior had been incomprehensible and unpredictable—no one had heard of bipolar disorder in those days—she would worry, also.

Claire had had a vivid imagination, but with time she had become increasingly pragmatic, modeling her behavior after her father's restraint, his control, his avoidance of emotion.

"Don't give 'em the satisfaction of seeing your disappointment," he'd said when, in high school, she had not been invited to be a cheerleader. "Lift that pretty head of yours high, and act as if you don't give a hoot. Set your sights on the future and move on to bigger and better things."

She had graduated as valedictorian of her class.

Claire had groomed herself impeccably, had faked self- assurance, and had faced the world with bravado, albeit with a lump in her throat. Her demeanor had served her well, and Phillip, too.

But now he was gone, and life seemed meaningless without a companion. Where and how would she find a man, especially in this small community? Then there were STDs to be concerned about. Yet the thought of sleeping alone, of living alone for the rest of her life anguished her deeply, and at moments, even brought thoughts of suicide—which because of her mother, terrified her.

On her next visit, Dr. Delanny leaned toward Claire. "Did you make that list I suggested?"

Claire nodded. "I started it."

"May I see it?"

"I forgot it at home. But the list hardly matters; I know why I left the retreat."

Dr. Delanny's eyebrows rose.

"It's so simple, really. All the other people at the retreat believed in God. That's why they were at a retreat in a former monastery. I don't believe in God." She crossed her arms over her chest.

Dr. Delanny made no comment.

"Don't you see?" Claire leaned forward. "I

was the only one without a religious belief in a religious setting."

"Are you sure it was a religious setting? The way I understand it, a silent retreat means silence, and can be held anywhere quiet. You weren't encouraged to participate in church services, were you?"

Claire crossed her arms again. "No, but it felt religious. There was a crucifix hanging on the wall of my room. I removed it and stuck it in a drawer. How could I be comfortable in a place like that? I felt like an outsider."

"Were your parents religious? Did you go to a church when you were young?"

Claire shrugged. "Now and then. They didn't go often."

Patients who avoided issues, who clung to denial, resisted assignments, wasted her time with platitudes, and were uninterested in growing and changing, were patients whom Mary Delanny eliminated from her practice. Claire Bennett's superficiality annoyed and bored Mary, yet she had continued seeing the woman. Was it pity, or a challenge? But they were getting nowhere.

"Your coming here is a waste of your money and my time," Mary said abruptly.

Claire recoiled in her chair. "What?"

"There are people in genuine distress who want desperately to understand and grow past their pain."

"I'm in pain," Claire said. "What do you think I come here for? I'm in terrible pain! Phillip is gone—"

"The man is *dead,*" Mary said sharply. She leaned forward. "Your husband is not gone. He is dead. Say it: dead."

Claire buried her face in her hands, then dropped them and lifted her chin. "I know that."

"Then say it."

"I don't choose to do so."

Dr. Delanny lifted her hands in exasperation and let them fall. "Look, Claire, I am here to help my patients ask and answer the hard questions: who they are, what they want, and help them cope with the reality of their lives. I consider your unwillingness to acknowledge your husband's death dangerous for your mental health. There's a normal process to grieving. After the initial shock, there's denial, anger, depression, and in time, acceptance and moving on with life. You are stuck in denial." She looked at Claire with intensity. "And you like it there."

Red-faced, Claire said, "I am not stuck in denial. I'm angry with Phillip every day of my life."

"Then express your anger."

"I do. At home, I kick things."

Dr. Delanny sighed. "What things do you kick, Claire?"

"The hassock in my bedroom."

The therapist leaned across her desk again. "I'm sorry for your loss, Claire. Where have your children been all these months?"

"Paul's in the navy, stationed on an aircraft carrier in the Mediterranean. He flew in for a few days for his father's . . ." She paused, then swallowed hard.

"His father's what, Claire?"

"Damn it, his funeral! Okay?"

"And your daughter?"

Claire waved a hand in a dismissive gesture. "Amanda came, of course, but we've always seemed to rub each other the wrong way. She adored her father. She stayed a week, sorted his things, chose what she wanted, and shipped them home. Then she went back to California."

"I'm sorry." Silence filled the room. "Who are you, Claire Bennett?

Claire gasped. "What do you mean, who

am I? I'm Mrs. Phillip Bennett. Everyone in the village knows that. Why, they've named the children's library after me and Phillip."

"I know you've been the primary fund-raiser for the library. Why did you do all that work? Was it because you're essentially generous of spirit? Did you do it for the glory of it, for praise and recognition, to prove to the world that you're tough and smart and don't have to grieve? Do you love learning or children with a passion?" The therapist came around her desk and sat in the chair across from Claire.

"Understand me; none of these reasons is wrong—but the answer might offer a clue as to who Claire Bennett really is. In these last several months, you've evaded every serious question I've asked. You give me platitudes. You avoid looking at me. You change the subject and ignore the work I suggest might be helpful to you."

"I didn't ignore it. I made a list."

"Why isn't it here?"

"I told you, I forgot it." Claire averted her eyes and studied the photographs of stones.

"We forget what we want to forget, Claire."

Claire looked back at Dr. Delanny. "It didn't

seem important, once I knew why I hated that retreat."

"Silent retreats are meant to be introspective. I explained that to you when I mentioned it as a possibility. I warned you that in those first few days the silence might be difficult, but that if you stuck it out, you might come to a place of peace. Things of great import could rise to the surface—like maybe an understanding of why you won't acknowledge that your husband is dead, or consider your future without him."

Claire hesitated, then said, "A man there reminded me of Phillip. I called out to him once, but he ignored me. I felt humiliated. How could I stay there after that?"

"Is that why you left? A man ignored you?"

Claire dropped her gaze. "I don't know."

"Didn't you just tell me you left because everyone else was religious and you weren't?" *One last try, and then I'm finished.*

Hands clasped in her lap, Claire stared at the floor. Then her shoulders slumped, and her chin quivered. "I don't know what to do," she said in a hoarse whisper. "I'm so afraid. I have no friends. My children hate me; they stay as far away as possible. I've made a mess of my life. After all these years living here, I feel as if I'm a stranger. I'm so afraid."

Mary asked gently, "What are you afraid of?"

After a long silence, Claire looked at her. "I am afraid that I'm not strong enough to cope with life by myself. I'm afraid of living the rest of my life without a man to share it with." Claire pulled a wad of tissues from her purse, and wiped her eyes. "Every day when I wake up, I fight off fear. My heart is so heavy, I don't know if I'm going to make it through the day."

"You're a strong woman, Claire, stronger than you imagine. You act with assurance, as if you're completely in control of your life. That in itself takes courage."

Claire gave a watery laugh. "You think that because I get up, get dressed, plaster a smile on my face, and proceed with the routines of my life, I'm brave?"

"Yes, I do. I believe you're strong and capable. The routines you mention keep you going. Some people can't even get out of bed. You do. Think of what you've done: you continue to run your business, and carry on with volunteer work. I'd say you haven't taken the time to mourn, or to consider what you might want."

Claire's shoulders rose, then fell. "I want a husband. I want a man in my life."

"Nothing else?"

Claire shook her head. "Nothing else. If I had a husband, I'd wrap myself in whatever he wanted."

"Are you saying that if he were a bird-watcher you'd become a birdwatcher, and if he liked jazz you'd go to jazz concerts, whether you liked them or not?"

"Certainly. I know how to please a man. I can make a man happy."

"Can a man make you happy?"

"Yes, of course."

"Did Phillip?"

The room grew silent. "I saw Phillip's potential when he was just a salesman. I know how to draw out a man's potential."

"Did your husband make you happy?"

"Yes. Most of the time, he did. He used to say, 'I'm a better man because of you, Claire.' That made me very happy."

Mary Delanny persisted. "So you would choose a man in whom you recognized unfulfilled potential, someone you thought could be better, richer, more famous, whatever,

than he was because of your encouragement? And you find that role satisfying?"

"Yes. Don't you see? I'd be identified with
his success, like a doctor's wife. I felt important being married to Phillip. He was an inter-
nationally respected antiques dealer. We'd
arrive at a hotel in Paris or London, and everyone scrambled to make us welcome and
comfortable."

"So you'll keep the business?"

"No. I'm selling it. It's nothing without Phillip. I can't go on trying to run it by myself."
Claire's voice dropped. "I feel invisible with
Phillip gone. It's humiliating walking into a
room without a male escort. I can't go to a
movie alone, or out for lunch—and certainly
not for dinner, where I'm a fifth wheel."

"What about Claire's potential, Claire's latent talents, gifts, skills?" Mary asked gently.

Claire lifted her chin. "My gift is to be a
muse, to inspire." Her head dropped. "You
don't understand. I'm . . . well, I'm nothing
alone."

"I reject the idea that you're nothing alone,"
Mary said. "You're a woman with great
organizational skills. You could run your business alone if you chose to."

Claire shook her head. "I can't. "

Mary sighed. "Unfortunately, our time is up. Let's talk about this again next week."

Claire rose from her chair. "You'll see me again?"

"Yes. Next week, same time."

5

Estrangement

Several hours after her session with Dr. Delanny, Claire phoned her daughter. "How are you, Amanda?"

"Fine. And you?" Amanda's voice registered caution.

"You've moved east."

"I wrote you."

"Yes, I was away," Claire said. "I just got your letter." There was a long pause. What had she expected from Amanda? "How do you like North Carolina?"

"It's beautiful. I like it."

"I'm going to sell the business," Claire said.

"You're going to sell Daddy's business?"

Claire bristled. "It's as much mine as his."

"What about Paul? Maybe he'd be interested."

"Paul's never shown any interest in antiques. How could a boy without an education, with no experience with antiques, carry on this business?"

"Oops, sorry, I forgot. Daddy's the only man who ever ran a successful business—with your help, of course."

Claire leaned against the doorframe and studied her fingernails. "When did you leave California?"

"Several months ago," Amanda muttered.

"And you're planning to marry that boy?"

Amanda's voice tightened. "That *boy*, Mother, is thirty years old and an architect."

"Don't architects work for large firms in cities? Whatever will he do in the country?"

"Mother, if you can set aside your stereotypes and prejudices, we'd be happy to have you at our wedding. If not, perhaps it would be better if you didn't come."

"I don't know where I'll be next spring," Claire said, regretting the words as she said them, yet driven to go further. "I may sell this house and buy a condo in Florida. A change of scene might do me good."

"Sell the house?" A pause. "Okay, you do what you want. Look, I have to get off the phone. And by the way, Tom has an office in Dad's house, and when the barn's renovated he'll work from home."

Amanda's words stung Claire. *"Dad's* house?"

"Tom's dad's house. He's great. He asked me to call him Dad."

"I see." *Get off this phone before you damage this relationship more than it already is.* "Well, I have to run, too. Goodbye, Amanda."

"Goodbye, Mother."

The clunk of the receiver reverberated through the quiet room. Claire sank into a kitchen chair. The antagonism between herself and her daughter dated back to Amanda's childhood. Claire had demanded tidiness: every book on the shelves in the den aligned by height, clothing hung by color in the closet, sheets and bedspread smooth within minutes of rising.

Conversely, Amanda flung clothing, books, and toys helter-skelter in her room and elsewhere in the house. She dropped food on the floor, spilled her milk, bumped into furniture, and left dirt trails on walls. It seemed to Claire that Amanda deliberately assaulted every room she entered.

A memory rose to haunt her: Amanda screaming, running down the hall to the den where Claire was reading. Claire had sighed, set down her book, and gone to the door.

Her face swollen, her shoulders heaving, Amanda stood with blood dripping down her hand onto the Persian rug. Terrified that she could not cope, probably a result of feeling helpless in the face of her mother's illness, for a moment Claire irrationally felt angry at her for being hurt and, insanely, angry that blood was dripping onto the expensive rug.

She had scooped up Amanda and tried to comfort her as she carried her to the bathroom to wash and dress the tiny hand. But once cleaned, it was obvious that the cut would require stitches. Claire had bandaged the hand to try to stop the bleeding, but blood continued to ooze through the bandage. Feeling helpless, wanting to weep, she wrapped Amanda's hand in a towel and drove to

Phillip's office. He had taken charge, held the child close, whispered in her ear, got her smiling, and carried her off to the emergency room.

But children sensed things. Her mother's hesitation, the way she'd looked from the rug to the child, had spoken the truth—and in that moment trust had been broken, and a chasm created that had never been bridged between herself and Amanda.

Talking to Amanda now unsettled Claire, and she struggled to push away the guilt. After all, what had she known about mothering? Mentally ill and often hospitalized, her mother had been unpredictable and capricious. Many nights, feeling alone and scared, Claire had cried herself to sleep. She felt that way now—scared and desperately lonely.

Suddenly the house seemed huge and almost sinister. If her housekeeper didn't live with her, if she hadn't installed an alarm system and a bolt on her bedroom door, she would never have been able to stay here all these months.

Claire made her way to the den and looked

at the furnishings as though appraising them for sale. Mahogany bookshelves lined two of the nine-foot-high walls. Between the windows hung original American Currier and Ives prints. The burled walnut and ash William and Mary lowboy had been purchased on their first, glorious trip to England. The Victorian chairs on either side of the fireplace were well scrolled and curved; they would bring a pretty penny.

What am I doing? I haven't decided to sell anything.

Claire sank onto a couch. Her mother had not been crazy. Today she would have been diagnosed as bipolar, and with medication, she could have lived a normal life. She would have been able to express love for her family. She would have cooked, and laughed, and been there for her children and husband.

Occasionally Claire had glimpsed happiness in her mother's eyes, occasionally a zest for life manifested itself. What effect had the shock therapy had on her? Did she commit suicide because of it? *I have to get out of here.*

Claire ran into the foyer, snatched her

jacket from the hall closet, and dashed from the house. A half hour later she had checked into a motel, and she slept that night in her clothing on an uncomfortable bed with a rocklike pillow. As she lay there crying, she thought, *This is where fear has driven me.*

6

Decisions

The next day, Olden Riverdale welcomed Claire into his spacious corner office with a friendly hug. "Sit. Sit, my dear."

Claire took the leather chair facing the desk from where she could see out into the street. Classical music played softly from concealed speakers. Olden sank into his swivel chair.

"How are you, Olden? Francine and the grandkids are well, I hope." *I can never remember those boys' names.*

Olden had lost his wife, Sarah, to cancer three years ago, and his recently divorced daughter, Francine, had moved from Massachusetts to East Hampton with her two boys to live with him.

"All's well," he said. "The boys are a bit noisy, but they're good kids. How are you, Claire? You've shut yourself away in that big house and I hardly see you. I worry about you. How about coming over for Sunday brunch, or for dinner some evening?"

"That's kind of you, Olden, and I will, I really will. I'll call Francine."

He nodded and folded his hands on the desk. His eyes were kind and caring. "So, what can I do for you?"

"I want to sell the house," Claire said. After she'd talked with Amanda, the idea of moving to Florida had fixed itself in her mind.

Olden's eyebrows shot up. "Why would you want to do that?"

"I can't bear to spend another winter in the freezing cold."

"You and Phillip invested heavily in your home. The antiques in your living room alone must be worth a fortune."

"Probably so. I'd sell some, store some, take some."

"Take them where, Claire?"

With her finger, she traced invisible circles on the top of the oversized teak desk. "I'm thinking of buying a condo in Florida."

He looked relieved. "You want to escape the winter. Can't say I blame you. Sarah and I had that condo on the ocean in Boca Raton." He looked at her, his eyes reassuring. "You'd like Boca Raton. It's got style, like you, Claire."

"Do you still have your condo?" *Maybe I can buy his, spare myself the Realtors, inspectors, and banks.*

Olden shook his head. "I sold it a few months ago. I hated going there after Sarah died." He paused. "It's never good to make important decisions too quickly after you lose a spouse."

Inwardly, Claire groaned. *For heaven's sake, don't start sounding like Dr. Delanny.* The room grew quiet. Across the street, the broad dark hands of a clock on another bank read two forty-five. A red leaf from one of the maples that lined the street drifted past the window toward the ground.

Claire gazed at Olden. He was a man of infinite patience, and she knew that he was waiting for her to continue. "I want to sell the business, too. I need your advice on how to price it and where to advertise it. Two warehouses packed with inventory, the business itself, and the contacts that come with it should fetch a pretty penny."

"I'm sure they would, but sell the business?" He waved his hand as if to dispel the idea. "Go to Florida, enjoy a warm, sunny winter. I'll help you locate a qualified manager to handle the business while you're gone. Don't be hasty, Claire, I beg you."

"I don't want a manager, Olden. You don't understand. I want out. I must . . ."—she swallowed hard—"get on with my life, make a new life." Claire's mouth went dry, and she hesitated. "Phillip isn't coming back. He's dead."

Olden cleared his throat. "I am well aware of that. But isn't it a bit rash to cut all of your ties in a place you've lived and worked in for thirty years?" His face flushed. "I'll do whatever I can for you, of course, but I beg you, don't be hasty."

"I want to sell."

"I'm sorry to hear it." His thick brows drew together over deep-set brown eyes. "In that case, we'll need to inventory everything and have it appraised: the business, your house, your antiques. How much time do we have?"

"Say, two months. I'd like to be settled in Florida before Christmas."

Olden whistled through his teeth. "Before Christmas? You'll miss the Christmas parade, the Christmas party at the club. What about your friends here?"

"Let's be realistic, Olden. Other than you, who might they be?"

"Susan Pelitzer?"

"A nice person, but hardly someone I'd stay here for."

Silence settled about them.

"What about me?" he asked.

"You are Phillip's and my dearest friend, and I'll be sorry to leave you, but I must."

"I'll . . . we'll miss you—the library, Susan, all of us."

She leaned toward him, the fingers of her hands pressed together as if in supplication. "Olden, try to understand. I need a change, a new life in a new place."

For a moment, he looked crestfallen.

Good Lord! Olden's not interested in me as more than a friend, is he? That's ludi-

crous. He's ten years my senior, too short, and he's balding. She almost laughed, but the earnest look on his face stopped her.

Olden coughed. "I understand more than you think I do." He reached for a pad and pencil and scribbled some notes. "Well, let me see what I can do. You'll need a realtor for the house." He leaned across the desk. "Claire, you'd be severing all your connections, burning bridges, so to speak. Why not rent your home? It would bring a good price. Is leaving like this what Phillip would want for you?"

Claire rose from her chair, rounded the desk, and placed a casual kiss on Olden's forehead. "I think he would. I'll wait to hear from you."

He reached for her hand and held it. "Claire, please, think this over for a few days. If you need to talk, call me."

Books had always been Claire's faithful companions. They had comforted her during her mother's interminable hospitalizations and soothed her when her sisters excluded her as they so often had. She had adored her father, and books had offered an escape from the pain she felt at his distraction and sadness.

She read copiously: Nancy Drew mysteries, and the Oz books, and graduated to Wordsworth, Keats, and Shelley; then Shakespeare, to the classical nineteenth-century novels of Brontë and Dickens, and on to Hemingway, Fitzgerald, and Faulkner. In high school she lost herself in Marcel Proust's *Remembrance of Things Past,* and André Malraux's *Man's Hope* and *Man's Faith*; his classic works on the Spanish Civil War and the Boxer Rebellion held her spellbound. These days she read science fiction, adventure thrillers, romances, and current bestsellers. Occasionally she bought a self-help book, but usually failed to read past page ten.

Tonight Claire opened a new science fiction book, but within moments it lay unread on her lap as her mind replayed her conversation with Olden. Selling the house and the business *would* be burning bridges. Would she regret this decision? Would she be cast up alone in some unfamiliar town in Florida as if she were flotsam? Claire pulled up the fine Egyptian cotton sheet and nuzzled her chin in its softness. Before going to St. Dunstan's she had purchased *The Stations of*

Solitude by Alice Koller. Drawn to it by the description on the jacket, she wondered if it was possible to transform loneliness into creativity. The author spoke about recognizing the extent to which a person can be alone: "thoroughly, unremittingly, and elementally." The last word stopped her. What did it mean? Her dictionary defined "elemental" as basic, rudimentary, and irreducible—all words describing the loneliness welded into her bones, into her very soul, from childhood.

The loneliness had not been assuaged, as she hoped it would be, when she married Phillip. He did not share her intuition, her sensitivity to nature, which she had all but extinguished over the years. He had loved her and tried to meet her needs; he just didn't have a clue what they were, no matter how she tried to tell or show him. So they buried themselves in the one thing they both understood, the business.

Dr. Delanny had asked her about many things, including her anger at Phillip for his sexual indifference, but Claire refused to go there. How did she know that she could really trust the woman with her deepest hurts and fears? But if she did not trust her, why continue therapy? Claire suspected that her unhappiness stemmed from a childhood redundant with uncertainty, loneliness, and fear, but it was too scary to go there.

After Phillip's death she had removed all of his photographs from their bedroom, but two months ago she had reinstated their wedding photo on her bedside table. Now she picked it up and spoke directly to her husband.

"I did love you, Phillip. Surely you knew that. Look at you—still handsome, even with the white hair that came after Terrance was killed. We never talked of Terrance . . . not then, not ever." Her eyes misted.

"In all our years of marriage, we were never truly close. So many unspoken issues hid behind our smiles and carefully pleasant voices."

Intimacy for them had been those hours sitting shoulder to shoulder poring over auction catalogs, or planning a buying trip overseas, or exclaiming over each exquisite item as it emerged from its packing crate. Their mutual pleasure at spotting a rare antique was . . . well, orgasmic. Working with a man, replicating those experiences, was what she wanted again. She would make this her quest.

Feeling better, Claire returned the photo to the table. That's exactly what she would do: go to Florida and have a look around. Satisfied, she promptly fell asleep.

7

Florida

The plane shivered when it touched the runway, then settled and slowed as it cruised toward the terminal. Claire waited until the other passengers had hauled their bags from overhead bins and departed before she reached for her bag and walked to the exit door. In the concourse, the frenzied rush of humanity jarred her, and she stepped back to avoid bumping into a woman hauling a resisting child by the arm.

The child hunkered down. "I got to pee-pee!"

"Later. Hurry up," the woman said.

Claire's heart sank, remembering that she,

too, had paid little attention to Amanda's or Paul's needs.

The woman holding the sign CLAIRE BENNETT was short and tan with wavy bobbed hair and large green eyes. Claire walked toward the Realtor from Boca Raton.

"Welcome to Florida, Mrs. Bennett." Renee Ormon lowered the sign and extended her hand.

"How do you do?" Claire replied.

Renee rolled her eyes. "Don't ask." She guided Claire along the concourse, past people rushing to or from flight gates. "Traffic was mean. Highway I-95's as bad as the Lincoln Tunnel when I used to drive into the city from New Jersey." Renee dodged a woman pushing a stroller and holding the hand of a whining child. She shrugged. "C'est la vie."

Renee walked fast and Claire, in high heels, hurried to keep pace. Renee slowed as they approached the escalator to the baggage area. "Sorry. I go too fast; bad habit."

Another of Claire's grandmother's adages struck her: "You can change locations, sell your house and everything you own, but you take yourself with you."

Once in the car, they exited the parking

garage onto a busy street, and after a wait at the entrance ramp that spewed into I-95 heading south, Renee plunged her Lexus boldly into traffic streaming along at seventy-five miles an hour.

"It was good of you to pick me up," Claire said. "I could have hired a limo. Is it far to Boca Raton?"

"Twenty minutes, unless there's an accident on the highway or you get behind some old codger who shouldn't have had his license renewed." She slowed to avoid the Cadillac in front of them, then changed lanes to maintain her speed. "Want me to drop you at your hotel, or shall we get started?" Renee patted the fat blue book on the seat between them. "I have several absolutely gorgeous condominiums to show you." She cast a quick glance at Claire. "You might want to rest, though. We can start tomorrow."

"I'd like to check in and freshen up a bit, then I'd be delighted to condominium-hunt," Claire said.

"Great." Renee maneuvered across traffic to the far right lane. "I'm going to take the ocean route."

They drove south on A1A at a considerably slower pace, and Claire began to relax.

Intermittently, for arm-to-arm condominiums blocked the view of water, she caught a glimpse of wide sand beaches, the ocean, and dunes. Something amorphous and tender quivered deep within Claire and stirred a wisp of memory: a beach, her mother happy, her father laughing, a brief golden holiday long, long ago.

"This is Highland Beach," Renee said as they drove through a tunnel of high-rise apartments. A short while later the view changed and she said, "Here we are in Boca Raton. Years ago, Boca passed a bond issue and bought up miles and miles of beachfront. That effectively stopped condominium construction on the ocean. The developers scrambled to buy oceanfront land in Highland Beach, and you've seen the result. Boca Raton has miles of pristine beachfront. It's one of the city's outstanding features."

Across from the water, on the right side of the road, stood a handful of attractive apartment complexes interspersed with heavily thicketed green tracts of land. "Those are very appealing condos," Claire said.

Renee pulled off the road onto a wide shoulder above the beach, in a spot where the sea grape trees had been cut low to expose a long view of sand and sea. Cream-white sand stretched in both directions. Banks of cumulous clouds cast shadows on the spar-kling blue water, while the swells breathed lace-crested loops and swirls along the shore-line. Out on the ocean, the passing ships were mere dots.

The beach was clean and sparsely occu-pied: several young girls in bikinis baked slim bodies in the sun. Two older women, their faces covered by floppy straw hats, lay on beach lounges. A couple strolled the shore hand in hand, avoiding two small children dip-ping their toes into the water and squealing excitedly.

Claire's concerns about living on the ocean—the sound of pounding surf, gusting winds, salt spray that dampened sheets and coated windows, corroded hinges and door-knobs—vanished. She pointed to a condo-minium set back from the road to her right. "I think I'd be quite content in one of those buildings."

"They're very nice—older, but you get larger rooms than in some of the newer places. Those apartments face the ocean in the front and the Intracoastal Waterway in the back, but you have to cross A1A to get to the beach," Renee said.

"I can handle that," Claire replied.

Days later, after looking at apartments in several buildings directly on the ocean, Claire made an offer on an apartment in the original building that had attracted her. The apartment faced west and overlooked the Intracoastal Waterway. Her offer, fifteen thousand dollars less than the asking price, was accepted, and Claire considered this a propitious sign. Her move and the location were preordained.

"I can walk across the street to the beach anytime," Claire told Renee, as they stood at the large window in the living room of the apartment. "From here, I can see sunsets and the lights of Boca Raton at night." For a moment, she felt unsure. Just buyer's remorse, she assured herself; it's done, signed, sealed, and delivered. Time to move on.

8

The Last Therapy Session

Back in East Hampton to arrange her move, Claire made a final appointment with her therapist.

"So." Dr. Delanny smiled at her. "How are you, Claire?"

Claire slipped into a chair. "Better than ever."

"How so?"

"I flew down to Florida and bought a condo in Boca Raton. I have an offer on my house here, so this will probably be my last session with you. I'll be leaving in two weeks and I have oodles to do."

"Leaving in two weeks! You've certainly

accomplished a great deal in a short time. Isn't it a bit impulsive?"

"Not at all. I've been thinking about moving, and Florida seems like a good place: warm weather year-round, with no more snow and sleet." She leaned forward. "You don't approve of what I'm doing?"

"It's not for me to approve or disapprove."

"But you do understand that I have to go somewhere new? Who will I ever meet here?" Claire suddenly needed reassurance. Had she been overly hasty? She could feel anxiety rising, and this she could not permit. What was done was done and she didn't regret any of it.

Dr. Delanny cleared her throat. "Claire, I hope in our time together you've come to understand yourself and your motivations better. I hope you feel you've made some progress along those lines."

Claire shrugged. Her single goal was still to marry a man into whose life she could bring glamour and success, and in whose light she could bask—regardless of what Mary Delanny thought or said. What she had gleaned from their work together were some memories of her childhood, and she did occasionally relate them to events in the present, particularly in regard to her children. "Yes, I have gained certain insights. Thank you for those."

"What insights would they be?" Delanny asked.

"About my mother, why I felt as I did about her, and why things were as they were at home, with her being mentally ill. I understand it would be different today."

Dr. Delanny did not respond.

"I'll find him, you know," Claire said confidently.

"Find whom?"

"A husband."

"I wish you all the best."

"I'll meet men at country clubs, art galleries, maybe I'll even take up golf." Claire's chin tilted upward. "Whatever I have to do to put myself in a position to meet the right man: attractive, healthy, and wealthy." Her nervous laugh faded fast.

"I wish you a safe trip and all good fortune."

Claire hesitated. She had sat in this chair almost every week for six months. Hadn't she found the right apartment in Boca Raton in just a few days? Hadn't her home here sold in three weeks? Those were good signs. Yet she was overcome with uncertainty. "Can we talk?"

Dr. Delanny glanced at the clock on the wall. "I wish we could, Claire, but our time's up. I'm sorry." The therapist flipped through her Rolodex and wrote a name on a pad. "If you ever want to see someone in Florida, here's the name of a friend of mine. Carol Ringer is a fine therapist in Delray Beach, just up the road from Boca Raton." She rose and handed Claire the paper.

Claire accepted it, and slipped it into her purse. "I'm sure I shan't need it. Well, thank you for seeing me all these months."

"Goodbye, Claire, and good luck."

Feeling dissatisfied and anxious, Claire walked out of the building into a cold, overcast November day. *Yes,* she thought, pulling her coat about her. *It'll be good to live in the sunshine.*

9

Boca Raton

Claire had always considered South Florida a tourist resort and a playground for the rich and famous. Driving through the sprawling developments west of I-95, she was surprised at how much of Boca Raton was given over to housing for families with children. And now the snowbirds were arriving, mainly retirees from the north who wintered down here. She detested the slow, heavy traffic, and since she had bought on the strip of land between the Intracoastal and the ocean, she impatiently had to wait for the drawbridges to the mainland to close as tall-masted pleasure boats cruised up and down on the Intracoastal

Waterway. And, by four-thirty each afternoon, long lines of older couples had already formed at the most popular restaurants.

"Avoid certain hours on the roads, go late for dinner, and you'll be fine," Renee had advised Claire.

On the plus side, Boca Raton's upscale appearance—its landscaped roadways, the ongoing influence of architect Addison Mizner's Spanish-inspired architecture with its rounded lines and warm sand and pink colors, the long stretch of open beach devoid of development—contrasted sharply with towns of lesser charm to the north and south.

Claire especially liked Mizner Plaza on Federal Highway, with its red brick paths and comfortable benches, its statuary, tiled fountains, and gazebo. She frequented its fine shops and restaurants, tucked inside arcades under the balconies of apartments above, and loved the small-town, old-world feel of the place.

"When I go to Mizner Plaza," Claire told Olden on the phone, "I wish I'd bought one of those apartments overlooking it. It's so alive, you can step downstairs at night and be part of the life stream, the music, and restaurants."

"You could sell your place and move," Olden suggested.

"Maybe later on, I will," she replied. "For now I'm settling into my apartment. I like living on the seventh floor. I feel safe. I enjoy sitting out on my terrace in the evenings with a glass of wine, watching the boats go by. People wave, I wave, and the sunsets are dramatic. And it's so close to the beach—I just take the elevator down, walk across A1A, and I'm on the beach."

"Well, I guess you can't have everything," Olden said.

"I guess not."

Claire didn't tell Olden how many mornings she awakened early feeling alone and afraid, and how many sunrises found her following the shifting surf along the empty shore.

Within three weeks of moving to Boca Raton, Claire had unpacked and arranged her old furniture in her new home. But the tall Edwardian armoire overpowered her bedroom, and the dark mahogany sideboard crowded the living room. Her oversized, traditional couch with its crushed-velvet upholstery appeared ridiculous in a tropical setting. Claire rented an air-conditioned storage unit for all the antiques she had so painstakingly selected and shipped. Then she had the apartment painted a pale apricot and shopped for new furniture. On a jewel-toned Persian rug, she placed a cream-colored contemporary sofa, and behind it a floral folding screen. She added a tall plant stand and topped it with a round bowl of white silk antheriums. Two marble-topped end tables served as a coffee table. The Biedermeier armchairs from her home on Long Island fit well on either side of the couch so she did not replace them, but she refurnished her newly painted blue bedroom in French Provincial.

Claire worked with alacrity and soon she had completely revamped and accessorized her apartment. Now she was ready to reinvent her life. She would join a country club, art museums, and a church for social purposes—but which church?

Her mother had been a disaffected Episcopalian, and her father a nonaffiliated Jew. There had been little of religion in her childhood other than the occasional attendance at the solemn church of her grandparents, where she had always felt chilled, and another church she sometimes attended with a girlfriend, with its awe-inspiring lofty arches and stained-glass windows that delighted her with its size and elegance. The temple that her father occasionally took her and her sisters to was white inside, with a high, domed ceiling and dark benches with deep blue pads. What had fascinated her was the cabinet behind the altar, which was opened during the service to reveal the Torah. "Inside the covering," her father had said, "are rolled scrolls comprising the first five books of Moses—our Hebrew bible." The Torahs were beautiful, ornately decorated with velvet covers, topped with silver crowns dripping with tiny tingling bells, and she had wondered why they would hide such a lovely thing away.

When her mother became seriously ill, her father had severed his limited ties to religion and castigated God. After her mother's death, the brightly decorated Christmas trees vanished, replaced by a small plastic tree, fewer gifts, and a dearth of gaiety.

For some reason, now that she was here in Boca Raton, Claire procrastinated on joining a church, country club, or museum. After all, she needed time to acclimate, to explore her new town, to roam the beach, to relax and watch the boats slip by. And when the wind was right, the voices and laughter of crews and passengers that carried to her seventh-floor patio made Claire feel somewhat less alone. She would sit for long periods of time thinking that maybe one day *she* would travel north to Virginia and beyond on that liquid highway.

One early morning, as Claire walked on the beach, a man walked toward her. Focused on his feet, he moved in a zigzag fashion, close to the water, then higher up on the sand, then to the water's edge. Absorbed, he would have ploughed into Claire if she had not taken a swift step out of his path.

Startled, he stopped and looked at her. "Forgive me. I was preoccupied."

"It's all right. I know how you can lose yourself walking on the beach."

His polo shirt hugged his chest and showed firm muscles. In each hand he carried a white tennis shoe stuffed with a sock. His face was tan, deep wrinkles spread from the corners of his eyes, and his hair was silver in the first rays of the rising sun. He was fifty-five or sixty, she thought, an appropriate age for her.

"You walk here much?" he asked.

Claire hesitated. "Now and then." Was he a tennis pro, a politician, a drifter? A woman must use caution. Then she spied a couple from her condo heading down the path to the beach. They waved, and she waved in return. *What the heck, I'm not alone on the beach. What can happen?*

"I live in Delray," he said.

Water swirled about their ankles. "That's a long walk from here," she replied.

"Yes. I hardly noticed the distance or the time." He looked at his watch. "My wife passed away just over a year ago from cancer. A long and painful illness to the end. Now I find I can't sleep, and walking along the ocean helps."

He spoke so openly of his wife's demise, while she still struggled to say that Phillip was dead. "I'm widowed." She swallowed hard. "It takes a long time to get over the loss."

"Yes. A long time. We were very close. I miss her terribly." He looked out at the horizon, then back at her. "Were you heading south? Mind if I walk along?"

The couple from her condo opened beach chairs and settled onto the sand above the waterline.

Claire shrugged. "I don't mind." *I'll keep that couple in sight.*

"I'm Jason Aronson," he said.

"Clara Benedict." *I'm not telling a stranger my real name.*

They walked in silence. The glaring sun slid above the thin line of the horizon and she felt its warmth on her arms and neck.

"Have you lived here long?" he asked.

"Not long. And you?"

"Almost thirty years. We came in the early seventies, when Boca was a village of maybe twenty-five thousand people. Everyone knew everyone. It's grown west almost to the Everglades now, and gotten so congested. That's why my wife and I moved to Delray a few years ago. I guess a lot of other folks felt as we did, for they've started moving north. Now that Rachel's gone, I'm considering relocating."

"Where to?" His stride was longer than hers, and she stretched her legs to keep up.

"A small town in Vermont, maybe. I'm originally from Northfield, Massachusetts."

"What do you do here?" Claire asked, thinking he was probably retired.

"I'm a pediatrician. I started my practice here."

Ah, a professional. Not some beach bum. Sea foam splayed between her toes. Behind them, the avaricious water swallowed their footprints. Then the boardwalk at Red Reef Park and the gazebo came into view. Soon they would round a bend, and the couple on the sand would be lost to sight.

"I have to be getting back," Claire said.

"Oh, yes, sorry." He looked at his watch. "I have to get back, too."

When they stood again at the place where they had met, Jason extended his hand. "It was nice meeting you, Clara." He started away, then turned. "Say, would you have dinner with a lonely chap some evening?" He pulled a card from the pocket of his shirt and handed it to her. "Habit," he said. "I always carry a card or two. My nurse will vouch that I'm a nice guy. Think about it, and leave a message with Miss Boggs if you'd like to kill an evening."

Kill an evening? How sad that sounds. Claire accepted his card and started up the sand toward the pathway.

"Morning. Lovely day," the woman from her condo said.

"It certainly is," Claire replied.

"You're new, aren't you?" the woman asked.

"Yes," Claire replied. "Sorry I can't stop to chat, but I'm late for an appointment. Enjoy the beach."

"We sure will," the husband returned.

Claire stripped off her T-shirt as she thought of Jason Aronson—a widower, available for dinner, and what else?

On Friday evening the condominium association threw a party, which Claire discovered was a quarterly event. They celebrated Hanukkah/Christmas with an ornately decorated tree in one corner and a menorah with Hanukkah candles as a centerpiece on the buffet table.

"We want our newcomers to feel at home," Laura Leggitt, president of the association, had said when she phoned earlier in the week to issue the invitation.

"I'd be delighted to come," Claire said. "How formal is it?"

"Informal—a pantsuit or a dress, nothing fancy. Be comfortable." A pause, then, "Is your apartment finished? I saw trucks taking your lovely, old pieces in and then out."

Antiques, not old pieces, you silly woman.

Laura continued, "Furniture from up North

never seems right in South Florida homes. Are you settled now? After the holidays, I'd love to see what you've done with your place."

"I'm not settled as yet. I'll let you know when I am." Claire shifted from leg to leg.

"Well," Laura said, "see you on Friday evening at six o'clock. Don't have dinner; there's always tons of food."

The salmon-colored linen pantsuit Claire wore to the party was casual yet stylish, and a French braid kept her hair off her neck. Many of the women were similarly dressed, while others were, in Claire's opinion, decidedly overdressed in velvet jackets or ankle-length gowns. They hung on to husbands as if their men would run away like wild horses if they could. Everyone introduced themselves and welcomed her, and Laura invited her to join her bridge club.

"Perhaps later, thank you," Claire said.

Mary Louise French, a retired librarian, invited her for mah-jongg.

"I don't know how to play mah-jongg," Claire said.

A shriek from Mary Louise, and Claire was surrounded by three ladies offering to teach her.

"Thank you so much," Claire said. "I'll think about it."

One of the women slipped a card into Claire's hand. "Please give me a ring when you have time. I'm on the fifth floor." The card read:

Sarah Slayer, Ph.D., Literature
Florida Atlantic University
Boca Raton, Florida

"I haven't had a new card made since I retired last year," Sarah said. "Maybe it's because being a professor at the university was my identity. My husband and I had big plans for traveling, but Joe died suddenly of a heart attack. Mah-jongg and the support from the women in this building saved my life."

"I'm sorry about your husband," Claire said.

"Do give me a call and let's get together," Sarah said.

Later that night, Claire settled into a lounge chair on her terrace. This was not what she had planned: there was no framework to her life, no sense of order or control. Was there anything wrong with just drifting for a while, being open to whatever came along? Yet habit urged her to take action now, to set concrete goals. Inactivity left her wondering if she had made the right decision, which created anxiety.

She recalled that Dr. Delanny had asked her who she was. One thing she was not: she was not like most of the women at that party. Many were older than she was and seemed focused on bus trips to theaters and museums, bridge games and mah-jongg. Another topic that had animated everyone was comparing early-bird specials and recommending restaurants to one another.

She had envisioned a much more glamorous life: museum openings, galas at the country club, and of course she would enter on the arm of some gorgeous man. So why hadn't she joined anything? What was this unaccustomed inertia she felt? Was it connected to her experience on the beach? Walking there before sunrise, she had felt fleeting moments of tranquility, feelings so unfamiliar they confused and disturbed her.

Claire looked up at the sky, whose stars were obliterated by the city lights. She missed a star-filled sky. She missed seeing the constellation of Orion slide across the sky.

But compromise was what life was all about. Without the city lights, without the life and energy implicit in the yachts and motorboats below, she would be utterly lonely. She needed a lift, a date. Jason Aronson, maybe?

Meeting him, hearing him speak about his wife, had forced Claire to consider that the wound of Phillip's loss did indeed need suturing, bandaging, and time to heal. But how was she to do that?

She shrugged. Enough sad thoughts! She had made this move to begin a new life, and her goal remained unchanged. She would phone Jason's office and arrange to have dinner with him, and she would make a must-do list. She would join the Boca Raton Art Museum, and find the right country club. Both were ideal milieus at which to meet Mr. Right.

10

Jason Aronson

Dinner with Jason Aronson at a rooftop restaurant, five stories above the Intracoastal Waterway, revealed a very nice man, thoughtful and seemingly honest.

"Have you dated much since your wife passed away?" she asked.

"No, not much. Dating's a whole new ball game for me. Friends invite me to dinner to meet eligible ladies, saying, 'I have the perfect person for you, Jason.' It's not worth the pressure I feel to be animated and witty, which I am not."

"How would you describe yourself, then?" Claire asked.

"Rather a dull fellow. I read a great deal, mostly nonfiction, autobiographies. My wife used to tease me about being too serious. 'You don't laugh enough,' she'd say." He leaned forward and looked deep into Claire's eyes. "What's been your dating experience?"

"I haven't dated at all, actually. You're my first date."

"You're kidding! An attractive woman like yourself? I'd imagine your phone would ring off the hook."

He's so personable and casual. I like him.

Their entrées arrived, and a three-piece band played oldies from the fifties.

"Do you like to dance? I'm quite adept at that, they tell me," Jason said.

Claire smiled. "I used to love to dance. It's been years."

He dropped his napkin on the table. "Then let's dance."

"Our dinners will get cold."

"You're right. After we eat, then?"

Claire nodded. And when they danced, she did not resist when Jason pulled her close.

Back at the table, she asked, "Would you remarry?"

"I'm nowhere near ready, but when I do, it'll have to be someone Jewish who keeps kosher, or my kids would kill me."

"Your children have that much influence on you, at this stage of your life?" Claire considered telling him that she was half Jewish, but keeping kosher? Goodness, no.

"My children are very much a part of my life. Wouldn't you consult your kids if you were going to remarry?" he asked.

"No. I don't think so. They live far away. They have their own lives, and I have mine."

"My family's very close. My two daughters live in Boca and my son is in West Palm Beach. I attend synagogue on Friday nights with them, and after the service we go to one of the girls' homes and have our own oneg."

Oneg. That sounded familiar, but it had been so long she wasn't sure what it meant. Her heart sank. She didn't know the simplest things about Judaism. "Oneg?" she asked, feeling foolish.

"After services, we share food and drink. There's always an oneg at the synagogue. We hang around a while for courtesy's sake, then we go home and do it again."

"And you're thinking of moving to Vermont?" she asked.

"In all honesty, no—but I try to get up there every October for the fall leaves. That's when I hanker to make a move. I could never leave the kids and grandkids, though. I have seven grandchildren, three boys and four girls. I'm teaching all but the baby to fish." His eyes brightened. "Maybe you'd like to go fishing with us some Sunday?"

"Thank you, but I'm a terrible sailor. I get seasick even with medication." The first day Phillip had taken her out on his yacht, she'd been seasick and miserable and had ruined the day for him, begging to be returned to shore. Though she wouldn't go out on Jason's boat, she wasn't averse to seeing him again. He might even become her first lover since marrying Phillip.

Jason Aronson escorted Claire, who had divulged her real name, to his home that night, and she spent every night from Saturday to the following Thursday at his lovely home on the Intracoastal Waterway. Jason excelled as a lover, approaching sex openly, unashamedly, with delight. Nothing between two consenting adults was odd, strange, or forbidden to him. Where Phillip had pulled away from her touch, protesting that it tickled, Jason encouraged her and reciprocated.

Phillip had been a missionary-position man. To Jason the entire body was a source of pleasure to be explored and enjoyed, and her total relaxation with him, marked by her uncensored moans of pleasure—Phillip had made love in silence and expected the same from her—reminded her of what she had missed all those years. It would be easy to fall in love with Jason, and it was hard to accept their affair for what it really was—unadulterated and delightful lust. But once Friday night arrived, Jason was no longer available.

11

Topsy-turvy

On Friday evening, brooding over their differences, Claire walked the beach alone. She reminded herself that passion waned in time and that sex was not the be-all and end-all of a relationship, though it was certainly important. Their disparate interests, Jason's family ties and insistence on maintaining a kosher kitchen, would never work. And his long-range plans after retirement included a stint volunteering for a United Nations clinic for children in a third world country. Still, it was better to see him five nights a week than to be alone.

Tears stung her eyes. *Damn Phillip for dying, for forcing me to live alone.* Claire stabbed her bare foot into the sand. *Damn him for leaving my life without meaning. It's hardly worth living.*

Overhead, a graying sky devoured the crimson sunset. A brisk wind kicked up whitecaps on the ocean, plastered her shirt against her breasts, and mussed her hair. Claire hunkered down close to the water's edge. Immediately, her shoes and the bottoms of her slacks grew wet and heavy. Dejected, she sat and stretched her legs toward the ocean. Water soon saturated her clothing almost to her waist. Feeling the pull of the tide, Claire half lay, half sat chest deep in water. Laughing bitterly, she threw back her head and felt the bite of wind against her face.

A wave struck her with such force that it dragged her underwater and away from shore. Her head struck the sandy bottom. As she struggled to right herself, to reach the surface and to breathe, gritty sand ground into her face and hair. Lifted up by a wave, she gasped cool fresh air. Before being dragged underwater again, raindrops splattered her face.

Yield. Let the sea dispose of me. No! I don't want to die. Amanda—Paul—I must

make things right with you. Dear God, help me. I don't want to die.

An incoming wave deposited her on the sand like a beached dolphin, and Claire gasped for breath and heaved up water. Through the cacophony of waves and wind, she heard her teeth chattering. Her lungs, her arms, her chest, her entire body hurt. Shivering and terrified, she crawled to higher ground as the steel-gray sky dumped rain on the desolate beach, blurring her vision, chilling her.

At the top of the dune, a street lamp's meager light indicated the path, and Claire's feet buckled when she finally reached a wooden bench. The rain gave no sign of abating, and as cars passed, their headlights glittered in the wet road, blinding her for a moment. The challenge of crossing A1A glued her to the bench for a time, and when traffic finally slowed, she rose and straggled across A1A, and she slumped against one of the stone columns at the entrance to her condominium complex. Using trees and the hoods and fenders of cars to support her, she slowly reached her building. Leaning against the elevator door, she nearly toppled to the floor when the door slid open.

In her apartment, Claire stripped off her

wet clothes, dried her shivering body, wrapped a towel about her hair, and collapsed into her bed. The huge emptiness that was her life struck with the force of the ocean waves.

I might as well have drowned. But she had fought to live, prayed to live. *God, I miss home. I miss the familiar rooms, streets, people. I'd give anything to be having brunch with Olden and his daughter and grandchildren, even to play bridge with Margaret Verey.*

"Phillip," she moaned. "Phillip's dead." Pain exploded within her, and Claire beat her fists against the bed. "Goddamn you, Phillip! I hate you, hate you!" Sobs choked her. Nausea rose in her throat and she staggered to the bathroom, where she lay curled up on the cold marble floor, her knees drawn to her chest, whimpering, "Phillip, I need you. I *need* you."

Moving to Florida had been a monumental folly.

12

The Proposal

Sunlight streamed into the bedroom window, and on awakening, Claire couldn't remember getting up from the bathroom floor, changing her nightgown, and getting under the covers. Feeling weak and hungry, Claire shuffled to the kitchen, where a cup of tea soon soothed her raspy throat.

Feeling unsubstantial, she stepped out onto her terrace and stared at the massive clouds changing shapes against a deep blue sky. She had read about Native American shamans who possessed the ability to shape-shift. If she could change her shape, what would she be?

Loneliness overwhelmed Claire and she sank onto a lounge chair, thinking of all the women in her building who might be sipping coffee with their husbands or chatting on the phone with friends, planning their days and evenings with other people.

That day and the next, Claire lay on her terrace and watched the clouds drift by. She idly counted boats as they glided past on the Intracoastal Waterway. When the sun baked the western side of the building, driving her inside, Claire drew the curtains across the glass sliding doors and watched reruns of *I Love Lucy, I Dream of Jeannie,* and *Golden Girls.* The days melted into nights, nights into days. Claire ate and slept little. She merely existed.

Sometime in that hazy limbo, the phone rang. She ignored it, then turned off the ringer and forgot to turn it back on. Three days later the need for people, for activity, for anything but her apartment, drove her to shower and dress. As she was preparing to leave the apartment, the doorbell rang and rang again.

To her shock, Olden Riverdale stood in the doorway. "Claire, my God, how are you?

I've tried for days to reach you. I was worried frantic. Are you all right? You're not; I can see it in your face." He took her hands.

Tears streamed down her face as she led him into her living room. "Olden, I almost drowned. I've been in a stupor these past days." She sat on the couch beside him and touched his hands and shoulder. "Dear, dear Olden. You knew something was wrong and you came. How can I ever thank you?"

"You never have to thank me," he said. "I was frantic when I couldn't get through to you."

Phillip used to say, "Pay attention to Olden. He's more often right than wrong." "Thank you, my friend, for coming. I needed you." Claire sat back and looked into his face. "I was about to go out. Have you had breakfast? Let's have brunch somewhere, shall we?"

Over eggs Benedict, Claire said, "I was drowning and I prayed to live, Olden. Me, praying—can you imagine?"

"Life-threatening situations will do that," he replied.

"I've been so depressed lately. I feel as if

there's no reason at all to be alive, and yet I fought for air. I wanted desperately to live." Claire reached across the table and rested her hands on his. "I'm so glad you came. Thank you."

Olden's face reddened. "Come home with me, Claire." When he lifted the coffee cup to his lips, his hand trembled.

"Is something wrong, Olden?"

He set down his cup. "Marry me, Claire. I know you don't love me the way I love you, but maybe you will in time. I'll take care of you. You could do whatever you want: keep the business, take on a partner, sell it, whatever. You shouldn't be here alone. You could have drowned, and I can't bear to think of that."

Claire's cheeks flushed as red as Olden's. "Olden, I love you as a dear friend, not as a husband. It wouldn't be fair to you."

Disappointment clouded his eyes.

She hated herself for hurting him, but the spark she'd felt for Jason wasn't there with Olden.

He leaned toward her, his tie barely missing the grits on his plate. "We could have separate bedrooms if you preferred," he whispered.

"You deserve better than that, Olden. I'll always treasure our friendship, but I can't marry you. I might never marry again." How odd the words sounded. Days ago, she'd been hell-bent on remarrying.

"If you ever—" He finished his coffee, his hand still shaking, then said, "If you ever feel differently, I'm here."

"Thank you, Olden. I appreciate your saying that so much."

Olden checked into the Boca Raton Hotel, and for the remainder of his visit he never spoke of his proposal. Claire expected to be bored with his company, but found that she actually enjoyed being with him. We have history together, she told herself, and I'm comfortable in ways I could not be with a stranger.

Olden knew Boca Raton and environs well. They drove north and strolled the boutique-laden streets of Palm Beach. They visited the Norton Gallery of Art in West Palm Beach, and on their return stopped at the Morikami Japanese Museum, where they walked through exquisite gardens.

They chatted about mutual acquaintances

in East Hampton. Lucille and Charlie Binder were divorcing; Charlie had another woman.

"Charlie's paying through the nose," Olden said.

"Perhaps he deserves it," Claire said.

They talked about Francine, Olden's daughter. "She's dating a young pharmacist who recently arrived in East Hampton."

"Do you like him?"

"I do, but more important, the boys like him." Olden related stories about his grandsons. "Georgie wanted a hole cut in his bedroom door and a tunnel built to crawl through. I was rather put off by that, but his mother had no problem, so Georgie has his tunnel. The deal is that once a week he's got to remove the tunnel and let the cleaning woman in."

"Kids get weird ideas," Claire said. "Remember when Paul was eleven and wore a sailor suit for a week, even slept in it? We ate fish that entire week, tuna sandwiches for lunch, fish for dinner, until Phillip put his foot down."

"I remember the week of the fish. That boy of yours was born with an affinity for the ocean. I wasn't surprised when he joined the navy."

A shadow crossed her face, and he fell silent. Then he asked, "What do you hear from Amanda? A beautiful girl, and so sweet. I've always been fond of her."

"She's in North Carolina now, and plans to marry the young man she's been living with. He's an architect."

"Congratulations. When's the wedding?"

"In the spring. She didn't give me a date."

Olden studied Claire for a moment. "You're going, aren't you?"

She sighed and nodded. "I guess so. How can I not go? It would only make matters between us worse. Tell you what—let's call Amanda! She'll be so pleased to hear from you." She clasped his hand. "Will you come with me to the wedding, Olden?"

He raked his teeth across his lower lip. "Well, if I'm invited."

They ate that evening at a waterside restaurant on the waterway in Deerfield Beach and watched the yachts glide by, their motors barely idling. People on board waved, and they waved back. When they returned to Claire's apartment, she phoned Amanda.

"Hello, Tom speaking," a friendly male voice said.

"Hello. This is Claire Bennett, Amanda's mother. I wonder if I might speak to her?"

"Why, yes. What a pleasure to talk to you. Amanda's right here. Let me get her." His accent was that of a Southerner who had lived away from the South for many years.

After a long pause, Amanda came on the phone. "Hello, Mother?"

Claire's palms sweated. *Damn,* she thought, feeling jittery. "I have someone here who wants to say hello, Amanda." She handed the phone to Olden.

"Sweetheart," Olden said. "How are you?" His eyes were bright as he listened. "Oh, I know, you're all grown-up, but you'll always be sweetheart to me." He laughed and settled into a chair, crossing one leg over the other. "No, I haven't moved to Florida. I'm visiting your mother, trying to talk her into coming back home." A pause, then, "No. She's determined to stay here."

Claire plucked a dead leaf from a plant she had neglected to water and tried to quell her sense of expectancy. Or was it hope that, mollified by having spoken to Olden, Amanda would speak to her, and that their communication would be as easy and loving as Olden's and Amanda's.

"Well, sweetheart, your mother has coffee for us." Olden listened for a moment. "Of course I'll come, I'd love to. What? That would be an honor. A great honor." He put both feet flat on the floor and sat straighter in the chair.

When he hung up the phone, Claire's heart sank. Amanda had not asked to talk to her.

"Amanda asked me to give her away," Olden said.

"Why, that's wonderful! You will, won't you? Phillip would be so pleased, as I am."

"I told Amanda I'd be honored." He rubbed his hands together. "Looks like I'll be your escort to the wedding."

Farther down the waterway, the Fortieth Street Bridge lowered. A ketch with a single mast had passed below, heading south. "That's what they opened the bridge for?" Olden asked. "One boat?"

"Yes. Imagine holding up so many cars while letting one boat through. You'd think they'd make it wait until there were several," Claire said.

"They need a new bridge, a higher one." Olden picked up the thread of their conversation.

"I'm really honored Amanda asked me to stand in for her father."

"Who else would she ask? You've been like a favorite uncle all these years. Did Amanda say when the wedding was?"

"April eighteenth or the twenty-first. She's going to let me know. Amanda says they've planned an outdoor wedding at his father's place, and that's a nice time of year. She wants me to wear a suit, not a tux. What do you think: gray, blue, or brown?"

Claire stiffened. "What kind of hippie wedding is my daughter planning?" Giving birth to a daughter had delighted her, and over the years she had dreamed of Amanda's wedding at the Episcopalian church in the village. Not that they attended church, but Phillip had insisted that they join, especially as they contributed funds for a glorious stained-glass window. In Claire's dream wedding, there would be a choir and a dozen bridesmaids. Amanda would be exquisite in satin and lace as her father walked her down the aisle.

But none of that would ever be. Phillip was gone, and Olden would give Amanda away. Claire's high heels would sink into grass and dirt, and the smell of manure would probably fill her nostrils. They would be lucky if it did not rain.

Olden seemed to read her mind. "You're disappointed. I'm sorry. But you can't make this decision for her, or control her choice of a mate." He patted her arm. "Just go with it, Claire. It's Amanda's wedding; make her happy. Now tell me, what color suit shall I bring? What will you wear, do you think? I want us to match."

Claire swallowed. "You're telling me to stop thinking of myself, aren't you, Olden?"

"Your words, Claire, but worth giving some thought to."

After she dropped him at the airport and drove away, Claire immediately missed Olden. It was then that she realized that Jason Aronson had not called in these many days. Restless, and dreading the empty apartment awaiting her, Claire drove to Mizner Plaza to a restaurant where she sometimes stopped for coffee. It was dim inside, paneled in dark wood like an English pub, and as she was just finishing her coffee she saw Jason and a dark-haired woman leaning across their table toward each other, their hands touching, their eyes locked, totally oblivious to anyone or anything.

A hard knot of rejection and disappointment twisted in Claire's belly. She left and sat on a bench in the park, trying to gain some perspective. Jason had made it quite clear that he wanted a Jewish woman who would keep a kosher kitchen. Her affair with him, the terrific sex they'd had, had been merely a way station in her quest for the right man. Her heart softened, then, and she smiled. He had been great for her ego, and had transitioned her from her celibate state of widowhood.

The bench vibrated as someone sat beside her. Claire stiffened and held her handbag closer.

A hand touched her arm. "Claire, where have you been? I phoned for days," Jason said.

"I had out-of-town guests. For a few days, the ringer on the phone was off. You didn't leave a message."

"I'm sorry," he said. "How have you been?"

"Busy," she said.

"Terrific. I wanted to tell you, I've met someone."

"Someone who can cook kosher, I hope?"

He smiled and nodded. "We met at synagogue. I know it's soon, but . . ."

Ten days ago we were making love, Claire thought. "I know how lonely it's been since your wife died. I'm happy for you."

"What you and I had was very special, Claire. I thank you for our week together."

She looked away, not wanting him to see the tears forming in her eyes. "Thank me?"

"Yes. You were the first since my wife died. I didn't know if I could perform, and you showed me that I could. If you ever need anything, Claire, please call. I'll always remember you."

Claire smiled genuinely. It had been shared enjoyment and ego gratification. "It was great for me, too, and I'll always remember you as well."

The woman came out of a store, looked around, shaded her eyes, saw them, and approached. Jason rose to leave. "Be well and happy," he said.

"You, too." Claire gathered up her purse and strolled casually across the street toward the parking garage.

That night, Claire dreamed that she stood alongside Olden high on a hill and watched waves crash against a rocky coast. They were dressed for Amanda's wedding, he in a tux, she in a pale blue gown, and Claire jolted awake, deeply worried that they would be late for the wedding.

13

And the Band Played On

After Olden left, the weeks slipped by. In February and early March, unusually cold winds gathered the ocean in virile arms and hurled huge waves against the beach with brutal force. Seashore erosion topped the local news. One blustery day in mid-March, Claire stood at the top of what was left of a dune and watched the ocean tear at the shore, reducing the width of the beach.

Deeply saddened, she turned from the ocean with a shiver and returned to her apartment. There she turned on the heat for the first time since moving to Florida. She missed having a fireplace, and mentally retraced each room and the furnishings of her spacious home in East Hampton. The following day the sun shone, the temperature rose, and life resumed its meaningless pattern.

Olden had offered Claire a return to the past, to familiar things and people. Jason had signified the possibility of change, the future as she envisioned it. To realize that future, however, she must reach out and begin to invest in the community.

The cultural season was in full swing. Claire had purchased season tickets to the Caldwell Playhouse but had attended only half of the plays. She joined her condo neighbors on a bus to the Fort Lauderdale Center for the Performing Arts for a stunning performance of the opera *Aïda*. As the bus filled with older, single women—many of whose faces were lined with wrinkles—Claire stood on the sidelines, and when she descended from the bus and walked into the theater she walked fast, hoping not to be associated with the cluster of chattering, white-haired women.

Then Claire finally called Sarah Slayer, who turned out to be cultured, educated, a person with a great sense of humor, and a gardener. Her terrace overlooked the waterway and brimmed with potted plants. Claire joined Sarah for a salad at her home; Sarah visited with Claire for cocktails, and then for cake and coffee on the terrace.

"My husband Jim was a stockbroker. He literally worked himself to death," Sarah told Claire. "Luckily, I've always had a life of my own. Besides my work, I'm a master gardener. I volunteer at the arboretum's nursery one day a week."

"What's a master gardener?"

"You take a course where they teach you all about plants, soils, fertilizers, plant diseases, bugs, and so on, and in return you volunteer at one of their projects. I chose to work at the plant nursery, but I could have been a phone counselor advising people who call in about fertilizers, pruning, and so on. Are you a gardener?"

Claire wiggled her thumbs. "Brown thumbs."

Sarah nodded. "I'm also membership chair at the Boca Raton Museum of Art. Have you joined yet?"

"I plan to."

"Oh, you must. I work there on Wednesdays, and we're a nice bunch of folks. With your background you'd be a terrific docent, or there are fund-raising projects. You'd be incredible, such an asset."

Claire had told Sarah about her background and that she and Phillip had traveled extensively. Here was someone who appreciated her skills and talents, who could open doors for her. "I'll be there on Wednesday," she replied.

Typical of the Mizner style, the Boca Raton Museum of Art was painted pink, and with its rounded windows and soft lines, it fit into the overall plan of Mizner Plaza. Inside the paintings and sculptures were displayed with the sophistication one would find in New York City. Claire joined the museum and checked the box indicating her interest in special projects. She would let Sarah tell them about her background; she would not boast. At last, her quest for the "right" man was under way! She received an invitation to the opening of a Georgia O'Keefe exhibit at the museum, and since Sarah had been called out of town due to a crisis with one of her children, Claire decided to go alone.

The O'Keefe exhibit generated great excitement; buses of visitors from Fort Lauderdale, Pompano, West Palm Beach, and Miami were lined up along Mizner Plaza and in the parking lot when Claire arrived.

The O'Keefe canvases filled five rooms.

Head high, ignoring the pounding of her heart, Claire meandered from room to room. Intent on a painting of a huge flower exploding from a canvas, she stepped back and inadvertently bumped into a man. He caught her arm, steadied her, and introduced himself as Fred Austerman.

"I'm Claire Bennett," she replied. "I am so very sorry."

"Nothing to be concerned about." He raised his eyebrows. "I've never seen you at one of our openings, and I'm a connoisseur of both art and beautiful women."

He was tall, with thick graying hair and dark, penetrating eyes. *A ladies' man,* Claire thought. *Stay clear of him.*

"Shall we have a look at the rest of the exhibit?" He took her arm and guided her toward the next canvas.

Instinct warned against him, yet, relieved not to be alone, she allowed him to conduct her into another room where four large desert scenes covered the walls.

"I tried to buy that painting several years ago," he said, pointing to one of them. "Another buyer, an old friend and rival, got to it first. I arranged its loan to our museum for this exhibit."

"You're a collector, then?"

"I pride myself on having a good eye. I've picked up a painting or two that has become quite valuable."

"Georgia O'Keefe?" she asked.

"Yes, two of them, actually. I admire her work—it's fierce in its intensity, filled with passion for the landscape." His eyes portrayed their own fierce intensity, and Claire felt the hairs on her arms bristle.

They circumnavigated the room. The empty eye sockets of a cow's skull stared down from a canvas. Fred leaned toward her, his face inches from hers. His proximity discomfited her, and she stepped back.

"Such purity and originality of style," he said. "I've always admired O' Keefe's courage, combining such precise and formal treatment of the landscape with flowers and especially animal skulls."

Claire had no comment; her taste ran to the French Impressionists. "Are you in the art business?"

"Not really. I'm retired. I dabble. If I happen across some exciting new artist, I pass the word along to the right people. Do you paint?"

Claire laughed. "No. I don't." She wanted

to ask Fred who these right people were and found herself saying, "My husband was an antiques dealer in East Hampton. We traveled and purchased for select customers." Why was she playing one-upmanship with this creepy man?

"Really? What's the name of the business?" Fred studied her with new interest.

"Antiques Unlimited."

"Phillip Bennett? I've heard of him. That's your husband? But you said *was*—has he passed away?" His eyes darted to her finger, where her gold wedding band marked her as married.

Claire's heart did not tumble. It *was* getting easier to say, "Phillip died a little over two years ago. We ran the business together."

"His reputation as a top-notch antiques dealer lives on, however. What became of the business?"

"I closed it. It's for sale, in the hands of a very good friend."

Greed and a cunning that revolted her gleamed in his eyes.

"Well, I just might have a buyer for you," Fred said.

Not you, she thought.

Fred gripped her arm in a way that brooked no argument and guided her along a thickly carpeted hall, which opened to a reception room that was splendid with crystal chandeliers and beautifully decorated tables piled high with food and drink. Women in stunning cocktail dresses chatted with men in tuxedoes. Claire suddenly felt inadequately attired in simple black with pearls, since every turn of a head or flick of a wrist made another woman's diamond earrings or bracelet sparkle in the light from the chandeliers.

"Caviar?" Fred pointed to the table.

Claire nodded and bent to cover a cracker with the minute black pearls.

"What will you drink?"

"Ginger ale."

"Recovering?"

She understood his question. "No. I've never liked the taste of liquor, or beer, or even wine."

"I'm a recovering alcoholic," he said. "Drinking just about killed me, and AA saved my life. I wouldn't miss my weekly meeting, even after all these years."

At that moment, Claire noticed a tall, fair-haired man across the room. He stood with his back to a wall, a glass in hand. His eyes swept the room as if searching for someone. His eyes met hers, and he smiled.

"I really must be going." Claire extended her hand. "It was a pleasure meeting you."

"Not so fast, little lady." Fred barred her way. He fished in his vest pocket, extracted a card, pressed it into her hand, and leaned close. Claire stepped back. "Your card?" he asked, eyebrows arched.

"I haven't any with me."

"I'd like to take you to dinner at my club," Fred said. "It's on the ocean. Very pleasant, if I say so myself. Excellent cuisine! Excellent music, too."

A club she might like to join? Instinct warned against it, yet she asked, "What day did you have in mind?"

"How about next Sunday? I'll pick you up about seven? Where do you live?"

Claire weighed his invitation against the prospect of a lonely Sunday evening on her terrace, and she nodded and gave him her address, which he wrote on the back of another of his cards. "I'll take my car and follow you," she said.

His expression indicated that he found her statement peculiar, even ludicrous, but he nodded and smiled. "Whatever you want."

Then he bowed slightly, a sardonic smile on his face.

Claire wanted to retract her acceptance.

"Seven it is, then, little lady."

She was not little, and hated his patronizing tone. She disliked him, but what harm could one dinner do? "Until next Sunday."

Claire left the museum and headed down the brightly lit street toward her car. A policeman standing on the curb nodded at her. Behind her she heard footsteps, and turned. The attractive man from the museum stepped off the curb and placed his hand on the hood of the car parked next to hers.

"What luck," he said, smiling at her. "Destiny." Before she could reply, or open her car door, he said, "I'm Andrew Allenby, attaché with the British ambassador."

His accent was British and refined.

"The ambassador couldn't attend this evening, so I came to represent him. I haven't much interest in art, to be honest." He spoke with quick, clipped words as if time was of the essence. "I saw you at the reception and noticed the gentleman hovering. Straightaway, I had the impulse to charge over and rescue you. You wanted to be rescued, am I correct?"

She laughed. "You're most astute. I prayed to be rescued."

"Would you honor me by having a night-cap with me?"

"Now?" she asked.

"Why not? It's only half past nine o' clock."

"I don't drink, but I'd enjoy dessert or a cup of tea."

"There's a French restaurant not far from here, and their pâtisseries are superb. My car or yours?"

"I'll follow you," she said.

The restaurant proved intimate and charming. When the waiter appeared with a tray of mouthwatering desserts, Claire selected a crème caramel and ordered tea, and was pleased when it was served in a delicate china cup, as tea should be served. Andrew chose a crusty shell, stuffed with chocolate cream and a cup of good, strong coffee.

"How long have you been in America?" she asked.

"Two years in Washington. The ambassador and his family are vacationing at the Boca Raton Hotel."

"So you'll be leaving soon?"

"Regretfully so." He lifted his cup as if to

toast her. "I hope you are not offended that I followed you from the gallery."

She shook her head. "I didn't know you'd followed me, but I'm glad you did." He was beautiful with a fine classic face, wide shoulders, and strong, square wrists. In the background, soft music played. She swayed slightly in her chair to the music. "Do you like to dance?"

"I adore dancing," Andrew said. "Would you accompany me to the hotel? There's dancing in the ballroom until midnight."

Claire laughed lightly. "What happens at midnight?"

"At midnight the magic begins. There's a full moon—magnificent on the water. I'd be honored if you'd share it with me."

Claire was captivated, although Andrew was clearly years younger than herself. She felt free and lighthearted and flattered that he was interested in her.

"I'd love to share it with you," she replied.

They danced until the musicians packed up their instruments and departed. Then Andrew took her hand and led her out onto a veranda overlooking the water. "We could drive over to the inlet," he said.

"Where is it?"

"Not far, across A1A. We could walk, but I'd rather not this time of night."

They walked in silence to his car, and minutes later crossed A1A and parked on a sandy spit of land. Moonlight rode ripples of water along a golden pathway to their feet at the shoreline. Andrew extracted a blanket from his trunk, from beneath a cooler, snorkel, and flippers. He shook it vigorously and spread it on the sandy earth below a cluster of trees.

"Sit, fair lady."

They sat, and she did not protest when he kissed her, but let that marvelous giddy feeling of youth envelop her. Andrew removed his jacket, rolled it, and laid her back until her head rested upon it. *What am I doing? Who cares? I'm answerable only to myself, and I want him.*

In the privacy of the trees, Andrew removed Claire's clothing and then his own. Moonbeams filtered through the leaves, casting patterns on his chest and arms, and Claire surrendered fully to the moment.

"You're so beautiful," he said. "Have you ever bathed in moonlight?"

"You mean at the beach, swimming?"

"No. I mean to stand naked in the light of the full moon."

A dreamy look came into Claire's eyes. "I never have."

He kissed her eyes, mouth, and neck, and when he lowered his lips to her breasts, she shivered.

"You're cold. Let me warm you." His long naked limbs covered hers, warming her body. Claire wasn't certain if the thunder in her ears emanated from their mutual pleasure or from the ocean crashing against the rock-lined shore. She floated.

After a time, he whispered, "Come, put the blanket over your shoulders and stand with me in the moonlight."

She smiled up at him, and he helped her to her feet. Hand in hand, they strolled to the edge of the vast ocean. In the distance, a speck of light signaled a lone ship. Claire wondered about the vessel's destination, and if a sailor on watch on deck at this very moment enjoyed the moonlight with them.

"Be naked. Bathe in moonlight." Andrew's voice sounded far away, as if in a dream. The blanket puddled at her feet. She looked at him, a golden god in his nakedness, and she his goddess.

"Breathe," Andrew said. "Close your eyes and breathe deeply."

Claire breathed. Air filled her lungs; her belly extended.

"Lift your arms to the sky," he instructed.

Mesmerized by the beauty of the night, Claire raised her arms. She tilted her head back and exhaled, then filled herself with fresh cool air again. Moonlight draped her body. She felt taller, wider, *more*, in every way than she had been a moment ago.

"Did you feel that tingling sensation?" Andrew asked. "It warms you, and makes you feel as if you can do anything."

She didn't feel quite that way, but loved the novelty of it, the loveliness of the man beside her.

"Can you see the woman in the moon?" he asked.

"Not a man in the moon?"

"No, look closely. See how tall the woman is: she's got long, streaming hair and she's carrying what seems to be a bundle of sticks on her shoulder. In ancient times, men worshiped the moon as a goddess. Can you imagine what it must have been like for early man, sitting in the mouth of his cave watching the stars move across the sky and the moon change shape, disappear and reappear? No wonder they associated her with fertility, planting, and the harvest."

Claire struggled to see the woman in the moon, but could not. A breeze made her shiver, and she bent to retrieve the blanket and cover herself.

"You're cold. I'm sorry," he said. "We should leave."

They drove back to the hotel parking lot, and he stood next to her car. "Thank you for a marvelous evening," he whispered, then bent and kissed her softly on her lips. "I loved being with you, Claire. I won't forget you." Then he turned and walked toward the hotel.

The ambassador and his entourage left Boca Raton the following morning, and Claire never heard from or saw Andrew again. He had gifted her not only with a new perspective on the moon, but had also enhanced her pride in her body and her confidence that she could and would attract the right man.

14

Dinner With Fred

On Sunday morning after breakfast on her terrace, she studied Fred's card, torn between dislike for the man and her dread of a long, empty evening at home. Why was she fussing about this? How important could one dinner be? She'd never have to see the man again, and what could possibly happen? They'd be in a restaurant with other people. Claire picked up the phone several times to cancel and then decided not to.

Wishing to appear staid and unapproachable, Claire selected a deep blue linen dress with a mandarin collar and a row of tiny pearl buttons down the front. She pulled her hair into a severe bun at the nape of her neck and chose simple pearl earrings to complete her toilette.

On the dot of seven, her doorman, Alex, buzzed and informed her that a gentleman was waiting. Fred greeted her with a smile and guided her to his Porsche.

"I'm taking my own car," she said, indicating the Volvo parked alongside.

"That's hardly necessary; it's such a short way."

She shook her head and pulled her keys from her small black evening bag. "I'll follow you."

They headed north on A1A. Whenever the barrier of trees and shrubs permitted a view of moonlight on the water, Claire thought of Andrew with delight and regret that he had vanished from her life.

Fred's Porsche turned into a driveway lined with royal palms. Instantly a valet materialized and accepted their car keys. Inside the dining room, the maître d' hastened to greet them.

"Good evening, Mr. Austerman." The maître d' nodded at her. "Madam."

"Table for two at the window, Roger."

Roger's palm closed over the folded bill

Fred handed him. "Of course, Mr. Auster-man." He preceded them across the dining room to the huge wall of windows. As they walked, the normalcy of the low hum of con-trolled voices, the light clink of silver on china, the soft background music, reduced Claire's apprehension.

The room cantilevered over the ocean. "It must be quite a job keeping all this glass free of salt spray," Claire said, more to herself than to Fred.

"The proletariat work to serve our plea-sure."

"An elitist attitude," she replied, liking him even less.

Fred ignored her remark and opened his menu. "The veal is superb, as is the tender-loin of pork."

Claire scrutinized the menu. "The veal sounds good," she said.

Since neither of them drank hard liquor, Fred ordered a bottle of sparkling cider. When the champagne bottle nesting in ice arrived and the waiter poured the bubbly liquid into fluted glasses, she looked at him, perplexed.

"We don't want to appear juvenile, so it's a cider-filled champagne bottle," Fred said. His eyes bored into her. "Now, tell me about your antiques business. Who's managing it in your absence?"

She shrugged. "I've closed the business. Better that than dealing with a long-distance manager."

"True enough," he replied. "But a closed business is easily forgotten, and could decrease in value."

"I'll take my chances," she replied.

The tables at the windows filled rapidly. Fred nodded and greeted several people, but no one approached their table and he introduced her to no one. Claire turned her attention to the beach.

In the twilight, as the tide retreated, skinny-legged birds pecked their dinners from the shoreline. The darkening sky leached the blues from the ocean, leaving it gray and forbidding, and a white strand of beach stretched south around a curve and was lost to sight.

"Fine view isn't it?" Fred asked.

"Indeed it is." The thin line of his mouth, the cynicism and steely hardness she read in his eyes, disturbed her, even though his smile softened his features. The smile seemed calculated, meted out.

"Do you have children, grandchildren?" she asked.

"I do, but they live in Germany. My daughter's husband is with the Foreign Service."

"Do you see them often?"

"No. Not very often."

"Are you of German ancestry?" Claire asked.

"Yes. My grandparents were German. I'm third generation. They spoke English badly. I learned barely enough German to be able to talk with them. But that's all the past; we live in the present. How do you like Florida?"

"When I hear about a storm and the snow piled up on the East Coast, I'm glad to be here, but there are times when I miss not having familiar things about me."

"You can always visit East Hampton. Florida can be whatever you want it to be: a dynamic, exciting place with dynamic and exciting people, or slow and laid-back. Which do you prefer?"

"To date, my life here's been rather on the slow side."

"It doesn't have to be." He turned to the sea and pointed out a passing ship lit up like a carnival. "Now, they're having a good time." He reached for her glass, topped it off, and handed her the drink. "I could make your life exciting."

The intensity and arrogance in his dark eyes made Claire uncomfortable, and she did not reply.

"Your boring life here," he repeated. "I can help make it exciting."

She raised her eyebrows. "I said slow and laid-back, not boring."

"I could introduce you to the right people—people who buy antiques and original art, people who hop a plane to Paris or London for a concert, or to Majorca for a weekend. People who know how to enjoy and relax, you understand?" He brought two fingers to his lips, mimicking a smoker.

"You mean drugs?"

He laughed and wagged a finger at her. "Only for pleasure, my dear, only for pleasure."

Claire felt in over her head. After a hard day's work and an early dinner, she and Phillip might take a short stroll or settle in to watch TV, and were in bed by eleven. They never drank and neither of them smoked.

With great flourish, the waiter delivered their meal and departed.

"Perhaps after dinner we can go to my place and relax," he suggested.

Claire began to say no, but caught herself.

After dinner she would shake his hand, thank him, and have the valet bring her car. In silence, she concentrated on her meal. The veal was delicious, but the cider left an odd taste in her mouth. The moon appeared on the horizon and for a moment, remembering Andrew, Claire closed her eyes and breathed deeply.

"Is something wrong?" Fred asked.

Opening her eyes, she saw that he was studying her intently. "No. Nothing." She hoped he did not sense her anxiety. "I'm just tired. I went through Spanish River Park today. I'd never seen banyan trees as large as those. Have you been?"

"No. The parks here don't interest me—not after Versailles and the grand parks of Europe. You must agree they are of a much higher quality there."

"They're different, but no less beautiful," Claire responded.

His next words shocked her. "You went somewhere after you left the museum." Fred reached for a roll and pressed the butter so firmly into its soft center that the roll crumbled in his hand. He seemed to catch himself then, smiled at her, and placed the knife and roll on a plate. "You went dancing."

A shiver raced through her. Claire set her fork down, pushed her plate away, and placed her napkin on the table. I hardly think it's any of your business what I do, or with whom."

"Forgive me, little lady. I'm a jealous man." His smile did not reach his eyes.

"Jealous? We hardly know each other. A brief meeting at an art museum opening certainly doesn't give you the right to spy on me or to question me." Claire pushed back her chair and rose from the table. "Thank you for dinner, but I must leave now." She raised her brows. "Please don't follow me."

Head aching and uncertain of her balance, Claire did her best to walk erect through the dining room and foyer. Later, she would recall stopping to ask the maître d' why the palms in the foyer were swaying and to request her car.

15

The Day After

Sunshine warmed Claire's cheek. She opened her eyes then quickly closed them as pain shot through them and lodged at the back of her head. She opened her eyes again to assure herself that she was indeed in her own bed, in her room, in her condo—for she had no memory of driving home, of coming upstairs and getting into bed.

The red light on the bedside answering machine blinked in the most irritating fashion. Claire groaned, pressed her hand to her forehead, leaned across the pillows, and pushed the button.

"Hi, little lady. Did you have as good a time

as I did last night? You were terrific. Sorry I tore your dress. Let's do it again soon."

Fred's voice made her skin crawl, and Claire clutched her stomach. She felt as if she'd been kicked by a mule. What had happened? Why couldn't she remember? Her arms and back ached. And what did he mean, he tore her dress?

Claire managed to reach the bathroom before retching. In the mirror, red marks stood out on her neck, and when she reached for her toothbrush, she was horrified to see bruise marks on her arm.

Cold fear washed over her. Something terrible had clearly happened. It seemed that since coming to Florida, she had lost her ability to think clearly or to make wise choices, and now she couldn't remember what had taken place just the night before.

Claire staggered from the bathroom, through her bedroom and living room, to the front door. The chain hung loose and the door, to her great distress, was unlocked. With trembling fingers, she locked and bolted it, then checked all her closets. With great effort, she kneeled and peered under her bed. No one was there.

She sat for a long time with her head in

her hands. She *must* remember. But her memories of last night ended when she had walked from the dining room into the foyer of the club. The palm trees had swayed; she did remember that. Had there been an earthquake? Had she fallen or fainted? Fred must have driven her home, and had he bribed Alex, her doorman, as he had the maître d' at the club?

Claire looked around. Sure enough her dress lay on the floor behind a chair. She picked it up. Buttons were missing and there was a long tear along the back. Dear God in heaven—the cider! Had Fred drugged her? Nauseated and with rising panic, Claire barely made it back to the bathroom.

She rarely took medication. One Tylenol relieved pain and put her to sleep. The smallest dose of whatever Fred might have slipped into her food or drink would have knocked her out.

Lathering with soap and scrubbing herself thoroughly in the shower did nothing to relieve the anxiety, the shame, the rage roiling in the pit of her stomach, nor did rubbing her body vigorously with a towel wipe away the sense of being violated.

Even after dressing in terry cloth sweats

with a turtleneck top, Claire felt naked. She walked with faltering steps into the living room and sank onto the couch. Everything felt skewed. Air! She needed fresh air.

But out on her terrace, the light stung her eyes and her head pounded. Fear and the enormity of her aloneness threatened to crush her. She had no friends here; no one to call, to turn to. Only Olden, who was far away on Long Island, and she could never tell him she had been so foolish as to ignore her instincts and what might have occurred.

Had Sarah Slayer returned? Claire stepped inside, reached for the phone, and stopped. She hardly knew Sarah. Shame overwhelmed her. She could never confide something as personal as this to anyone.

A cup of hot tea did nothing to calm her, nor did a hot bath, although after a while she was able to reassure herself that whatever had happened, at least she was home and not seriously hurt.

Of two things she was certain: Fred Austerman had drugged her, and he must have attempted to violate her. The bruises indicated that she had resisted, but all details eluded her.

When the phone rang, Claire froze. The ringing stopped before the machine picked up. She must get information, but from whom? Maybe the doorman had heard or seen something. She would have to swallow her pride and ask him. It was after one P.M. so Alex, who worked the late shift, would have arrived.

He *was* there, and from the embarrassed way he looked at her and quickly away, he clearly knew something. But would he tell her? Perhaps, if she told him the absolute truth.

"Alex," she began. "This is very hard for me."

He nodded, his eyes kind.

"I accepted a date with a man I met at the museum. We went for dinner at his club in Delray last night. I was somewhat apprehensive about going, but I went." This was so hard, so humiliating. "We had cider that tasted odd, and I had veal for dinner. I had driven my car, and when I began to feel woozy, I left. That's all I remember. I woke up this morning with bruises on my arm and feeling as if I had been drugged or drunk, but I do not drink. Can you help me fill in the blanks? Did you see or hear anything?"

"I'm sorry, Mrs. Bennett; I am sure it was a most unpleasant experience. It was for me."

"What happened? Please tell me." She was crying now, and he led her into his small office, where a TV monitor recorded the goings and comings of anyone in the lobby. He offered her a seat in his swivel chair and took the straight one.

"I was sitting right where you are at eleven last night. I saw you stagger into the lobby. I assumed you had had a tad too much to drink, but then a man followed you to the elevator, grabbed you and tried to kiss you. You slapped him, tried to fight him, but he shoved you into the elevator. I realized something was amiss, and I took the service elevator up to the seventh floor. When I got there, I heard you screaming, 'No! Leave me alone!' and him laughing. The door to your apartment was unlocked." He paused and his shoulders rose, as did his chin. "I pulled my gun from its holster, then I slammed open the door. That man had you on the floor and was tearing at your clothes. He saw me and jumped up fast. That's when your dress tore. He raced out of there, pronto. I helped you to your bed and left you sleeping. I'm deeply sorry you were put through such a terrible experience. How do you feel, Mrs. Bennett? Should you see a doctor for your bruises?"

Tears rolled down Claire's cheeks. "I don't know what to say." She blew her nose on the tissue he offered her, and tried to regain some composure. "I don't drink, Alex. I never have. Something was in that cider he ordered, or in the food. He knew the maître d' well and tipped him handsomely when we arrived. I don't even remember driving home."

"You didn't, Mrs. Bennett. Your car is not in its place or anywhere in our lot. I think perhaps you could not drive."

Claire's hands covered her face. "He must have driven me home. I can't thank you enough for what you did for me, Alex. God knows what you saved me from. I'm so humiliated and so sorry to have put you through this." Claire gave him a rueful smile. "It's certainly not your job."

"On this job, one never knows what one may be called upon to witness"—he pointed at the monitor—"or to do. I'm glad I could be of help to you."

Claire returned to her apartment, resolved to leave today. But for where? East Hampton? Where would she stay? She'd been a fool to sell her house.

Then she thought of her daughter. Would Amanda welcome her? Maybe. She certainly couldn't tell her daughter what had happened, how foolish she had been; she would just have to arrive unannounced. Amanda wouldn't turn her away.

Yes, she'd go to North Carolina. She'd rent a place in that Weaver-something town and hide like a wounded animal until spring. Amanda needn't even know that she was in the area, and perhaps by April she'd have recovered sufficiently to face her daughter and the wedding.

Claire hauled out a suitcase and began to pack haphazardly; she'd buy anything else she needed when she got there. When the suitcase was overflowing, she zipped it closed.

Action brought a sense of calm and control, the first she'd felt since awakening. Claire wrote checks for the next three months, estimating the cost of electric, phone, and credit card bills, and added a hundred dollars to each as a safety measure. She owned her apartment outright, as well as her car. Her car! It was at the club. She would give Alex the spare keys, and pay him for picking it up and bringing it here. She didn't want to take a chance on someone at the club seeing her and reporting back to Fred; he might have connections and have her followed. She'd buy a new car and head north right away. She wrote Alex a check and a note thanking him for his kindness.

Claire looked around. She wanted to take her Danish Bing and Grøndahl figurines of Balinese dancers, her Waterford crystal candlesticks, and a sterling silver water pitcher. It was ridiculous, craving material things at a time like this. Or was it? She was driving, not flying. Claire hauled out another suitcase, wrapped the items she cherished in towels, and wedged them between other towels to cushion them. Later she would return, perhaps with Olden, and clean out the place. Until then, she would arrange to have the locks on her door changed.

Claire reached for the phone to call Renee, her former Realtor. When she knew what she wanted to do, after she and Olden emptied the apartment, she would ask Renee to list it for sale.

Renee's phone rang four times.

"I am so sorry to bother you," Claire said. "I have an emergency and I'm leaving in a few minutes. I'll leave my keys with the doorman. Sometime today, would you pick them up, and have my locks changed?"

"My God," Renee said, "you sound upset. What's happened?"

"It's my daughter. She needs me. It's serious."

"I am so sorry and hope she'll be all right. Yes, I'll take care of getting the locks changed. Do you need a ride to the airport?"

"No. I'm driving." That didn't sound right, if she was traveling to an emergency. Claire shrugged as she hung up. She had no destination; rest and time to digest what had happened were what she needed.

Claire called a cab. She dragged the heavy suitcases to the elevator and, once downstairs, gave the envelope addressed to Renee Ormon to Alex. She then pressed the envelope addressed to him into his hand. He resisted, but she insisted. "You have been more than kind. Please, Alex, don't embarrass me by refusing."

Alex nodded and carried her luggage to the cab. "I wish you the best," he said.

"And you, too. Again, thank you."

The cab dropped her at a Ford dealer, where Claire purchased a Taurus. Within an hour, she was headed north on highway I-95.

The trucks and cars crawled along, squeezing into one lane at several construction sites. Impatient, Claire gripped the steering wheel and tried to relax. Four hours later, unable to keep her eyelids open, she pulled off the highway and found a motel on the ocean near Melbourne.

16

Heading North

Claire awakened disoriented and uncertain of her surroundings, and she realized that she was in a motel room. As memory flooded back, anguish speared her. Burning with shame and anger, she buried her head in the pillow and sobbed. Finally, drying her eyes, she rose, walked to the window, and opened the curtains. Bright sunlight assaulted her. The beach here was wider and flatter than at Boca Raton. Seaweed lay in drifts on the sand, and terns pecked for food along the shoreline.

Claire slumped into a chair, then returned to bed and fell asleep again. A loud rapping at the door awakened her, then a female voice with a thick Spanish accent said, "Señora? Sorry I wake you up."

Claire rolled over and stared at the supply cart filled with towels, toilet paper, and cleaning products. A heavyset, olive-skinned woman stood beside it.

"You no answer knock," the woman said as she pulled her cart back toward the door.

"Wait," Claire called. She had taken Spanish lessons the year she and Phillip had gone to Spain, and searched her memory for a word or two. "Wait, *un momento.*"

The woman stopped. *"Sí, señora?"* This was followed by a barrage of words that were incomprehensible to Claire.

"No comprendo." Claire shook her head. She beckoned the woman, who walked slowly toward the bed. *"Café, por favor?"* Claire made the motion of drinking.

"Sí, sí." The woman turned and left the room.

Her head aching, Claire lay back. She needed something to eat—a cup of coffee, a glass of juice, a roll and butter. Why had she tried to ask the cleaning woman for food, instead of calling the front desk? Claire reached for the phone by the bed and dialed 0.

"Front desk," the crisp male voice said.

"I'm not feeling very well. I wonder if you have anyone you can send to room . . ." She paused, unsure of the room number. "This is Mrs. Bennett. I can't remember the number of the room. Can you find it?"

"Just a moment, please."

Then she heard another man's deep voice. "May I help you?"

"Yes. This is Mrs. Phillip Bennett. I checked in last night. I'm not feeling well, and I need a cup of coffee and a glass of juice. Is that possible?"

"Of course. I have Luscita right here; she was trying to explain. I'll have her bring it right up."

"Thank you." Several minutes later came a light knock, the sound of the key slipping into the lock, and Luscita's voice identifying herself. The woman carried a small tray with a white Styrofoam cup of coffee, several packets of cream and sugar, and a small plastic glass with orange juice.

"*Gracias.*" Claire dug for her purse under the clothing thrown on a chair, and moments later a smiling Luscita departed room 204 with a five-dollar tip in her pocket.

The coffee and juice refreshed Claire and eased her headache. Checkout was at eleven, so there was time for a short stroll on the beach. Maybe the fresh air would help clear her mind.

Claire never tired of beaches. The sand differed in color from one beach to another, sometimes white, sometimes cream, sometimes yellow, and it differed in texture from as rough and grainy as rock salt to as soft and pliant as powder. This day, a wide ribbon of pale cream sand reflected the morning light, and the ocean beyond shifted from shades of gray in the distance to bands of blue-green close to shore.

Barefoot, Claire shared the beach with terns who scuttled along, gobbling tiny creatures deposited by the retreating waves.

The ocean lay placid and peaceful, hiding its potential for fury. She remembered her sadness while watching the storm devastate the beach in Boca Raton. Humans built dams that harnessed millions of tons of water, yet they couldn't stop the awesome power of an ocean roaring out of control. Some people are like the ocean, she thought. They appeared calm, their veneer covering God knows what kind of violence or evil.

She remembered Fred and shuddered,

then thought about Phillip. He had visited their doctor for his annual physical and been pronounced in perfect health. At three the next afternoon, he had complained of indigestion.

"Mix me an Alka-Seltzer, will you, Claire?" he'd asked.

Glass in hand, Claire had returned to their office to find Phillip slumped over his desk, his wire-rimmed glasses twisted beneath his cheek. A pillar of ice, Claire had stood at the door, unable to speak, cry, or move. She felt that way now—frozen inside and out, unable to think rationally, to organize her thoughts, to even push on toward North Carolina.

Perhaps it wasn't safe or prudent to continue her journey at this moment. Perhaps staying here at this motel, resting and walking the beach for a day or two would be helpful and restorative.

A wooden, slatted chair stood in front of the motel. Claire ambled toward it and sat. The wood, warmed by the sun, welcomed her body. She leaned forward, elbows on knees, chin on clenched fists, and stared down at her naked feet. Her toenail polish was chipped. Wiggling her toes, Claire dug them into the sand, wonderfully warm on this late-March morning. She shut her eyes and tried to imagine herself at the beach at East Hampton in summer, but instead, she saw her house and garden.

A family with three small children had bought and now lived in her home. When summer came and the lavender wisteria vine draped the trellis to the east of the kitchen, would anyone stand at the sink and relish its beauty, as she had done for so many years? Would those people appreciate her roses, pick and bring them into the house as she had? She was no gardener, but Mr. Hanson was, and he had cared for her yard almost from the beginning. She had recommended that they keep him on, but they seemed indifferent, and she regretted selling them her home. But it was too late now.

Claire moaned and leaned forward. Why hadn't she stayed in East Hampton and done the grief work her therapist insisted was essential? She had chosen to leave everything familiar, and for what? To begin a roller-coaster ride of sleeping with men she did not know? How could she have put herself in a position to be assaulted by a man? Things like this happened to tramps, women who became involved with criminals like drug dealers.

Jason and Andrew had been good men, but she hadn't known that in advance. She had been lucky with them. But she hadn't even liked Fred Austerman. It was time for her to face reality. Because she rejected the company of women, she had isolated herself, and rather than face an evening home alone that Sunday, she'd ignored her instincts and agreed to dinner with Fred. A terrible price to pay for male companionship.

Claire covered her face with her hands. Who *was* she, after all, and what was she going to do with her life? Surely not what she'd been doing these last few months.

A man was approaching. From the corner of her eye, Claire noted the creases of his black pants as they fell over well-polished, black shoes and heard the crunch of sand beneath his feet on the concrete pathway. Instinctively she drew back and crossed her arms about her chest.

"Good morning, Mrs. Bennett. Sorry if I startled you. I'm Murry McIverson, the manager. Checkout was at eleven. Luscita went in to clean the room, but your clothes and suitcases were there. She saw you on the beach. She was worried."

"That was kind of her," Claire said. Tears

rose to her eyes, and she fought them back. "I'd like to stay on for a few days. Have you a room for me?"

"We do, and we're glad to have you. There's a packet of menus from nearby restaurants in the desk drawer in your room, as well as sights to see in the area. We're close to Cape Canaveral and there's a shuttle launch this evening. We have a list of places where you can park and have a splendid view."

"Thank you," Claire said.

"I'll leave you then, Mrs. Bennett." He walked away, his shoes crunching sand.

Overhead, a small plane droned. Claire watched the glitter of sunlight on its wings as it flew out over the ocean, saw it shrink as the throbbing sound of its engines faded. Behind her in the motel courtyard a low, husky voice sang in Spanish. On the street beyond, a car door slammed. A motor sprang to life, a car drove away. Then there was silence.

17

The Shuttle Launch

Claire strolled along the beach until the heat of the sun drove her inside to rest, then she lunched at a 1950s-type diner across the street from the motel. In the afternoon, she watched a rerun of Oprah. The program dealt with reuniting adopted children with their birth parents, usually a mother, followed by tears, hugs, apologies, and promises. Claire wondered how the adoptive parents, stoic smiling souls sitting bravely in the audience, really felt after all the years of loving and nurturing the child. She could not have been one of those parents.

At five, as the credits for the Oprah show

rolled on the screen, she decided to go to the space shuttle launch, scheduled for six-thirty P.M. From the diner across the street, she bought a sandwich and soda, then headed up A1A to the site the manager of the motel recommended. There she found a space between a pickup with two men in overalls and two boys about ten or eleven, and a sedan in which an older couple sat shoulder to shoulder. Cars with license plates from Maine, Alaska, Oklahoma, Illinois, Georgia, and Florida lined the foggy banks of the Banana River and the crowded roadside lookouts.

Claire envied the families and couples in nearby vehicles. If only Phillip were here to share this experience with her. But in her heart, she knew that if Phillip were alive they would never have come. Work had consumed their lives, work had *been* their life.

The newspapers predicted thirty-five thousand spectators. Claire stepped from her car and turned her attention across the marsh, where floodlights shot rivers of light into the darkening sky. Helicopters and jets laced in and out of the light beams as they flew above and around the giant structure that supported the shuttle.

The air quivered as launch control counted down, and then a glint below the booster rocket turned into sparks, which burst into fire. White clouds and flame spewed in all directions. The world shuddered, and the shuttle lifted off.

The shock waves set her teeth chattering. Her skin prickled and itched, and the hair rose on her arms and the back of her neck. The smell of mineral ash drifted over the mesmerized crowd as firemen doused the launch pad and surrounding area with water. The marsh and the river turned the color of brass.

Filled with awe, she watched the man-made clouds emanate from earth rather than from the heavens, and birds, moths, dragon-flies, and gnats, driven by terror, swarmed upward, circling around and around. Claire's eyes followed the flow of flame and smoke, and the golden halo surrounding the shuttle, higher and higher.

An older man explained to the awestruck boys standing in the bed of the pickup, "Once they get into orbit, the sun's gonna rise every hour for them, imagine that."

"Wow," one of the boys exclaimed.

The man's arms circled the boys' shoulders.

"Watch now. See those two red spots up there? Those are the solid fuel rockets breaking free. Soon we're not gonna be able to see the shuttle."

"Awesome," the other boy said. "Grandpa, I'm gonna be an astronaut when I grow up."

"That's a fine idea, Timmy," his grandfather said.

"Just six minutes and it's out of sight," the other man from the pickup said. "A pretty amazing sight."

The older man nodded. "Out of this world, you might say."

The boys laughed. "That's where I want to go," one of the boys said. "Out of this world."

The older man climbed down and into the cab of the truck, while the boys hunkered in the back as the engine started. The man backed the truck from its space and out into the line of traffic.

Waiting for the traffic to thin, Claire slipped a CD into the player, turned on the car engine, and locked the doors. The strains of a Mozart string quartet calmed her mind, which brimmed with images of the launch and awe for the science and the men who catapulted other men into orbit beyond the earth.

In such a setting, her own problems paled.

She realized, for the first time, why people thronged to football, baseball, hockey, basketball games, and music concerts. All her life, she had avoided events that drew huge crowds of strangers. Now she realized that the power of the shared event enhanced the experience. She understood why her passion for opera was more intense in a theater than while watching a video of the performance at home.

The launch experience also set Claire thinking about creation, about the significance of life, the infinitesimally short time she had on this planet, and what she was meant to do or be during that time. Perhaps it wasn't all about being with a man.

"You are too much alone," her grandfather used to say when, as a young girl, she had buried herself in her room with her books.

"I like to read," she had replied.

"Remember, child," he would tell her in broken English, "man was not meant for to live alone."

As she drove back to the motel, Claire seriously considered her life. What was important? Work? Love? Passion? Husband? Children? Money? Hope? Some people lived happily without spouses or children. Some folks chose not to work a steady job. Passion faded, and love degenerated into routine—she knew that all too well. Money was made and lost.

But hope engendered dreams and possibilities. "Hope is necessary in every condition," Samuel Johnson wrote. When she and Phillip had started their own business, she had clipped that quote to the refrigerator. Hope had sustained her in that first rough year when the business lurched from side to side and money was tight.

As Claire swung the Ford into the parking lot of the motel, she heard Phillip's voice. "Take heart, Claire. Don't give up because you've made mistakes. Be hopeful. Find something you enjoy doing, and do it well."

Claire's heart stuttered. "Phillip!"

No one answered. His voice evaporated, leaving her with goose bumps, a thudding heart, and, for the first time, a measure of hope.

18

Continuing the Journey

Claire awoke from her nightmare perspiring. The dream pitted Fred against Phillip in a tug-of-war, with her as the prize. Pulled this way and that, she had hung suspended between a dark turbulent sea and an equally forbidding sky. When they loosened their holds, she floated in weightless space, oddly unafraid.

Energized by a shower, Claire decided to resume her journey. She'd stop along the way wherever she chose, in total control of what she did. That would banish the terrible sense of helplessness that Fred Austerman had caused.

Hope is necessary in every condition, she reminded herself.

Adept at leapfrogging over grief and pain, she stood before the mirror at the bathroom sink, put on her makeup, then dressed.

As she packed she thought of Olden, and a stab of guilt reminded her that he did not know her whereabouts. Like an overprotective mother, Olden had phoned every other day. If he was unable to reach her, he might hop a plane to Florida again and find her gone, which could unleash a chain of most unpleasant events. If she had a cell phone, which she had refused to get, he could call her anywhere, anytime.

Before checking out of the motel, Claire called Olden. He was in a meeting, but his secretary, Mrs. Norton, insisted that he would want to talk with her.

"Claire, what's wrong?"

"Olden, I am so sorry to bother you in a meeting. I just wanted to say I'm on my way to Amanda's, and I realized I hadn't called you. Yes, I'm fine. I spent the night in Melbourne, and last night I saw the shuttle launch. It was a wonderful experience." She kept her voice light.

"Seeing the launch is very powerful. One

doesn't forget that sight in a hurry. You're okay? Going to Amanda's, you say?"

"Well, to the Asheville area. It's supposed to be lovely. I thought I'd stay there until the wedding. I'll call you when I have a place."

He hesitated. She knew he doubted that nothing was wrong, but couldn't pursue it at the moment. "Well, take it slow. And call me. I'm sure you'll find a lovely place to stay in Asheville. I've heard the Grove Park Inn is a great hotel; try that."

"I will. I'll call you."

"Don't drive too fast, and stop when you're tired," Olden said.

"Don't worry, Olden. I'll phone every night, and when I arrive at Amanda's."

They said goodbye, and Claire hung up. Since she had refused his proposal of marriage, he had increasingly assumed the role of a solicitous parent. It irked her, yet she obviously encouraged it, or at least permitted it. After all, she had turned to him when she wanted to sell her home, and to handle her business affairs. She had been delighted to see him in Boca Raton, and enjoyed his company more than she'd imagined. He was her closest friend and ally, and perhaps the only person in the world who truly cared for her.

Unfortunately, he lacked the glamour and ex-citement she liked in a man.

Claire tucked a twenty-dollar tip in an envelope and left it on the dresser for Luscita, then wheeled her suitcases down the hall, mulling the value of glamour and excitement.

Claire drove north on A1A until red lights and heavy traffic made it slow going, then turned west toward I-95. When a siren shrieked be-hind her and blue lights flashed, she had no notion why the policeman was stopping her.

He strode to her car and asked in a no-nonsense manner for her license. "Ma'am, the speed limit's sixty-five miles an hour, and you were doing eighty."

"Eighty? Are you sure?"

He nodded, handed her back her license, and wrote out a ticket, which she accepted without comment. When he drove away she remained on the shoulder of the highway, fighting hot, embarrassed tears that burned her eyes. A naughty child could not have felt as reprimanded.

After a time, Claire wiped her eyes, took a deep breath, and looked for a radio station with country music. Not that she liked coun-try music especially, but it had a beat, and she needed to stay awake and attend to the road. She'd never speeded at home, had never gotten a ticket, and it took her a long time to stop quivering inside.

Claire waited for a gap in the traffic, got back onto the highway, and set her cruise control to sixty-five. Though it felt as if she was crawling, the slower pace calmed her after a while.

At two P.M. she congratulated herself for making it is as far as Jacksonville. Since it was way too early to isolate herself in a motel room, she stopped for coffee and pushed on. When the sign WELCOME TO GEORGIA appeared, Claire sighed with relief. Perhaps she could reach Savannah before nightfall.

Eventually she pulled into a motel just off the highway, and once in her room, she ordered in a pizza from a menu on the desk. When it arrived, she sat cross-legged on the bed to watch the evening news.

As she pulled the slices from the box, Claire realized that she couldn't recall what the newscaster said a moment after he'd said it. She felt brain-dead, yet when she tried to sleep, it eluded her. After hours of numbly watching TV, she finally drifted into an uneasy, dreamless sleep.

19

Jekyll Island

Jekyll Island would be her next destination, Claire decided. Friends had raved about it, and she and Phillip had talked about vacationing there. Once the private playground of the Rockefellers, Pulitzers, Astors, and Vanderbilts, it was now owned by the state.

She drove east past marshlands to reach the island, and crossed a low bridge over shallow, dark water and tall reeds as far the eye could see. When she reached the island, a guard directed her to the Jekyll Island Club Hotel. As she drove under moss-draped oaks, the coastal road offered a clear view of the

Intracoastal Waterway and the city of Bruns-
wick on the far shore. Victorian mansions called
"cottages" appeared on her right. An ochre-
yellow house with dark green trim and a wide,
front porch caught her fancy, and intending to
tour the place, she made a note of the name,
Moss Cottage.

When Claire pulled her car into the lot in
front of the turreted Queen Anne mansion
that housed the Jekyll Island Club Hotel,
Cadillacs, Mercedes, and other luxury cars
dwarfed her Taurus. Intimidated by this and
at the idea of checking in as a single woman,
she considered leaving, but she squared her
shoulders, lifted her head, and strode to the
registration desk.

"How long will you be staying with us?" the
desk clerk asked.

"A few days. I'm not sure. Can I let you
know?"

"Certainly, madam." Then he said, "High
tea is served on the patio at four o'clock each
afternoon."

"Tea sounds charming. Thank you."

"The clerk nodded. "Dinner dress is formal
in our dining room, with jackets required for
men. Our indoor tennis court and pool are at
your disposal. Enjoy your stay."

Claire smiled and accepted the old-fashioned key he handed her.

After the bellhop delivered her bags to the pleasantly furnished bedroom, Claire sank into a flowered chintz-covered armchair. Since Phillip died, she had made a mess of everything. She had abrogated work, the most meaningful activity in her life, burned her bridges, and indulged in appalling behavior.

Arms wrapped tight about her shoulders, Claire stared out the window until hunger pangs reminded her that she must eat. Sunset bathed the sound in gold, and for a moment, lifted Claire's spirits.

"You're a capable, creative woman," Dr. Delanny had said.

"Yes, I am," Claire reminded herself as she headed for the bathroom to shower. She dressed in a simple turquoise sheath and put on her diamond earrings, a gift from Phillip on their tenth wedding anniversary. But her self-confidence deserted her when she stood at the entrance of the elegant pink and white dining room and realized that nearly everyone in the room were couples. Her hands turned clammy, and she found it impossible to enter. Stepping back, she hastened to the elevator, convinced that the porters, the diners, and the maître d' were staring at her and laughing. Back in her room she ordered room service, determined to leave in the morning.

20

The Downward Path
to Wisdom

Claire awakened feeling as downhearted as she had yesterday. "Still," she told herself, "it would be best to stay and rest for another day." Talking to herself was becoming a habit. "I don't have to eat in the dining room. I might as well see a bit of this place and visit Moss Cottage. Then I'll decide what to do next."

Thus resolved, she tied her hair back with a ribbon, went light on the makeup, and dressed casually in khaki slacks and a long-sleeved cotton shirt. Over her shoulders she draped a pale blue cashmere sweater, for the weatherman reported a chilly morning in the low sixties.

A porter directed her to the Café Solterra, an eatery in the hotel. As she entered, Claire noted that only a few tables were occupied: several men in business suits engrossed in conversation, a middle-aged couple intent on their breakfast, a man oblivious to all but his morning newspaper. A woman sat by herself near the window. Beyond her Claire could see tall oaks, underpinned by low bushy palms. People strolled casually about the grounds, stopping periodically to inspect a tree or read the signs attached to every plant in the hotel's landscaping.

The waiter led Claire to a small table near the window, and she settled into a captain's chair and ordered pancakes and scrambled eggs. The other woman, sitting nearby, attracted Claire's attention. She was dressed in jeans and sneakers and a tie-dyed T-shirt, and her head was crowned with dark brown braids. Her eyes, when she glanced at Claire, were astonishingly green, and when she smiled, Claire involuntarily smiled in return.

The woman rose and approached Claire's table. "As we are two women alone, perhaps we can breakfast together?"

"Please, do join me," Claire replied.

The woman waved to the waiter, who immediately gathered up her cup, her plate of toast, the butter, and her purse which hung over the back of the vacated chair. Seating herself across from Claire, she introduced herself. "I am Zora." She offered no last name.

"Claire Bennett."

"A lovely name, Claire. Isn't that a Latin word that means 'bright, shining like a full moon'?"

"I don't know." Claire thought of Andrew, bathed in the moonlight.

"Zora's a Slavic name that means 'dawn.'" She dropped her napkin onto her lap and smiled. "Together, our names suggest a bright shining dawn, so we were clearly meant to meet."

That's one way to reason, Claire thought, as the waiter set her breakfast before her.

Zora said, "You are traveling alone, and I take it you don't much like it?"

"I find it uncomfortable. How can you tell?"

"I observed that although you were dressed appropriately, you chose not to enter the restaurant last night. After I was widowed, walking into a restaurant without my husband was grueling and humiliating. It was as if I wore a scarlet *W* for 'widow' on my chest. I thought the men were all appraising me suggestively, and all the women were looking at me with pity or scorn." Zora shrugged and smiled. "In time, you will not care what anyone else thinks."

"I don't see how that's possible," Claire said.

"Oh, but it is." Zora smiled. Her tanned, slender face warmed, and her lovely eyes drew Claire in. "Do you perchance ride a bicycle?"

"A bicycle?" This woman certainly changed subjects quickly. Claire's mind traveled back to a two-story brick house, a paved sidewalk, and her father calling, "Steady, girl, focus on balance." A smile curled the edges of her mouth. "A very long time ago." Then her heart sank. She hadn't ridden one since Terrance's death. "A long time ago."

"I ride every morning. Will you ride with me? It will all come back to you, I assure you. I will be happy to show you the island."

"I don't know." Zora's invitation seemed precipitous and her speech odd, lacking contractions. And hadn't she come here to sort things out, to try to bring clarity to the haze that was her life? Yet there was something appealing about Zora. Claire found herself challenged at the idea of riding a bike again.

"I hope you will join me." Zora turned to the window, and a faraway look settled in her eyes. "I came here once to evaluate my life and make decisions. It was lonely and difficult. I wish there had been someone I could have talked with then." She sighed. "It seems to me that life circles and circles, and hopefully leads to one's own center, where things become clear. Do you not think that we recycle behaviors that do not always bring us happiness?"

Claire hadn't expected a psychology lesson with breakfast and was interested.

"I'd like to go bicycling with you, but you'll have to be patient while I get my bike legs back."

"I am glad you will join me, and we will go slow," Zora said. "In our fast-paced world, slow is better."

Claire straddled the thickly padded seat of the rental bike, and was surprised at how quickly she gained confidence as they rode away from the hotel and started down an oak-shaded road.

"We will go first to the Moss Cottage," Zora said. "They like people to take their regular tour, but they do not have one today. I sometimes lead tours, though, and I have access."

Heavy shade dimmed the brightness of the sun, and they rode past one restored "cottage" after the other, some as tall as three stories and one designed in the style of an Italian villa.

On reaching Moss Cottage, they propped their bikes against a tree and walked up the steps onto the porch, which faced the sound.

Zora knew Moss Cottage well. That was clear as she opened the front door with a key and led Claire into a large foyer from which rose solid stairs that quickly formed a landing, then turned and proceeded to the second floor. The room on the left appeared to have been a den or game room, with its bearskin rug, chess table, and small writing stand. To the right, the dining and living rooms were furnished simply with mahogany antiques and filled with framed photographs of stern-faced men and unsmiling women of the late 1800s and early 1900s. The kitchen lay behind the stairs, a large room with central counters and glass-fronted cabinets stacked with china and glassware.

"There is a room behind the kitchen where they say the hunters brought their kill for the cook's helpers to skin and prepare for cooking," Zora said.

Claire imagined freshly shot rabbits suspended from hooks, and on a tin-topped table, a deer, its legs rigid, awaiting the butcher's knife. She refrained from looking into the room.

Returning to the foyer, they climbed the stairs to the bedrooms, which were furnished with mahogany spindle beds and handsome chests and armoires. From a window facing the street, she caught glimpses of yachts and motorboats in the sound. It reminded her of Boca Raton, and for a moment, feeling slightly faint, Claire leaned against a tall dresser.

"Is something wrong?" Zora asked.

"I guess I'm not accustomed to riding a bike. I'll be fine."

"If you can manage, I would very much like to show you the beach. I especially adore the beach. It is different. Very wide, with gray sand," Zora said.

Claire took a deep breath. "The beach. Yes, I'd like that."

Zora said that they were taking a shortcut, but by the time they reached the beach, Claire's leg muscles ached from the strain of pedaling, and her breath came fast. With great relief, she dismounted and set the bike stand.

Low dunes housed mainly scrub oaks, and steel-gray sand stretched out of sight to the south. High concrete walls, probably barriers to wind and water, fronted the motels, and a barrier of enormous sharp-edged gray rocks between the walls and sand added further protection from the avaricious ocean.

The day had warmed, and Claire deposited her cardigan over the handlebars of her bicycle. Would the water be icy if she walked across the smooth, gray sand to dip her toes? "Isn't the water cold this time of year?"

"It is to the natives, but folks from Maine find it manageable. People flock here in winter," Zora replied. "I am always amazed at the toughness of those who venture in. However, they do not stay long in the water. I have watched them lift their heads, square their shoulders, and race into the ocean. Minutes later, they are scrambling back onto the sand grabbing for their towels. It must give the heart a jolt, would you agree?" She shrugged. "For me the water is too cold. The indoor pool at the hotel is heated and that is good enough."

A nearby tree, whose twisted bark and stunted growth spoke of the salt air and persistent winds, provided the only shade. Claire sat beneath it and welcomed the cool ocean breeze on her face and arms.

"The first transatlantic call was made from this island," Zora said.

"I didn't know that."

"Most people do not know that, or much else about this island," Zora said.

They did not speak for a time. Pelicans circled, then dove into the water. With their huge bills, the brown pelicans appeared cumbersome and graceless to Claire until, in flight, they metamorphosed into graceful denizens of the air, circling, then plunging to garner their hapless prey.

"I love islands," Zora said, interrupting

Claire's train of thought. "I adore the smell and sound of the ocean, the birds, the way the wind shifts from warm and comforting in summer, to rough and wild on a cold wintry night."

"I've never seen sand this gray before," Claire said. "Do you live here all year?"

Zora stretched her arms above her head and arched her back. "I live on a small island off the coast of Maine, in a fishing village where I have a trinket shop for tourists. It does well, and it pays for my winters on Jekyll Island."

"Why this island?"

"It reminds me of the old times, and I enjoy the laid-back atmosphere," Zora replied.

"What do you do here all winter?" Claire asked.

Zora smiled, and her gaze drifted to the ocean. "I bike. I walk the beach. I watch the birds. I do a little writing. I befriend strangers, and we part as friends. There is a good bookstore on the island. I browse and visit folks hanging out there."

"And that's enough for you?"

Zora nodded. "It is enough."

"God, I wish such simple needs were enough for me."

"I first came here ten years ago after my husband died. The moss hanging from the enormous oaks depressed me. I hated the place, but I stayed, and after a week or so I began to relax and started to live in the present. It takes time to learn to live in the here and now. You have to hang on past the bad times, and there are plenty of those, as you well know. If you do hang on and do not run from your life you discover that you have more control of your thoughts and feelings, and of your life, than you believed possible. You learn to quiet your frantic mind, to downgrade your expectations of things and people, find pleasure in solitude, and finally discover who you really are." Zora stood and brushed the sand from her jeans. "Are you up to walking the beach?"

Claire rubbed her tired calf. "I think not. I'll just sit here in the shade and wait for you." She watched the slim woman move briskly down the beach. Zora lifted her hands to her hair and unpinned her braids, which tumbled to her waist. Occasionally, Zora kicked the water with her canvas sneakers, seemingly uncaring as to whether they were soaked and cold.

What a different kind of woman. Yet

something about Zora touched a deep, unexplored place in Claire. Was Zora a psychic, or some such thing? Was she writing a book about people who came to this island? Did she collect people to help her pass the time?

A crab scooting along the sand caught Claire's attention, and in an electric moment she became aware of the minute holes that studded the dune and the scrambled bits of sand tossed about by scurrying claws. She brushed away a strand of hair that tickled her cheek and listened as wind swooshed in off the ocean and rustled the leaves on the scrub oaks, whose movements cast mottled shadows on the sand near her feet.

"The beach is a haven for crabs."

Zora's voice broke into Claire's thoughts, and she looked up, wondering when the woman had returned. "I guess I lost myself watching them, and it's been an amazing exercise in concentration. They diverted my mind. I feel more relaxed than I've been in months."

"What has it been like for you, in those months?" Zora seated herself, then rewound and pinned her braids into a circle about her head. She slipped her feet from her wet shoes, set the shoes in the sun, and wiggled her toes in the warm sand. She smiled at Claire. The relaxed slouch of her body and her green eyes—calm, attentive, and car-ing—encouraged intimacy.

Claire talked as she had to no one, not even her therapist, about her uncertain and confusing childhood: her mother's deepening mental illness, her father's increasing depres-sion as his wife slipped further and further away from the family and from him. She spoke of her life with Phillip, of her unsatisfac-tory sex life, and cried over her disappointing relationships with her children. She spoke of her decision to leave East Hampton, and blurted out the story of her trysts with Jason, Andrew, and finally, throat knotted, she told Zora about Fred Austerman.

"I was so humiliated and frightened that I fled from Boca Raton the very next day." Claire bit her lower lip and looked away.

Zora touched Claire's hand. "Do not chas-tise yourself. You, my friend, are on what I call the downward path to wisdom."

Claire bristled, mortified at having revealed so much and to have it all summed up so briefly. "The downward path to wisdom? What does that mean?"

"There are times in our lives when we find

ourselves descending into a deep, dark unhappy place. We are stuck there for a time, wallowing in the ashes of our misery until we gain knowledge. You might liken it to a phoenix dying and being reborn. Saint John wrote of it and called it 'the dark night of the soul.'"

Claire frowned. "I don't understand."

"Look at it like this: we live blindly. We repeat the same mistakes by rote until an emotional punch to the gut brings us up short. Losing your husband was such a punch. Sometimes it requires intense pain before we can take a good hard look at ourselves, before we ask the important questions."

"Which are?"

"Who am I? What is important? What do I believe? What do I want?"

"You've been in this dark, deep place?" Claire asked, thinking again how peculiar it was that Zora never used contractions like "don't" or "I've."

"I have," Zora replied. "That is how I recognize where you are."

"I'd never have described my situation in those terms."

"Few people do. Sometimes one needs another to hold up a mirror."

Claire mused over that for a while. "My therapist asked me who I was."

"What did you say?"

Claire shrugged. "I didn't know. I still don't."

"What do you want?" Zora asked. Sand she had scooped into her hand drained between her fingers and scattered on the wind.

"A man. I want a man to twine my life with and to build a new life with. I remember telling my therapist that I was nothing without a man." Claire's eyes avoided meeting Zora's.

"Do you really, honestly believe that?"

"I don't know. I don't know what I believe." A wave of annoyance went through Claire. *Who is this Zora, anyhow? How dare she presume to question me like this? What the devil does she know?*

Zora spoke slowly, as if measuring each word. "I have a theory. Within the first twenty years of our lives, before we are really adult, we make choices motivated by insecurity, fear, and other people's expectations; certainly not guided by clarity and wisdom. We plod along for years living with the wrong career or spousal choice, in a location we did not choose and perhaps do not like, and much more. One day we wake up restless and confused, and acknowledge that we have no agenda of our own, and that we have been living someone else's passion, their dream." Her eyes went to the far horizon. "Living someone else's life, in fact.

"Sometimes this crisis comes with menopause for women, sometimes with the loss of someone, or sometimes, it just comes. Then we need time to evaluate our lives, to retool, perhaps. Whatever we do or think, it is never easy. We feel alone, abandoned, and misunderstood. We begin the slide down the path to wisdom. Is that clearer?"

Claire nodded. "I think I understand. When I chose Phillip, I saw our marriage as a partnership. Based on my college encounters with men, I believed sexual attraction was doomed to fade. I knew before we married that my sex drive exceeded Phillip's, and I chose to ignore that." She smiled. "But I was right about the partnership. That did prosper."

"And when he died, you realized that you had no genuine interest in antiques?"

Claire gasped; she felt like a kid caught stealing. "How did you know that?"

"Based on what you have said today. If you love something, you do not walk away from it as you tell me you did. You could have gone on with your business, or taken a partner. It would have provided the stability and comfort you needed after your husband died."

"There was much about the business that I didn't like. We traveled a great deal, and I hated traveling by plane. I couldn't get on one without tranquilizers. I never told Phillip that; I just took a pill and boarded. We traveled first class, which made it a bit easier. It's certainly more comfortable."

"I imagine it is. So the question is, Claire, what do you do now? Do you make a life for yourself, or do you find another man and live his dreams? I am not saying it would not be good to meet a nice man and build a life with him. I do think that if you first know what you want and who you are, you can have a more balanced, a more equal relationship, and not one in which you are living *his* dream and subjugating your wants to his. An equal partnership in which each respects the other's interests and beliefs, and so forth."

Claire stared at Zora. "Are you some kind of mind reader?"

"What I have said makes sense?" Zora asked.

"It makes sense, but it's not comfortable to hear it said like that."

"Well," Zora replied. "You have much to consider, then, do you not?"

"Yes. Especially after what happened in Boca Raton, and particularly the way I've run away from life itself these last two years."

"Sometimes we need to step away from things to gain perspective. You are a gutsy lady. It is not easy to say 'I need help' and then to get it. Deciding to go to a therapist took guts," Zora said.

"You think so?" Claire detested how much she needed reassurance.

"Of course. You would think so, too, if you stopped to consider it," Zora replied.

Why was it so easy to confide in this stranger? "I've always avoided the real issues, I guess," Claire replied.

"Moving through life with blinders on works if the road is smooth and easy, as it essentially was when your husband was alive." Zora reached for another handful of sand. "But now you have come to the ruts in the road. Stones and other obstacles require that you pay attention to them—move around, step over them, or stumble across." Zora brushed her hands clean. "I am very hungry. How about you?"

Taken aback by the abrupt change of topic, Claire felt dismissed, yet realized that she was ravenously hungry. They had lunch at a small cafe nearby, then bicycled back to the hotel.

Later that evening, Claire met Zora at the entrance to the elegant dining room. She took a deep breath, lifted her chin as they entered, and followed the waiter down the carpeted aisle flanked by columns to a table halfway down the room. It was hard walking into the room with another woman. Would people think they were a lesbian couple? Was that her fear in befriending women? It shamed her to consider how many times she herself had wondered about two women together.

Once seated, Claire began to relax. Soft music from the grand piano and the soft lighting added to the luxurious ambience. Over salad, Claire asked, "Are you a therapist?"

Zora threw back her head and laughed. "Not at all. I am interested in some people that I meet, and you are one of them, and I have been told that I am a good listener.

People are starved for someone who will listen to them, do you not think?"

"Yes, but why do I interest you?"

"Have you never met someone and taken an instant liking or dislike to them?" Zora asked.

Before Claire could reply, the waiter removed their salad plates and placed their entrées in front of them: veal picatta for Zora; chicken cordon bleu for Claire.

"This looks delicious," Zora said. She picked up her fork and knife and began to eat.

As if by agreement, they spoke no more of personal or philosophical matters. Rehashing her life, spilling her deepest feelings and fears, had left Claire emotionally drained, and Zora produced a repertoire of silly jokes that kept her laughing.

That night Claire slept well and awoke lighthearted, anticipating breakfast and another day with Zora. Disappointment followed, however, when after seating her, the waiter explained that Mistress Zora had been called off island and would be away for several weeks. He handed Claire an envelope that smelled of lemon blossoms. As she read Zora's note, a lump formed in her throat and the bright, cheerful café seemed to grow dim.

Dear Claire,
   My apologies for leaving so abruptly, but urgent business calls me away. It was a pleasure meeting and talking with you. You are at the nadir of the downward path to wisdom. There is no place to go but up. Good luck in making wise choices, choices from your heart.
   Zora

Claire read, reread, and tried to find meaning beyond the words of the brief communication. She was still trying to fathom the concept of a downward path, and Zora was saying that she was on her way up.

After breakfast, Claire returned to her room, packed, and checked out of the hotel.

"I hope you enjoyed your visit on our island," the clerk said as he handed her the receipt. "Thank you for staying with us."

Minutes later, she was settled into the bucket seat of her car, and the hotel vanished from her rearview mirror as Claire headed for the bridge leading across the sound to the highway north.

Setting the cruise control at fifty-five miles an hour, Claire recalled the pride she'd felt regaining balance on a bike after so many years. She remembered the crabs squiggling into holes less than half their size, the pelicans diving and surfacing, their prey wriggling furiously from the edges of their bills, but mostly she remembered the quiet calm of Zora's green eyes.

21

Limitations

Claire spread a map out on the table in Denny's and studied the route to Asheville. She had passed Savannah and appeared to be half an hour from Interstate 26, which turned west and north toward Columbia, South Carolina. She could check into a motel near Columbia, or stop for dinner and good, strong coffee and drive through the night. The need to reach her destination bubbled within her like water boiling in a pot.

She really must call Amanda. She found a phone booth outside the restaurant and dropped in coins. A message machine answered, informing her that Tom and Mandy were out and to please leave a message. "Amanda. This is your mother. I am on my way from Florida and thought I'd stop by sometime tomorrow. Hope that's not too inconvenient for you. Mom."

Claire bought two audio books in a Barnes and Noble, a Danielle Steel novel and one by Isabel Allende. She slipped a cassette into the slot, and as the opening bars of introductory music began and the narrator announced the title and author of the book, she was once again on the highway.

It was one A.M. when Claire drove past the Biltmore Square Mall south of Asheville. Following carefully memorized directions from a gas station attendant, she crossed the bridge over the French Broad River and moved to the left lane, which merged into highway 19 and 23.

The city of Asheville rose in the distance, its lights glittering above a plateau surrounded by mountains. Dark against a moonlit sky, the mountains took Claire's breath away and her spirits rose. This had been a good idea. She struggled against the urgent need to sleep, though, and at the next exit she spotted a Days Inn. Claire pulled off the highway and checked in.

Morning brought tiers of flame-colored clouds on the eastern horizon, while to the west, layer upon layer of mountains rested among misty pillows. Today she would visit her daughter, then find a place to stay in Asheville.

When she dialed the number, Amanda picked up on the second ring.

"I'm here," Claire said, uncertain how she would be received. "I'd love to drop in and see you, but I need directions."

"We got your message and wondered where you were. I'm glad you decided to stop, Mother. I'd like you to meet Tom and his dad, Larry. Let me put Tom on. He's much better at directions than I am."

Following the directions, Claire soon found herself on Reems Creek Road in Weaverville. Tom had a nice voice, she thought; strong and pleasant.

Mountains stretched before her, but rather than feeling hemmed in, Claire felt protected. She drove slowly through the long, lovely valley. Expecting pastures with grazing cattle or sheep, ramshackle farmhouses with peeling

paint, weathered porch chairs, and dilapi-
dated barns, she was surprised to see developments and homes tucked back from the
road behind screens of trees.

The valley ended, and so did the paved
road. Ahead of her an unpaved road stretched
uphill. Since it was early, Claire decided to
explore. She turned onto the dirt road, which
wound steadily upward amid thick stands of
pine and deciduous trees. Occasionally a
narrow dirt road straggled off to the right,
hinting at a home tucked high on a hillside,
or on the left, a house clung to the steep side
of the hill.

At the summit a surreal scene, the after-
math of a fire, marked the landscape. The
fronds of fresh green ferns sprawled among
the charred remains of fallen trees, while
fungi and lichen extruded from the crevices
of cracked and fissured bark. A bright red
cardinal rose from the ground to perch for a
moment on a sagging wire fence; then he
spread his wings and flew deep into the
blackened cemetery of trees. With regret,
Claire watched him disappear; then she
headed back down the mountain.

22

And the Mountains
Are Dancing

Three miles down the road, Claire saw SOUR-
WOOD LANE on a sign that hung from a post,
and she turned left into a narrow entrance. A
small bridge crossed a modest creek; then a
gravel road, one car wide, headed up the hillside. Claire shifted into low gear. The climb,
steady and steep, seemed interminable as
the road crooked and turned. If there was a
view of the valley below, it was hidden by the
forest of evergreens.

Suddenly the road entered a clearing so
lovely, so pristine, that Claire's mind flew back
to a springtime visit to a college friend, a
medical student in Lausanne, Switzerland. In

an Alpine meadow, much like the one portrayed in *The Sound of Music,* they had
walked hand in hand, stopped to pick wild-
flowers, and gazed at the rugged, majestic
mountains across the lake.

She had stayed in his two-room flat above
a bakery, and they had shared fresh-baked
bread each morning and dinners at La
Pomme de Terre, a restaurant as old as
Napoleon. She salivated, remembering the
exquisite mushroom sauce ladled in lush
cascades over chicken or steak. At long
tables, she and Louis had joined in conge-
nial camaraderie with strangers, mainly
old men and university students. What
would her life have been like had she married Louis? She would never know, for she
had returned to the States, and he had
married a Frenchwomen after finishing his
medical training.

Claire looked about her. The mountains
rose on three sides of the meadow, not as
imposing as those in Switzerland, but impressive enough. Claire turned off the motor
and stepped from her car. Stiff from her long
trip, she stretched her arms high above her
head, then bent from her waist, first to one
side and then the other.

Neither cows, nor horses, nor sheep trod the carpet of smoothly mowed grass that hugged the meadow. No sound broke the silence. The mountains seemed fingertips away. Stepping into the meadow, Claire reveled in the thick grass that compressed beneath her feet. Lifting her arms to the sky, she threw back her head and laughed. The mountains seemed to echo her pleasure and return her laughter.

Claire raked her fingers through her hair, setting it free to fly about her face. An accumulating sense of pleasure impelled her to move, to twist and turn, and then to dance. Propelled by joy, she waltzed—one-two-three, one-two-three—then stopped counting as her mind and body, released from the corset of convention that had for so long confined her, moved to its own rhythm. The meadow became her stage; the mountains her partner. Claire danced slowly at first, then faster, and the mountains whirled about her, echoing her cries of delight.

How long she danced she did not know, but finally, breathless, she collapsed onto the dewy carpet of green. As she rested, catching her breath, a tall, gray-haired man stepped from the woods. Claire froze. Breathing hard, alert and alarmed, she sat up straight and hastily tucked in her blouse. Had he been watching her? Had he seen her cavorting about the meadow like an idiot?

The man walked casually toward her across the grass.

"Larry Harden." He extended a hand.

Tom Harden was Amanda's fiancé. Was this his father? How awful, meeting him like this!

"You must be Amanda's mother. We're expecting you. You probably drove right past the sign to the houses."

"Then you're my daughter's father-in-law-to-be. I didn't see the sign, I'm afraid. Sorry!" Claire tried to smooth her hair, all in disarray, and felt the tangled strands about her face. She must look a frightful mess. She straightened her shoulders.

"No problem," he said. "Nice to see someone enjoying the place."

"I don't usually frolic in meadows."

"Sometimes it just seems the thing to do, doesn't it?" He extended a hand again. "May I help you up?" As she accepted his hand, she noticed that his fingernails bore the grime of hard work. They walked toward her car, where she turned to face him.

"How do I get to my daughter's place?"

"Go down the hill a bit and take the first right. There's a small sign on a tree; I've been meaning to get a bigger one. It'll direct you to the barn."

"Thanks." Feeling at a distinct disadvantage, Claire slid into her car. With quivering hands she started the engine, turned the car around, and headed down the road where, after less than a quarter of a mile, she saw the sign that pointed to the right. THE BARN it read, and she followed crusty tire tracks through the woods.

The barn sat in a clearing. Its roof was red, its siding also red with white trim. White shutters flanked mullioned windows on either side of the front door. Towering above a small white sedan, a red pickup truck's tires rose nearly as high as the car's roof. Claire pulled alongside the vehicles and took several deep breaths. She adjusted the rearview mirror and rummaged in her purse for makeup. Before she could run a comb through her hair, Amanda exited the front door and ran toward her. Claire opened the car window.

"Mother! We were expecting you later, but welcome." She stopped. "You look flushed. Are you all right?"

"Yes, just a bit windblown," Claire replied. "I got lost and ended up in the meadow."

Amanda opened the car door. "People often miss our turn and find our meadow. Welcome to Sourwood Acres. Come on inside and meet Tom. He's making breakfast. We'll get your luggage later."

Her daughter's light brown eyes were serious and guarded; her silky, ash-brown hair had grown long, and a thick single braid hung down her back. Claire wanted to tell Amanda that braiding her hair would split the ends, but she smiled instead. "It's good to see you."

After all the years of tight-lipped withdrawal or bursts of hostile disagreement, she and Amanda had arrived at a truce that allowed for small talk and trivialities. Serious matters—fears, longings, uncertainties, future plans, even one's dreams—could be explosive topics and were assiduously avoided.

Claire sat with her daughter at the U-shaped breakfast nook in the big kitchen. Tom was shorter than his father, square and woodsmanlike, with thickly muscled arms and shoulders. He wore a checkered apron around his waist as he flipped pancakes.

"Isn't Dad coming for breakfast?" Amanda asked.

"He's working on one of those old trucks of his. Called to say he'd be over later." Tom swiped the back of his hand across his forehead. "Another pancake, Claire?"

"They're delicious, so light and fluffy. Maybe one more, thanks."

"I hope you don't mind my calling you Claire," Tom said.

"Claire is fine." She had never called her mother-in-law by her first name, or even Mom. "I called your grandmother Mrs. Bennett," she said, looking at Amanda.

"Nanna hated that."

Claire fought back irritation and was silent.

Amanda prodded, "You didn't like Nanna at all did you, Mother?"

"No, but it was mutual."

"I don't think so." Amanda's voice grew strident. "She never said a mean word about you to me."

"Isn't the lady dead?" Tom asked. He turned off the fire under the griddle. "Why fuss about someone who's gone? There's enough stuff here and now to bother about."

"I quite agree with you, Tom," Claire said, feeling smug.

The front door slammed, and the tread of

a man's footsteps on wood floors grew closer.

"Dad." Amanda rose to greet Larry Harden.

He kissed the top of her head. "Well, my girl, how are you this fine day?"

A wave of humiliation swept over Claire and she avoided looking at him.

"Dad, this is my mother, Claire Bennett."

"Welcome, Claire Bennett. Glad to meet you."

She waited for him to comment on their encounter in the meadow, but he strode to the table, settled into a chair, and accepted a stack of pancakes from his son. "Tom makes the best flapjacks," he said.

When he smiled, Claire noticed that two of his front teeth overlapped slightly and she wondered why he hadn't had them straightened. Her daughter, her future son-in-law, and his father were all a bit too casual for her in their faded jeans, T-shirts, and sneakers. And their laid-back attitude annoyed her. She had barged in on them practically unannounced, yet no one asked how her trip had been or why she had come weeks before the wedding.

Claire picked up the maple syrup and

inadvertently poured too much of it, covering the pancake with syrup that dripped over the edge of her plate. She dabbed at it with her paper napkin, but Tom was on his feet, and a moment later a damp towel removed the excess syrup and its stickiness.

She would not stay with them, and after she left to find a nice place to stay near Asheville, would Larry Harden tell them about their meeting in the meadow? Would they discuss it and laugh at her?

She lifted her chin. "Your father and I met a short while ago, Tom."

"Really?" Tom glanced at his father, but Larry's face remained bland, almost disinterested.

"I got lost and ended up in the meadow."

Larry smiled. "I found your mother dancing—and most gracefully, I must say."

"Dancing? You never dance, Mother."

"I used to dance quite a bit when I was young."

"Really? *I* never knew." Amanda crossed her arms.

Tom shrugged. "What's the big deal, Mandy?"

"She never dances. Never."

"Well, she did today," Larry said.

She? They were speaking of her as if she did not exist. With deliberation, Claire folded her napkin and laid it on the table. She turned the prongs of her fork down and placed it on the plate with her knife, indicating that she was finished. "I'd like to freshen up. And have you a phone book, Amanda? I need to reserve a room at a bed-and-breakfast or a motel, something closer to the city."

"Well, now, we needn't stand on ceremony," Larry said. "I've got a big old farmhouse with four bedrooms, a great front porch for rockin', and lots of space to ramble about in. I'm not around much, and Mildred, my housekeeper, is a great cook."

"Thank you, but I couldn't possibly burden you with a guest for so long. I've heard so much about this area, and thought it would be nice to rent a place and spend some time in Asheville."

"It's ridiculous not to stay with us. You can explore anyplace you want from here. It's only about ten minutes to Asheville."

Amanda, her face flushed, blurted, "I feel so frustrated. It's so hard to talk to you, to understand you, Mother. Why can't you just relax and stay here? Maybe we can get to know each other."

Claire wanted that, too, but she hadn't a clue how to begin. All the recent decisions she had made so hastily clouded her mind. *I am so alone. I'm mentally exhausted, physically tired—and why is it so hot in this kitchen?* Perspiration filmed her forehead, and when she tried to push away from the table and rise, her legs seemed rooted to the oak floor.

"Mother, what's wrong?"

Claire gave her daughter a vacant look. "Nothing's wrong. I'm just tired." She pressed her palm to her brow.

Amanda's voice reached Claire as from a distance. "Let me take you to my room. You need to lie down and rest."

"That would be nice," Claire murmured. "If I could just lie down for a few minutes." She lowered her arms to the table and rested her head on them. "Just for a few minutes."

From somewhere, she heard her daughter's voice calling, "Mother. Mother!"

It was evening when Claire opened her eyes. A small light glowed in one corner of an unfamiliar room, and moonlight pierced the lace curtains at the double windows. Claire stretched her legs. The bed was comfortable, the pillows soft. How odd! She had just had breakfast and now it was night. She remembered lowering her head onto her arms for just the tiniest moment.

A cool breeze from a half-open window brushed Claire's face and she touched her nose. It was cold, like the nose of a healthy dog, but she was warm beneath the covers. She rolled over, snuggled one of the soft pillows to her chest, and closed her eyes.

Claire next opened her eyes at the sound of a knock. Sunshine bounced off soft yellow walls. Amanda entered the room carrying a bed tray. A spray of greenery waved from a slim vase, and a fat little teapot sat under its quilted tea cozy.

"Good morning, Mother." Amanda's hair was pulled back in a ponytail, and wisps of damp curls snuggled at her temples. She wore a limp green sweatshirt, gray pants, and worn white sneakers. "Did you sleep well?"

"What happened, Amanda? Did I fall asleep at your table? How embarrassing." Claire pushed up in bed.

Amanda rested the tray over her mother's legs. "It's all right. The trip from Florida wore you out. You were overly tired and needed to rest. How do you feel now?"

"Much better." Claire studied the tray: orange juice without pulp, toast, slightly brown, the way she preferred it. Blueberry jam, her favorite, in a small round glass container. *Amanda remembered what I like for breakfast. Amazing.*

Amanda lifted the tea cozy. Steam curled from the spout of a little pot, and the aroma of coffee wafted through the room.

Claire poured herself a cup. "I am hungry," she said. "Did you and Tom have to carry me here, or did I manage under my own steam?"

"Larry carried you. You're in his house, in a guest room."

Claire was startled. "Why am I in his house? Why not in yours?"

"Mother, I told you, we don't have a guest room yet."

Amanda walked to the windows and drew back the curtains. A bank of mountains, a gorgeous view, filled the space. At any other time, Claire would have delighted in the sight.

Her coffee cup hit the plate with a clink. "Don't change the subject," she demanded "What happened? Did I fall asleep, or did I pass out? Answer me."

Amanda turned from the window. "One minute you were sitting at the table, the next you were saying how tired you were, and then you rested your head on your arms and fell asleep. Did you faint? I don't know. You didn't fall on the floor or anything like that."

"I'm sorry. I hadn't meant to impose on you, on your father-in-law-to-be, like this. Did you call a doctor?"

"Larry checked your pulse, your eyes, and your breathing. He said you were asleep."

"He determined my medical condition?"

"He was a paramedic in the army. You weren't sick, Mother—you said so yourself! You were exhausted."

"Well, I could have been sick."

"Good Lord, Mother. Why does everything have to be so complicated? You're human, like the rest of us. You had a long and tiring trip, and then the kitchen was hot and you fell asleep. Big deal! Now you've had a good, long rest and you're obviously fine."

Claire lifted her coffee cup to her lips and drank, then spread jam on her toast.

Amanda sank into the chintz-covered armchair near the windows. "You haven't changed, have you? I thought maybe after Daddy died . . . Oh, well, forget it."

"After Daddy died, what?"

"You might have mellowed, being alone and all."

Claire sipped coffee until her cup was nearly empty. They were silent a long time before Amanda spoke.

"You're still so beautiful, Mother, even without makeup. When I was a girl I was totally intimidated by you. You were elegant, poised, so sure of yourselff. I felt . . . less than, diminished in your presence. I had to get away to find myself."

"That's silly. You're just as pretty in your own way." Claire brushed back straggles of hair from her face. Then she realized she had not acknowledged but denigrated her daughter's feelings, had turned the conversation to who was prettier. She remembered Dr. Delanny saying that she ought to take a hard look at her own self-centeredness.

"No—I'm wrong. It's not silly at all," Claire said. "Parents don't always realize the effect they have on their kids. That is, *I* didn't realize." She filled her cup again and added cream.

Amanda looked at her quizzically. "Well, it's all in the past, isn't it? That's what Tom says; forget it, it's in the past." She leaned forward in her chair. "But doesn't the past make us who we are? Don't we have to examine the past so we understand why we do things?" There was anger and uncertainty in her voice, and her chin trembled.

"I suppose so." Claire thought of her mother's suicide, her father sobbing, and the icy knot in her stomach. How could it possibly be helpful to remember that?

"They say an unexamined life is not worth living," Amanda said.

"Who says that?"

"If I recall, it was written over the entrance to the oracle at Delphi."

"That's one point of view. Perhaps it's best to leave the past alone," Claire replied. They were silent again, then she said, "Back home, I saw a therapist for a while."

Amanda gave a funny, hoarse little laugh. "You went to a therapist?"

"After your father . . ."—she hesitated, then plunged ahead—"died, I had a difficult time. For a long while, I couldn't even admit that he was dead." She shrugged and pulled back from the brink. "I needed to talk to someone, that's all."

Amanda's eyes softened. "If you feel well enough, Mother, Tom and I are driving to

Johnson City in Tennessee to do some shopping today. Want to come?"

Surprise registered on Claire's face. "You're going to another state to shop? For what?"

"Sheets, towels, lamps. We can get it all in Asheville, but it's a beautiful ride. We'll take a picnic lunch and make a day of it." She waved an arm. "You're probably not interested."

"I'd like to come. I'd like to buy you something special for a wedding present."

Amanda's eyebrows arched. "Tom won't tolerate anyone else paying for things like housewares, so don't start with him when we get there, okay?"

"But it's such a small thing. A few sheets—"

"Don't do this, Mother," Amanda interrupted her.

Claire lifted both hands. "Okay. I won't."

"Fine. We'll pick you up, say, at ten?" She checked her watch. "It's nine-fifteen now. Does that give you enough time?"

"I'll need to get my suitcases from the car."

"Tom and Larry brought them in last night. They're right over there." Amanda pointed to where the suitcases sat alongside the dresser.

"I'll take a shower and get dressed. Why don't I wait for you on the porch?"

Amanda nodded. "Fine."

"Where is Mr. Harden? I'd like to apologize for the trouble I've put him to and thank him for his hospitality."

"Dad's gone to Asheville to pick up a part for an old truck he's working on. He collects classic trucks and restores them—that's why he always looks so grungy. Millie fusses that she can't get the grease out of his pants, but he ignores her. You may run into Millie. She's off at the market but might be back before we leave. She's not much of a talker and she won't bother you." Amanda slipped from the room and closed the door behind her.

Claire looked about. Her trained eye recognized the dresser, with its bow-shaped drawers, as an antique. "Up. Up," she urged herself. "Not much time." But she didn't budge, for the welcoming yellow room, with its lace curtains moving slightly in the morning breeze, was charming and comfortable. Maybe rather than going with her daughter and Tom, she would loll about the place, rest and read.

Dr. Delanny had once asked, "Do you always shoot yourself in the foot?"

Then, Claire had pretended not to understand what the therapist meant. Would she shoot herself in the foot again, this soon, with her daughter? Amanda had reached out, invited her to join them today. Not to go would be a missed opportunity.

Claire rolled out of bed and headed for the bathroom.

23

Over the Mountain

"The sky's clearest in the wintertime," Tom told Claire as they drove past the exit to the town of Mars Hill. "There are days in the summer when you can't see the mountains, for all the pollution."

"Pollution? Here?" Claire asked. "I always thought this area of the country was pristine. Didn't people come here to cure tuberculosis?"

Tom speeded up and swung past a lumbering truck. "That's how it was, but things have changed. Too many cars and trucks and factories to the west of us without pollution controls. The wind blows from the west and we get all their crap." He explained that in July and August, the mountains were usually shrouded in haze.

"Well, let's enjoy today. It's gorgeous," Claire said.

Tom nodded. "It sure is."

To their right, between the road and the steep, heavily wooded hillside, a narrow field bordered a sliver of a creek. A man trudged behind a motorized tiller, churning up the dark brown earth. Celery-green leaves, light and airy, announced the coming of spring. On their left, in contrast to the delicate beauty of nature, enormous concrete pillars rose to support the new highway bridge that stretched across gaps between the mountains.

"The new road's gonna bring a lot more traffic into Asheville. It's a hell of an engineering job. It'll cut the driving time over the mountain in half."

"Has your father lived in Weaverville all his life?" she asked.

From the backseat came Amanda's giggle. "Good gracious, no. Dad's got a Ph.D. in British history. His field's the Plantagenet period: Henry one, Henry two and his amazing wife, Eleanor of Aquitaine, Richard the

Lion-hearted. He taught at UCLA in California and later at Miami University in Ohio."

"Then his passion for classic trucks got the better of him," Tom said. "When Grandpa died, Grandma Alice was alone. I think Dad used that excuse to resign his professorship and come home."

"And he's satisfied with this life?" Claire wondered why a man as educated as Larry would enjoy spending his days under old trucks.

"Seems to be." Tom slowed behind an eight-wheeler straining up the hill. When the road widened to three lanes, he zipped past the truck, then reduced his speed to a steady fifty-five. The road grew steeper and twisted as the mountains closed in on them.

"My father was an architect," Claire said. "He worked from home."

At that moment, they crested the mountain and the scene changed. WELCOME TO TENNESSEE the sign said. The road widened into a four-lane highway. The mountains receded. Cows grazed in pastures that ran in long sweeps from valley to mountaintop. Homes with gardens dotted the landscape, as did idyllic white churches with tall steeples.

"It's beautiful country," Claire said.

"We're lucky it's in the sixties, warm enough for us to have our lunch by the river in Erwin," Tom said.

"Erwin's a small town on the way to Johnson City. Tom and I enjoy detouring there when we make this trip," Amanda said.

Claire slid her window down a crack. Certain smells in nature always pleased her: fresh-turned earth, the scent that rose from the hot earth after rain, honeysuckle.

They drove for a while without speaking, and then Claire looked across the front seat of the car at her daughter's fiancé. Did he and Amanda have any idea that marriage meant giving up things, compromising in ways you never imagined? Perhaps it wasn't worth the effort, the stress and strain involved in finding a new husband—yet being single had proved bleak and empty.

Tom turned from the highway onto a two-lane, then onto a single-lane dirt road, and parked near a rushing river under an old and spreading dogwood tree.

"This is the Nolichucky River," Tom told Claire. Bountiful from the spring rains, the river shot plumes of white water as it raced over protruding rocks. "It's one of our favorite places. Since it's a bit early for lunch, why don't we take a walk up the hill? There's a meadow you might enjoy seeing."

Claire found the climb steep and required frequent stops to catch her breath. But the exertion was well worth it, for at the top, a meadow sprinkled with white and yellow wild-flowers opened before her, with mountains all around.

"Isn't it lovely, Mother?" Amanda asked.

"It surely is," Claire said.

Whispering to each other, hand in hand, Amanda and Tom wandered off.

Claire thought of her honeymoon in the Caribbean, the balmy nights, the air scented with jasmine. They had walked barefoot on white sand beaches and made love in a sheltered cove. Seeing her daughter now, in love and happy, brought back the ache of Phillip's loss.

"Ready to go back, Mother?"

Claire was lying on the ground staring up at the clouds, her mind and body at rest. Had it been five minutes, or a half hour? She sat up and brushed off her slacks. "Yes, I'm ready to go."

Back at the river, Tom spread blankets, and Amanda unpacked cream cheese and cucumber sandwiches, asparagus wrapped in ham, white wine, and plump grapes from a large wicker basket.

Claire ate slowly, savoring the flavors, then leaned back on her elbows. The sky was a flawless blue, and the tips of new growth on the branches above stirred in the breeze. Claire's memory went to a day when, at seven years old, she and her father had strolled hand in hand along a country lane. He had stopped that lovely spring day to break a sweet-smelling bough from a blossoming apple tree and presented it to her. "For you, princess," he had said.

Claire remembered clutching that bough to her chest and giggling.

"Big trout in the stream," Tom said. "See how they camouflage themselves between the rocks?"

Claire rose and walked the few steps to the river's edge. "I see a tail wiggling." She laughed, thinking that her father would have loved this place. "The year I was seven, we lived in the country. My father used to take me fishing at Lower Lamper Stream. We'd sit on the bank and fish, and we hardly ever talked. 'It spooks the fish when we talk,' Dad told me."

From somewhere close by, a bird sang and another answered. "That same year, my father taught me to recognize birds: cardinals, blue jays, chickadees. 'With cardinals,' he said, 'the male's always brighter than the female.' When I asked why, he said, 'Because the female chooses her mate, and the poor fellow's got to look terrific to get her attention.'"

Propped up on their elbows on the grass, Tom and Amanda seemed as content as young lovers ought to be. "I never knew that you were close to your father," Amanda said.

"I guess I never talked much about my childhood."

"Somehow I got the impression it was incredibly unhappy."

"In many ways it was. My mother was ill a great deal, and that colored our lives. I guess it outweighed the good times." Claire looked away. "Well, now, how about telling me about your wedding plans?"

Amanda's eyes brightened, and she sat up and folded her legs beneath her. "The almanac promises us a sunny day. I'm going to wear an ankle-length, cream-colored dress and low heels. Be sure you wear low heels, Mother, so you don't get stuck in the grass."

As the details of the wedding unfolded, Claire refrained from commenting. This was not at all the wedding she wanted for her daughter. The tent, Amanda said, would be blue and located in the meadow, which was quite a distance from a kitchen or running water. The service composed of their own words was much too simplistic, Claire thought, and smacked of New Age claptrap.

"We want to keep it simple and easy. No tuxedos," Tom said. "Dad and I will wear blue suits."

Amanda skipped from item to item. Tents and chairs would be delivered the day of the wedding. Food would be catered and would be largely casseroles and salads. At least, Claire thought, they have not mentioned paper plates.

It was two o' clock when they packed up their leftovers and left. As they drove through Erwin, Claire noticed the mix of graceful white frame houses with wraparound porches and new brick and glass buildings. From every side street, one could see the hills and higher mountains that surrounded the town. Lines from a poem she had learned in high school by the poet e. e. cummings came to mind: "And the mountains are dancing are dancing."

In Johnson City Claire wandered about Target while Amanda and Tom shopped. She would buy their wedding gift in Asheville when they were not around.

Soon after they returned to the farmhouse, Millie rang a bell and everyone converged on the dining room.

"This is Mildred, without whom this place would fall apart." Larry put his arm about the woman's shoulders.

Millie, as everyone else called her, smiled at Claire. Claire judged her to be in her sixties, five feet tall and slightly overweight. Millie's blue eyes welcomed Claire with a sincerity that warmed her heart.

"Glad you're with us. Hope you'll stay a while." Millie gestured toward the table. "Dinner's waiting."

As he pulled out a chair for her, Larry whispered to Claire, "You'll probably be surprised by dinner. I never argue food with Mildred."

The table was set with a white lace-edged tablecloth, blue Wedgwood china, Waterford crystal, and slender white candles in silver holders on either side of a Baccarat bowl brimming with lilies. The meal consisted of a huge golden turkey with all the trimmings.

When she brought in the turkey, Millie announced, "This is a day of thanksgiving to welcome Amanda's mother. You all enjoy your supper now."

Larry raised his wineglass and toasted, "Welcome, Claire. We're delighted you came." He nodded at her glass. "Mandy told us you don't drink. Is ginger ale okay?"

"Perfect," she replied.

With the enthusiasm of a small boy, unruly hair falling across his forehead, Larry talked about trout fishing in the many rivers and hiking in the mountains on well-marked trails.

Tom spoke of their day and their climb up to the meadow in Erwin.

Claire noted the shy smile that touched the corners of Larry's mouth. "What is it about your meadows? I felt like dancing again," she said.

"And did you?" Larry asked.

"No, of course not."

"Why not?" he asked. "You should show this daughter of yours that you can dance."

Later, when they were finishing the pumpkin pie, Tom said, "So, Claire, you'll spend some time here with us?"

"I . . . don't know," Claire responded with a quick glance at Amanda.

"Do stay," her daughter said. "You slept well last night, didn't you?"

Larry waved away her doubt. "Stay, stay. My wife, Olivia, decorated that room. She had a way of making things welcoming." He pushed back his chair and crossed his legs. "Olivia was a licensed midwife."

"Mom was a terrific midwife. Women loved her," Tom said. "She always laughed a lot, and this place used to be full of people."

"She glowed around people," Larry said. "I used to enjoy just sitting back and looking at her." He fell silent for a moment. "She was a good woman, Olivia."

Tom said, "So many people attended her funeral, and so many spoke about her being their best friend."

"Olivia certainly made a contribution to other people's lives," Larry said.

It made Claire wonder how she might be remembered, and by whom? She'd been known as a tough businesswoman who sold antiques to rich people, a person generally considered aloof, even unfriendly, except by Olden, who'd always seen to the very heart of her.

What kind of wife had she really been to Phillip? Supportive? In business, yes, but in personal matters she had often been impatient and critical. Loving? Early on, yes. But over time, having to always initiate sex and uncertain of his cooperation, she had been edgy and overly sensitive in their private moments. Mainly they had been a team. Overall they had had a pleasant-enough life; certainly to the world it seemed that way.

It was a relief when Larry said, "I was telling you about the room you slept in last night, Claire. Anyone who sleeps in that room reports that they've slept like a baby."

"I certainly did," Claire said. "Thank you for being so kind. I'd like to stay another night, if that's all right."

"Stay as long as you choose," Larry said.

Millie brought dessert and coffee, which they ate in comfortable silence. Then Larry stood, stretched, and yawned. "Tomorrow I have a heck of a busy day. Off to bed with me. Night, all."

Moments later, Amanda and Tom pushed back their chairs. Claire did the same, thinking that they might sit on the porch a while. Instead, Tom slung his arm about Amanda's shoulders and they bade Claire good night.

"I'm glad you came with us today, Mother," Amanda said. "This was the nicest day I can remember that we've spent together, wouldn't you say?"

"Yes, the nicest day."

"Daddy would be happy we did this, don't you think?" Amanda asked.

"Come on, Mandy, don't press your mother," Tom said.

"Yes," Claire replied. "Your father would be quite pleased."

"Pleased isn't happy, is it, Mother?"

"I meant happy. He'd be very happy. He loved you very much, Amanda." *Can't I say anything right?*

They were in the hall now, and Tom had taken Amanda's arm and was gently nudging her toward the front door.

Amanda leaned away from him. "Mother, I've been meaning to tell you. Paul was able to get leave, and he's coming to the wedding. I didn't know that when I asked Uncle Olden to give me away."

"Olden was so flattered and happy when you asked him. You're not going to—?"

"Mother, stop it. I'd never do that to Uncle Olden. Paul understood."

Paul. Olden. Amanda. I can't cope with all of them together. Claire reached for the wall to steady herself.

"If you're worried about Paul coming, you don't have to do anything but be polite to him. He has no expectations."

Claire's face grew red; she began to tremble. "He should have expectations. And so should I. I thought he was somewhere near Japan."

Amanda retreated to the shelter of Tom's arms and told him. "See, I told you. I shouldn't have said a word. She hates Paul."

Claire leaned against the wall for support. Hate her son? Did Amanda really think that? "I didn't mean . . . It was so unexpected— that's all." She straightened. "It's just that I was deeply hurt when Paul dashed in and out after your father . . . well, you know." She fought back tears. She had needed Paul desperately after Phillip died, but he had avoided her, had seemed repelled by her. She in turn had responded with cold indifference. They had never talked. What could she say to him now?

Wrapped in a blue bathrobe, Larry descended the stairs. "What's going on here?"

Amanda, in tears and clutching Tom's arm, said, "I'm sorry. I never should have told my mother that my brother's coming for the wedding. It's going to be awful, and spoil our wedding."

"No such thing," Larry said. "Everything will work out just fine." He approached Claire.

"You look exhausted. Let me help you to your room. You can discuss this in the morning." With a nod, he dismissed Tom and Amanda.

"But I should explain to Amanda. She's upset. I—"

The door closed behind the young couple.

"There's tomorrow, and tomorrow, and tomorrow." Larry guided Claire upstairs. At her bedroom door, he said. "It'll all work out. You'll see. Now, sleep well."

"Thank you," Claire whispered, relieved that a man had taken charge. "I am tired. I must apologize to you for last night. I can't imagine how I could have passed out like I did. To arrive and intrude into your life like this—I'm very sorry. I've had so much on my mind. You've been most kind."

"There's nothing to apologize for. You were exhausted from a long car trip."

"It was more than that—stress, feeling unsettled since my husband died . . ."

"I know the feeling. Sometimes things pile up and we hit overload. Sleep well, Claire. See you tomorrow."

24

Kindness Rendered

Tomorrow arrived, bringing a debilitating cold that pinned Claire to the bed for a week fighting fever, joint pain, and a racking cough that left her limp.

Millie and Amanda took shifts tending her. She vaguely noticed their faces bent over her as they placed cool towels on her forehead, the gentle nudging and rolling of her body as they turned her to change her sheets so that they would be fresh and cool against her fevered skin. Millie made chicken soup, and Amanda sat beside her bed and insisted that her mother finish at least half a cup of the healing broth. When Claire was able, they helped her to the chair by the window.

When the fever broke, when the glare from the sun no longer pained her eyes, the curtains were opened so that she could enjoy the mountains.

"If anything'll revive you, them there mountains sure will," Millie said. She was a countrywoman, plain, short, and broad-shouldered with rough, red hands that were amazingly gentle when they sponge-bathed Claire, or helped her to or from the bed. "Ain't no one ever been sick in this room," Millie said one afternoon as she changed the sheets.

"I haven't been sick in years. Not even a cold," Claire replied.

"Too much worry and strain can make a person sick. Lowers your resistance, seems to me." Millie smoothed the sheets. "I could tell you came here with plenty of aggravation inside you."

"You're a wise woman," Claire said.

"I been around a while, that's all," Millie said. "And I watch people."

Somehow, Claire trusted this woman. "Since Amanda's father died, it's been very difficult. I've done one stupid thing after the other; my life's a huge ball of confusion."

"Sometimes a person needs to stay still and not do nothing. Step back and gather up your senses, and your insides gonna tell you what you need to know."

"Perhaps that's what my body was telling me. But my Lord, this last week's been miserable." Claire turned her head to the window. "Why do I feel so comfortable and safe in this room? I almost hate to get well and leave."

Millie smiled. "You ain't got to leave. You're a fine, strong woman. Before you know it, you'll be tramping them hills and runnin' about that meadow like you'd always been here."

Claire laughed. "I can't stay in Mr. Harden's house indefinitely."

"He don't care." Millie cocked her head. "This house has been too empty, too quiet since the missus died. Do him good to have another body here for a bit."

"We'll see." Claire started to rise from the chair, then hesitated. "Will I ever get my strength back? Millie, will you help me back to bed, please?"

"You'll be fine, just takes some time, that's all." Millie helped Claire ease from the chair and into bed. "It's time you come down to eat—use your limbs, get the blood moving."

"I'll try tomorrow." Claire fell back against the pillows Millie had fluffed. When Millie left the room, Claire allowed her thoughts to drift. What would she do next? Where would she live? What would she say to Paul? To Olden? She fell asleep, woke, had lunch from the tray Millie brought, and slept again. By evening she felt considerably better. *I'm getting stronger,* she thought. And as nice as it is, I'm getting bored being in this room.

Tom helped her downstairs for dinner. Though she clung to his arm and grasped the railing with the other, the descent made her dizzy. "Don't look down," Tom said. "Fix your eyes on one spot on the wall and trust me."

She did as told and made it to the dining room table, where she managed to eat some soup and drink a cool drink flavored with coffee. The effort of coming downstairs drained her, and she gratefully accepted Amanda and Tom's offer to help her upstairs.

"Uncle Olden called," Amanda said. "He's called every day since I told him you were sick. He's worried about you. He's coming earlier than planned."

She probably asked him to come to buffer whatever she thinks is going to happen between Paul and me, Claire thought. Well, it will be good to have him here. "Olden is looking forward to your wedding," Claire said. "And I'll be happy to see him."

"Have you ever considered marrying Uncle Olden? He's always been crazy about you, and you have years of history together."

Claire laughed. "Don't be silly; he's just a good friend. And besides, I like tall men."

"He's not that short. You could wear flats and he would seem taller." Amanda held up her hands. "Just kidding."

Did Amanda know about Olden's proposal? Claire decided it best not to delve too deeply into the source of Amanda's suggestion.

Later that night as she was reading, a light knock came and Larry's head rounded the door. "Just thought I'd check on you. Can I get you anything?"

Claire pulled the comforter high across her shoulders. Her toes under the covers were nice and warm. "Would you mind opening the window about five inches, please?"

"Sure." The loose floorboard she had learned to step over creaked as he walked across the room. He lifted the sash, then looked up at the sky. "Magnificent night full of stars." He retraced his steps. "Sleep well."

"You, too, and thank you," Claire replied.

When he was gone she sat up in bed, eased her legs over the side, and waited for the slight dizziness to pass. Her toes felt for her slippers, and Claire walked slowly to the window. The windowpane was cold to her touch.

Claire pressed her forehead against the cold glass and looked up. Stars as numerous as sand on a beach! She could see the constellation of Orion cresting a hill. How wonderful! After a time, Claire shuffled back to bed feeling sweetly content.

When Millie came into the room the following morning, she said, "Well, bless your soul—you're dressed! What'd I tell you? You're gettin' better. Let me help you, and we'll get you right down to my kitchen. Nothing like a good breakfast to give you strength."

Claire slipped into a chair at the oak table in the kitchen and sipped her coffee as she watched Millie scramble eggs. "Has Larry eaten and gone?"

"He's an early riser," Millie said.

Claire looked at the clock above the refrigerator: ten-thirty. Piles of finely chopped tomatoes, cucumbers, celery, and onions covered the chopping block. "What are you making?"

"Fixin's for a salad for lunch," Millie replied. "Now you eat on up, and don't drink too much coffee. Better to take tea these first few days."

Claire ate the eggs. "What day is it?" She looked at the calendar. "I can't keep it sorted out. And everyone seems so busy."

"They always are," Millie said. "Ain't nothin' we can do to hold 'em back. Your daughter's off to Asheville."

"Amanda worries about her brother coming. She's afraid he and I will have words." She found herself telling Millie about Phillip's funeral and her estrangement from Paul, and about how he had broken his father's heart by joining the navy.

"Funerals and weddings bring up all kinds of feelings. Your son mighta been feelin' real bad at that funeral, what with disappointing his father like that. If kids don't tell you nothin', how you gonna know what's goin' on in their heads, I ask you?" She set her hands on her hips and looked at Claire. "People don't act natural at a time like that. Grief gets a hold of you and you act different. Can't hold what a body says or does at a time like that against them."

"I don't remember much about the funeral. Just the way Paul acted, and how I felt." She handed Millie her empty plate. "Licked clean. Is that good enough for you?"

"Eat like that, you'll be up and out in no time," Millie replied.

While Millie rinsed her dish, Claire leaned her elbows on the table. "Well, Amanda need not worry about Paul and me. I'd never make a scene at her wedding."

"I would think not," Millie said. "You're too much of a lady for that."

That's a laugh. If Millie could have seen me in Florida, she'd think differently. "Can I help you with anything?"

"Mr. H. likes his salad greens chopped up real fine. I got three lettuces here. You could chop 'em for me and put 'em in this bowl." She set the lettuce on a board, handed Claire a knife, and set a shallow wooden bowl on the table.

"You can set your watch by Mr. H.," Millie said. "He'll stomp into this kitchen at eleven-twenty lookin' for his lunch. He'll lather up his hands and scrub 'em all the way to his elbows, like you see them surgeons do on TV shows. Pay him no mind if he grunts, eats, and gets him back to work. His mind's far off under some nasty old truck."

Lunch was indeed a silent affair, and his behavior was exactly as Millie had described. Larry barely greeted Claire and Millie. He bolted down his food, shoved back his chair, and strode from the room.

His behavior stirred painful memories for Claire, of lonely, silent meals and the frightening emptiness that had dominated her life during her mother's last illness. Visits to the hospital. Her mother's unsmiling face pressed against the glass window behind the grill of iron, watching them as her father drove the car up the beautifully planted drive.

Bright flowers had offered a startling contrast to the washed-out gray room in the institution, the washed-out gray face, the hunched shoulders and averted eyes of the woman who was her mother. Inadvertently, Claire shuddered. The phone call had come at three in the morning, on a Tuesday. In the nadir of her mother's life, she had hung herself.

A long, dark summer had followed. Frozen dinners eaten in frozen silence, and so many anxious days and nights. She had had no summer job that year. No one noticed. Her father turned somber and lackluster. He rarely left the house and for weeks dressed in a bathrobe and hardly shaved. He had more grunted than spoken to his children.

"What you thinkin' about, Claire?" Millie asked. "You look real sad."

Claire looked up at her. Millie was wiping her hands on her apron. "Nothing."

"Nothing don't put a look like that on your face. I gotta get me some fresh eggs from the henhouse. You be all right?"

"I won't move from this spot."

Millie returned with downy feathers clinging to her right arm. The egg she handed to Claire was still warm. "Now here's an egg for you. Can't get nothin' big and beautiful like this at them markets, can you?"

Claire weighed the egg in her palm. "No, you can't." She was grateful for the quiet of the kitchen, the steady sureness of Millie. "You like to cook, don't you?" Claire asked.

"Guess I do. You should have seen the cookin' went on here when the missus was alive: parties, picnics, barbecues, cars comin' and goin', people chatterin' and laughin'. The missus played an old piano and they'd gather round and sing the night away." She took a step back and studied Claire. "You look peaked, Claire. Best to rest this afternoon. You overdo it and you'll be flat on your back again."

Claire was sitting by the window reading that afternoon when Larry knocked on her door. "It's me," he called.

Claire closed her book. She wanted to say "Go away," but said instead, "Come in."

He smelled of pungent soap or strong aftershave, and his hair gleamed wet. "Finished that transmission I was working on. Mind if I sit a minute?" He drew up the chair from beside the small vanity and plunked into it. The chair seemed to mutter in protest beneath his weight.

Claire's fingers traced wide looping circles on the arm of the rocking chair. "I'm on the mend. In a couple of days I'll be out of your hair."

"We'd all like you to stay, Claire. With the wedding so close and all, and your friend Olden Riverdale and Paul staying here, why move? Besides, you're family now."

"Family? The kids aren't married yet."

"They will be soon. It's my intruding on your privacy, isn't it? I'm sorry; it's rude of me to come in like this." He slapped his palm against his leg. "It won't happen again. Stay with us. You need to be close to your children now."

"You haven't offended me. You've been nothing but kind and I appreciate that. It's Amanda—she doesn't really want me here. And Paul probably won't talk to me."

"Now you're having a little pity party," he said.

"Maybe I'm due a little pity." She smiled. "But you know what they say about overstaying one's welcome: after three days, fish and house guests . . ."

Larry laughed, and Claire suddenly felt as if she'd known him for years.

When Larry rose, she was sorry to see him leave. "You needn't go," she said.

"I've got a couple of things to take care of. Now you think about staying with us a while."

"Thanks. I will." Claire relaxed and closed her eyes. He was kind. Millie was warm and mothering. She wanted to stay.

25

Paul

The cab driver pressed his hand on the horn. No one appeared. "Ain't nobody home, mister."

"Doesn't matter," Paul said. "Someone will come along. I'll wait." He paid the driver. "I'm sorry it was so difficult finding the place. I had no idea it was this far from the airport."

"Me, neither." The driver shrugged and accepted the fare and the large tip Paul handed him. "What the heck, it's all in a day's work."

Paul exited the cab, heaved his duffel bag over his shoulder, and started toward the farmhouse as the cab reversed and departed.

He dropped the duffel bag on the porch, strode along the row of white chairs lined up like sentinels, and selected one halfway down. This was good—better than if they'd all been home and rushed out to welcome him. He needed a bit of time alone to collect himself.

What would he say to his mother? It was so long since it had been easy to talk or be with her. Sometimes, in that place between sleep and waking, he remembered being very small and her tucking him into bed and reading to him. Or was that imagination, hope, longing? What could he say to her now, feeling the guilt he still felt?

He had been upstairs, his eye glued to his telescope, scanning the horizon for passing ships when he heard the screech of brakes, the high-pitched scream, the thud as his brother's body hit the pavement. He heard it still at night in his dreams, heard his mother's gut-wrenching sobs. When he dreamed this dream, he invariably awakened sobbing.

He had only to close his eyes to bring to mind the twisted bike, Terrance's body lying on the ground. Terrance's body had been broken, and Paul's heart had been, too. It was all his fault. Had he done as asked and taken care of his brother, rather than locking him out of the attic and telling him to get lost, Terrance would be alive, and his mother's heart would not have frozen. The image of his parents' ravaged faces haunted him still.

The navy, the hard work, the distance from home, finally had brought a measure of relief. But when his father died, all the guilt and pain had resurfaced and nearly overwhelmed him. He had not been able to look at his mother, to speak more than a few formal words to her.

And soon he would have to face her—his unknowing accuser. Paul's palms sweated and his throat tightened. Tears blurred his vision, and he regretted coming.

But how could he ignore his sister's wedding? When Amanda had first shared her good news, he'd lain in his bunk on the ship and prayed that his mother would not be there. How could he think she would not come? He had stalled replying to his sister for so long that she had asked Olden Riverdale to walk her down the aisle. What a fool he'd been. But it was done, and he would smile, be pleasant, and manage civilities with his mother until the wedding. Paul dropped his head into his hands.

It was Millie who came upon the young naval officer. His head was down and his shoulders shook. Millie tiptoed away and returned to hand him a cold washcloth. She placed a glass of sweet iced tea on the railing of the porch and disappeared before he could thank her.

Paul wanted to run after her, fling his arms about her and weep on her shoulder. He wanted her to rub his back and whisper that everything would be just fine. Instead, he wiped his face, drank the tea in long swallows, and grew calm. He was, after all, a grown man. A navy man.

He sat and listened to sounds that were not of the sea: the buzz of a chain saw, a car on a road far below, the wind hissing through trees, the chirp of crickets. Wind gusted, cooling his flushed cheeks.

Finally he stood, picked up his duffel bag, and rang the doorbell. Soft footsteps approached and the door opened to reveal a short, stout woman who smiled up at him.

"I'm Millie," she said. "I'm the housekeeper. You must be Amanda's brother, Paul. Welcome. Your room's right up those stairs, first on the left. I started a hot bath for you, thinkin' you might be needin' one."

"That was very kind of you," he said. "The washcloth, the iced tea, everything. Thank you."

"Travel will wear a body down," she said, patting his shoulder. "I ain't done nothing more than one body ought to do for another. We're meant to help one another in this here life."

As he headed toward the steps Paul looked into the living room, shadowy in the afternoon light. A Tiffany lamp lit the highly polished surface of a mahogany end table, and across the hallway in the dining room he could see a table set for five, lovely with china and crystal glasses. Tall candlesticks waited to be lit. The runner on the stairs appeared to be pieces of a well-worn Persian rug. At the top of the stairs he followed Millie into a large bedroom with a sleigh bed, two armchairs that faced a fireplace, and windows with views of the side lawn. Beyond the treetops, the peaks of mountains were visible.

"You just come on down whenever you like," Millie said. "There's always a pitcher of iced tea in the fridge and cake on top of the fridge. Help yourself."

Paul dropped the duffel and stripped off

his clothes. In the adjoining bathroom, the tub had been filled with hot water. He folded his clothes and laid them across the back of a chair, then lowered himself into the deep claw-foot tub and relaxed. His mind quieted, and after a time he almost fell asleep.

"Hey, Paul—stop lazing in that tub and get on out here!" His sister's voice teased from beyond the door.

"Give me a minute to dry off and get dressed," Paul called back.

"Casual dress," she said. "I've got great people for you to meet."

When Millie told Claire of Paul's arrival, the countdown to the encounter with her son began. Nervous, Claire had retired to her room where she lay on the bed, trying not to think and taking deep breaths to quiet her pounding heart. Then she showered, dressed, and sat by the window—listening for the door across the hall to open and close, listening for her son's footsteps in the hall or on the stairs. Time passed. Had he closed his door so quietly she hadn't heard it? Had his footsteps been muffled by the runners?

When Millie rang the dinner bell, Claire realized that she had been sitting and picking at her fingernails for half an hour. She had grown accustomed to the tinkle of the silver bell, to a table laden with bowls of cholesterol-saturated fried chicken, macaroni and cheese, buttered beans, fried okra, and mashed potatoes with gravy. Meals in this household differed in ambiance, in the character of the food, and the attitude of the diners, from any she had ever known. Over the past days she had begun to relax and enjoy the easy banter between Larry, Tom, and Amanda without feeling obliged to participate.

To her surprise, Paul met her at the foot of the stairs. He held out both hands to take hers; they did not kiss or hug.

"Mother, you look well."

"And you look so handsome and grown-up." It was as if she were seeing him for the first time, and a thrill of pride raced through her. "How tall you are. How much you look like your father."

He laughed. "I was such a scrawny kid, remember?" He offered his arm to lead her into the dining room.

"Just a moment, Paul."

They stopped and she turned to face him. She longed to throw her arms about him, to hold him close, to tell him how much she loved and missed him. But he was not her little boy any longer. He was a tall, handsome man and something in his eyes stopped her. "I'm awfully glad to see you," she said. "I'm so glad you came."

His eyes held hers. "I'm glad to see you, too, Mother." What was it in those eyes that she could not read?

"It's good to see Amanda so happy, isn't it? Tom's a very nice young man. His father's been most gracious having me here and they've been so kind, especially Millie," Claire said.

He nodded. "She seems like a kind woman." He shifted from one foot to the other. "Shall we go in? The others are waiting."

He's as uncomfortable as I am. Claire took his arm. "Yes, let's go in."

The tone of the evening was as bright and cheerful as the table setting. Larry entertained them with stories about his great-great-grandfather, who had arrived from Scotland in the mid-eighteen-hundreds and immediately joined a party of immigrants headed west.

"His name was Quincy Lawrence Harden, and he worked for a time for one of his traveling companions from Charleston. One day, Quincy went hunting with an old hound dog that had attached itself to him. He trusted that old dog's nose. But the hound smelled something in the woods and vanished, and Quincy wandered about, got lost, and found himself smack-dab in the middle of your meadow, Claire." He cut his shirt apart, broke a branch from a tree, tied his banner to it, and planted his stake."

"What became of the dog?" Amanda asked.

"Once he built his cabin and settled in, the old hound showed up with a bitch in tow and a trail of puppies. He kept them all. They kept him company until he got him a wife and kids."

"A dog, and a wife, and a good, good life," Tom sang.

They all laughed, and a comfortable silence settled over the room.

"How many acres do you have here?" Paul asked.

"A hundred and thirty-two," Larry said. "From the top of the mountain behind this house down to Reems Creek Road, and about five miles along Reems Creek. Been offered plenty for it by developers. A lot of the land's steep, but more of it's easy land, and real pretty, too. I'll show you, if you don't mind a bit of hiking. Got two strong streams running through the land and plenty of trout. You like to fish?"

Paul grinned. "I sure do. I'd like that."

"Claire's father used to take her fishing when she was seven," Tom said.

"I didn't know that." Paul turned and studied his mother.

Before she could respond, Larry said, "Great age, seven."

"When I was seven, I was riding horses bareback. And, remember that time, Dad, when I was seven, and I fell from that big oak and broke my arm?" Tom asked.

"I can't even remember being seven," Amanda said.

Claire had been happy at seven, living in the country, taking walks with her father. And Terrance was . . .

Claire grasped the arms of her chair. "Stop! Enough of seven!" Her explosion stunned them into silence, extinguishing the joviality of the evening.

Millie stuck her head in the door. "Ready for dessert?"

No one replied.

Millie studied one face and then another and retreated to the kitchen, shaking her head and muttering, "What's happened now?"

How incredibly insensitive they are to keep talking about being seven years old. They all know that Terrance was seven when he died. For the first few years afterward, Claire had crossed out the seventh day of each month on her calendars.

"I'm so sorry, Claire," Larry said. "How stupid of me."

"Mother, I'm sorry," Paul said.

Tom coughed.

Amanda and Paul stared at one another across the table.

Claire looked from one to the other. "I'm so sorry for over-reacting like that." Her voice, small and trembling, broke the awkward silence. "That was very rude of me. I've not been myself lately."

"It's all right, Mother," Paul said.

"It's like that for mothers," Larry said. "Olivia and I lost a child, stillborn, a couple of years after Tom was born. Olivia grieved for that infant the rest of her life. Millie believes grief ate away at her over the years and lowered her immune system, so that when she got cancer, she couldn't fight it." He looked suddenly old, the wrinkles shirring about his eyes and mouth. "Mothers never forget." Then he lifted his face and clapped his hands once. "But hey, people, we're here to celebrate. Let's have dessert and then go into the den to shoot some pool or play some gin rummy."

The next morning when she went down for breakfast, Claire ran into Amanda in the hall. She was gathering up her purse and slipping her arms into a sweater. "I'm off—lots of things to do today in Asheville."

"Where's Paul?"

"He's gone fishing with Dad."

The door closed behind Amanda, and her car motor started. Claire watched her daughter's car's tires scatter stones in the driveway, and listened to the rumble of the vehicle diminish as Amanda rounded the first curve.

"I don't belong here. I don't belong anywhere," Claire muttered. "She knew I was here alone. She could have asked me if I'd like to go into Asheville with her."

The following day brought more of the

same. Everyone rose earlier than Claire and dispersed before she came downstairs: Amanda and Tom on some last-minute business pertaining to the wedding, Paul hiking or fishing with Larry.

Millie said, "You might want to drive about and see some of the sights. Ain't good for a body to be sittin' around mopin' like you're doin'. Plenty things out there in this world need tendin' to by an intelligent woman like you."

"Like what?"

"Like kids at the schools who need help with their schoolwork. Manna Food Bank in Asheville was on the radio the other night, askin' for help packin' up bags of food. Yes sirree, plenty things out there need doin'. Busy people are happy people."

Claire resented Millie's words. There was hardly time for her to get involved in things like that here. "I think I'll go for a drive, see some of the country."

"There are plenty of pretty places to see," Millie said. "Plenty places to get lost, too, so watch the roads real good."

As Claire drove down the hill to Reems Creek, her mind replayed Millie's words. How impractical to think that one could just walk into a classroom and announce, "Here I am. Give me a kid to tutor." Besides she'd done her volunteering, raising that huge sum of money for the children's wing of the East Hampton library. Of course, Millie didn't know that.

What did any of them really know about her life? She had arrived in a muddle and fallen ill, and then Paul came and she'd made a fool of herself. If anything, she needed to separate herself from them all until the wedding. And after the wedding? What would she do then?

Without thinking, Claire exited to the right off Reems Creek Road and started up a narrow, twisting lane through the deep woods. Luminous slants of sunlight penetrated the lush canopies of trees. Wisps of fog rose from the forest floor. Claire stopped the car. The trill of a bird from deep in the woods was met by a response close at hand. All living creatures, even the birds, shared their lives with another—except her. The sky overhead darkened and concerned that there would be a storm, Claire started back down the mountain.

The headlights of her car had come on and

ricocheted wildly across the tree trunks on the left. To her right, a rugged wall of rocks seemed dark and foreboding. What had been enchanting earlier seemed suddenly sinister. *Perception,* she thought. *It's all how we think and feel about something.*

On the straight road below, peopled with houses on either side, open fields, and low hills, everything seemed less disturbing, and Claire's mind drifted to thoughts of her father. She had spoken of him more since arriving here than she had in many years. *What sustained him through my mother's tragic illness?* Whatever his feelings were, however he neglected his work or himself, he never faltered in his care of his children: up early each morning to feed and get them off to school, with a snack ready for them when they came home. He had been the single, steady presence in their home, and had attended the basketball games she played in high school. *How had he done it?*

Sadness filled her as she remembered how, after his daughters were educated and married, he had withered away mentally and physically and vanished from their lives like a puff of smoke in a light wind.

Claire hadn't seen much of him during that last year, and when her sister Marjorie, with whom he lived, phoned her to come, she was stunned to see the hollow shell of a man. He was dying, and there had been little time for goodbye. How had she let that happen? She had loved him so much—why had she not visited more often? It was one of the biggest regrets of her life.

And now Amanda was to be married. It ought to be a joyous time; why had she resurrected such painful and ancient memories?

Light rain sent mist rising from the road, and the heavy gray clouds massed on the horizon threatened a heavy downpour. With relief, she turned into the driveway up to the farmhouse.

When she arrived, no cars were present. Before entering the house, she called everyone's names. No one answered.

On the kitchen table, a note in Millie's bold handwriting said: *No one knew when you were coming back. The family went to Weaverville for lunch. I had to babysit my grandchildren. There's a salad for you in the fridge. Millie.*

The house seemed eerie. A gust of wind

lifted the curtains at a window and blew a door shut somewhere.

Claire grabbed her purse and raced down the front steps to her car. She would go to Asheville, go to a bookstore, have dinner, maybe a movie, anywhere. She could not stay here.

26

Olden Riverdale

It was growing dark when Claire returned from the city, where she had walked from one end of the mall to the other and back again. Cars were lined up before the farmhouse, and for an instant Claire hesitated. Moments later, the front door was flung wide. Olden Riverdale appeared and started down the steps, his arms open to greet her. Claire stepped from her car and, with great relief and a sense of having come home, returned his hug.

"Olden, I'm so happy to see you! When did you arrive? Why didn't I know you were coming today? Who picked you up at the airport? How are you?"

Later, after coffee and cake, after Amanda and Tom had bade them good night and departed, after Paul and Larry had turned in, Claire and Olden sat side by side on the porch swing and talked.

"I was worried about you. Why did you leave Florida so abruptly?" he asked.

"I wasn't comfortable there. It's steamy hot one day and cold the next. That's how they say their winters are. After you left in February it got really cold, and when I left in March, it was already close to ninety degrees. I'm not sure Florida is where I want to be, anyway."

"What will you do? Will you come home, Claire?"

She heard the plea in his voice. "My house is sold. Where would I live?"

"That house was too big for you to be rambling about in by yourself. A nice condo or a smaller house, perhaps? You could stay with me until you found a place and got settled."

"I can't seem to make plans or do much of anything, right now. The travel wore me out. I've been relaxing here, trying not to think, not to make decisions."

"I've never been to this area," he said. "Why don't we do a bit of exploring and sightseeing the next few days? I picked up some brochures at the airport."

"That would be nice. I'd like that."

"For starters, let's go into Asheville tomorrow, and have a look around." He stretched and yawned. "I guess the trip's catching up with me." Olden brought the swing to a halt. "It's very pleasant here. They're expecting a cold snap on Long Island, with a last late frost."

Claire stepped away from the swing. "And you want me to go back there?"

"Maybe we both ought to pick up and move here. It's about time I started thinking of retiring."

The next day they lunched at a restaurant on Pack Square in the center of Asheville, then wandered down Patton Avenue, admiring the beautifully preserved Art Deco buildings. They strolled up Haywood Street to the Haywood Park Hotel, then set off down Wall Street, a pedestrian street with brick sidewalks and iron lampposts, where the magnificent, blown-glass objects in the window of a shop drew their attention.

Inside, Olden beckoned the saleswoman, an older woman with short gray hair. Claire watched as he attended to the woman the way a therapist might a client: interested eyes fixed on hers, questions designed to elicit information and express concerns. "Really, it took that long to make?" he asked when she held up an elegant glass vase. "What a talent the craftsman has. Have you ever seen him work?"

After she had replied in some detail to his questions, he said, "I'm looking for a wedding present. Something *very* special." His tone was conspiratorial.

Obviously stirred by his interest, the saleswoman spread a green velvet cloth on a display table; then she placed goblets, vases, a round pitcher with a slender neck, sculptures, and bowls on it for their perusal. She smiled at Claire and Olden. "I may have just what you're looking for in the back. Two absolutely magnificent bowls arrived today."

The delicately designed bowls were deep, fifteen or eighteen inches in diameter and fluted around the edges, and the colors imbedded within the glass swirled and moved like waves, or ribbons, or dancers, depending on the angle of view.

"The artist is Jake Jowers. He brought them in himself. He lives in the hills in Madison

County. I've never seen a creation of his that wasn't beautiful."

"Mr. Jowers's work is very fine," Olden said. "I can understand your enthusiasm for it."

He circled the table and studied each bowl from all angles, then selected the larger of the two. "This seems perfect for Amanda, don't you think?" he asked Claire.

"Yes. Perfect. She'll love it."

"Or do you think this other one suits Amanda better? The bigger one is lovely and its colors are softer, as if Monet selected them." Olden stepped back and studied both bowls again. "The brighter colors remind me more of Amanda. She was a feisty little kid." He handed the saleswoman the second bowl and his credit card, and she processed the sale, then began to carefully wrap the bowl.

"I have a box in the back that I think will fit this. The bride will love it, I'm sure. Is she your daughter?"

"My goddaughter, and this good lady is her mother. Thank you for showing us the bowl," Olden said.

Over the next few days, Olden planned excursions. At Biltmore Estate they skipped the house and walked through gardens brilliant with azaleas. They browsed the antiques shops in Black Mountain. The Folk Art Center on the Blue Ridge Parkway hosted the work of local artists, which they admired. They drove an hour west and south to the Pisgah Inn on the parkway, and lunched in a glass-walled dining room with a panoramic view of the mountains.

Over coffee and dessert, Claire leaned across the table. "I've had a lovely time these last few days. Thank you so much, Olden."

"You and I have always had a good time together. Remember how we used to dance at the club, while that stick-in-the-mud husband of yours played poker with the guys he sailed with?"

"And Sarah sat and chatted with her girlfriends," Claire said. "Thank God neither of them was jealous."

He nodded. "Indeed."

"Remember how Phillip hated the circus?" Claire said. "That first summer it came to town, you and Sarah took Francine, and I took my kids."

"Sarah loved the rides. She was like a kid that way."

Claire nodded. "And Amanda leaned too far into the petting zoo area and fell into it. Where was Phillip that day?"

"Sailing, I think."

"Oh, yes, there was a race."

"What was Amanda, five, six?" he asked. "Gave her quite a scare, if I recall."

"An excuse to scream her head off." Claire laughed.

Paying little attention to the road, Olden exited the parkway too soon and they found themselves driving alongside a creek past a sagging greenhouse surrounded by waist-high weeds that sat in a small section of flat-land across from the water. A short distance farther on, they came upon a gray wooden stand with a sign advertising fresh apple ci-der.

"How could it be fresh this time of year?" Olden asked. "Fresh apples reach the mar-ket in the fall."

Quilts for sale hung on a clothesline near the stand. A man and a woman sat in folding metal chairs, their legs extended, their arms crossed over their bellies.

Claire was relieved when Olden turned the car around and returned to the parkway. "Getting lost makes me nervous," she said.

"I know. That's why I turned around."

He knows me so well, and he's very kind to me. Amanda had asked, "Why don't you marry Uncle Olden?" *Because I don't love him. I like him very much, but I don't love him.*

Olden said, "I've been worried about you, Claire. From the day you asked me to sell your home and business, I've wondered what you were doing and why."

"It's not been easy since Phillip died."

"You keep saying that. It's more than two years, Claire. Have you given any thought to what you might do with your life?"

"Not really," she said. "Olden, could you turn up the air? It's stuffy in here."

He did so, and she welcomed the cool air on her cheeks and forehead.

They exited the parkway and slid into traffic on the 240 bypass around Asheville. "This'll take us to the exit to Weaverville," he said.

"How do you know that?" Claire asked.

"I studied the map before we started."

It was a beautiful day—warm, with the mountains clearly visible, the sky blue, and few clouds. Claire relaxed and enjoyed the layered mountains that circled Asheville.

Olden said, "I had a call just before I left home from a Fred Austerman in Florida. He represents a conglomerate of antiques dealers and called to make an offer on your business. They want the inventory and the name, though not the location, of course."

Claire gasped. "No! Not him."

"Why? Do you know him?"

"I met him at an art opening and I took an instant dislike to him. He seemed a Mafia-type person. I'll give away everything before I'd sell to him or anyone connected to him."

"This isn't like you, Claire. You're a sensible woman. You don't want the business. There hasn't been a decent offer on it to date. What difference does it make, whether you like the buyer or not? And it's not as if he's moving to East Hampton to take over the business. Once the deal's done, it's done, and I'll handle it. You never have to—"

"No! Please, Olden, I will not sell to him. Let's not discuss this anymore."

"As you wish. Maybe you'd consider coming home and liquidating the inventory yourself. Storage is going up again next month, and it's coming straight out of your capital. You can't go on like this."

Claire avoided his eyes. "I can't think about this right now; I have this wedding to get through."

"Okay." In resignation, he lifted both hands from the steering wheel.

"Olden! For God's sake, pay attention to your driving. Why is it taking so long to get back to Weaverville? Everything around here is such a long drive."

For a time, they drove in silence.

Olden coughed, and Claire looked over at him. "I'm sorry for being so snappish."

"Weddings are stressful times," he said.

"That's part of it," she replied. "I wish Amanda would include me in some of it. It's as if she dashes out before I'm up in order to avoid asking me along." Claire crossed and uncrossed her legs. "Sometimes I'm glad not to be involved in the wedding planning, other times I feel hurt. If I packed up and left, it would be days before they even noticed."

"Now, that's not true, Claire. The children love you. They know you've had a rough time. They don't want to burden you, I'm sure."

"You don't have to sugarcoat this, Olden. They don't like me a whole lot. I suppose I deserve that, but I'd like to put an end to this anger, this distance. I'm determined not to let Paul leave without our talking, and I'm not going anywhere until Amanda and I are on a decent footing."

"Why not just tell her you'd like to help with her wedding?"

Claire was silent. "I'm afraid she'll brush me off, and that would hurt even more."

"Nothing ventured, nothing gained."

"That's such a tired cliché, Olden."

"Just an idea. I guess you won't be coming home with me, then." He looked at Claire across the short distance that separated them.

Olden saw himself as a man of considerable importance in his town. Being bald and five feet eight inches tall did not impact his business life, but it influenced his options with woman, and he knew that. He had married his college sweetheart and been faithful to her, but the truth was, he had lusted in his heart for, of all people, Claire Bennett. When they had both lost their spouses, he had hoped that she might see him for what he was: a man of substance who loved her, accepted her totally, and would cherish her for the remainder of their lives. He felt stricken when Claire said, "I may never return to East Hampton."

Swallowing his disappointment, Olden

tightened his grasp on the steering wheel and drove on. "We'll soon be back at the Harden place. Tomorrow we'll go to Lake Lure; Millie says we shouldn't miss that. And in a few days, we have the wedding."

That evening, the entire family dined at a lovely restaurant in South Asheville, and Claire found herself seated at the head of the long table with Larry and Olden flanking her. Conversation was lighthearted, with champagne toasts, and they had flaming cherries jubilee for dessert. The younger people went on to a party somewhere, and Claire returned to the house with the men, and joined them on the front porch for a while before excusing herself and going up to bed.

She was neither sleepy nor tired, and would have enjoyed going dancing. So why hadn't she suggested it? Amanda had looked happy, Paul too, and playing at being a happy family had been nice. If only it had been real. She would have liked to have been a fly on the wall and spent the remainder of the evening just watching them. Claire expressed these feelings to Olden the next day while driving to Lake Lure.

"Reach out to them, Claire. Saying I'm

sorry and telling them that you love them could go a long way."

"Would they believe me? Do you think they'd stop long enough to listen?"

"I guess it depends on how you say it, and when you talk to them. If they're dashing off somewhere, then no."

"What if they don't believe me? I'll have made a fool of myself," she replied.

"Why is this so hard for you? You love them. Children don't want to dislike their parents."

"I think they believe that I never loved them, and God knows I did, and I do. And I need them so much."

"Say that to them, Claire. Speak from your heart, like you're speaking to me now. They'll hear the truth of it."

Claire gave a deep sigh. "Thanks for listening to me, Olden. There's no one else in the world I could have shared these feelings with. Your advice is always so wise, and I trust you."

She leaned her head back and closed her eyes. "I want to make things right with my daughter before the wedding."

Olden nodded encouragingly. "Find a quiet moment and just do it."

"Okay," Claire said. "I'll try."

"That's my girl." He reached over and squeezed her hand. "We've got the rehearsal coming up, then the wedding, and then I go home."

She turned toward him, her eyes wide. "You're leaving the day after the wedding?"

"Right after the wedding, actually. I have to get back."

"Olden, no! Not that soon. I'm going to miss you."

"You know how I feel about you, Claire. You know where I'll be. Whenever you come home, I'll be there."

I've taken this good man so for granted, Claire thought.

Silence floated between them the rest of the way home.

27

Breaking the Silence

"I thought you'd gone for the day, Mother," Paul said as Claire settled into the rocking chair beside his.

"We left after the boat ride on Lake Lure." She took a deep breath. "I'm glad you're here; I've been wanting to talk to you. I've planned this in my mind for years, and now I hardly know where to start."

"I've thought about us talking, too," he said. "There's something I must tell you."

She looked at him, her eyes questioning.

"Do you mind if I go first?" he asked.

"No, not at all."

He swallowed hard and avoided looking

directly at her. "The day Terrance was killed, do you remember you asked me to keep an eye on him? You had an important appointment."

She remembered. The important appointment had been the beauty parlor. She had been irritable and annoyed with the children, who had the day off from school. She recalled her determination to get out of the house, if only for an hour. Paul's voice yanked her out of herself.

"I was hell-bent on going up to the attic to look at the ships through my telescope. Terrance got into things and pestered me when I took him up there, so I locked him out. He banged on the door and cried, and I told him to stop being such a baby and go ride his bike."

An abyss opened before Claire, and her heart plunged.

"It's my fault that Terrance died, Mother. If I'd watched out for him as you asked me to, let him into the attic or played a game with him downstairs, he'd never have been in the street with his bike." His jaw quivered as he turned to look at her. "I'm responsible for his death." His voice turned hoarse. "I killed my brother. I couldn't bear to tell you and Dad. I didn't want you to hate me. I already hated myself." Tears rolled down his cheeks.

A swell of pain swept through Claire. "Oh, no, Paul! *You* weren't responsible. If there's fault, it's all mine—not yours. You were a twelve-year-old boy, and I saddled you with a demanding seven-year-old. It's my fault, not yours. I wanted to get out of the house, to go to the stupid beauty parlor. It was selfish and self-centered of me, shallow and vain. It's not your fault at all."

He reached for her hand and she clasped his tightly, unable to hold back tears. "Can you ever forgive me for dumping my responsibility on you that day?"

"I do," he replied. "Do you forgive me?"

"There's nothing to forgive, but if it makes you feel better, I do. I know what it's like to suffer regret. And I am so sorry that we never talked, never grieved as a family."

Paul knelt before her and rested his head on her lap, his shoulders shaking.

"I love you, Paul. I love you so much. I've missed you so much." She smoothed his hair.

"Forgive me for being so cold at Dad's funeral. It was Terrance's funeral all over again."

"I felt the same way—double the loss, double the pain."

Neither spoke for a time. Paul finally rose and sat beside her again, and she rested her hand on his arm.

"The day I arrived here, I got lost and ended up in the meadow where the wedding will take place tomorrow. It was awe inspiring: the circle of hills, the velvet carpet of grass, the absolute quiet. It seemed to demand something of me, some kind of tribute to its sheer loveliness. I danced. I hadn't danced in years."

"When I was little," Paul said, "I couldn't sleep one night. I heard music downstairs. I remember holding my teddy bear and creeping downstairs. You were dancing alone in the living room, with a pillow. I wanted you to throw down the pillow, pick me up, and dance with me. But I thought if you saw me, you'd shoo me back upstairs, so I stuffed teddy's ear into my mouth and watched. It's my very special memory of you."

"Oh, my precious Paul. Afraid that I would shoo you away? You should have felt free to rush into my arms. I'm sorry for the mother I wasn't." She was silent for a time. "When Terrance died, I stopped dancing."

"I'd dream about you sometimes, out there

on the ship. In all my dreams, you were dancing. I'd wake up crying."

"In the meadow I danced until I couldn't
take another step, and my heart felt lighter
than it had in years."

"I had to join the navy," Paul said. "Before
I left for training, I visited Terrance's grave
and talked to him. I begged his forgiveness. I
felt that Terrance gave me his blessing."

He leaned forward, fists clenched, and
turned to look at her. "I had to join up. I needed
to get away from home, from you and Dad,
from everything that reminded me of Terrance. My knees were shaking when I walked
into that recruiting office. I knew I'd be disappointing you both, and I'm sorry. I just had to
go."

"Do you regret your decision to enter the
navy?"

He shook his head and sat back in the
chair. "No. I love the navy."

"You always loved ships and the sea. I
used to say a mermaid came through the
hospital window and handed you to me."
They both laughed. Claire felt lighter inside,
relieved. "I'm glad you're doing what you love
to do."

"I have a degree now in information technology. I operate complicated computer networks on warships the size of three football fields."

"I'm impressed—and very proud of you."

Paul's rocker resumed its slow movement. "God, I'm glad we talked. It's been a weight on my heart for too many years."

"I'm glad we've talked, too," she said. "Now we can begin to heal."

From behind them came the sound of voices and the front door opening. Amanda appeared with Tom.

"I'm going to freshen up." Claire stooped, kissed Paul's cheek, ran her hand lightly over his hair, and was gone.

"What's that all about?" Amanda sat beside him.

"We were talking. It was amazing."

Amanda waved to Tom, who was headed for the barn. "I'll be home in a jiffy." Then she looked at her brother, and it occurred to her that they had never been close, never shared confidences. It wasn't until he left for naval training that she had realized how much she missed and loved him. Gently, she poked Paul's shoulder. "About what?"

He told his sister about his conversation with their mother, and what a relief it was to unburden his heart. "I guess when you bottle things up inside you, misunderstandings pile up, and the distance between you grows."

"I imagine my thing with our mother started as the usual mother-daughter, teenage rebellion. It escalated into blaming her for everything that happened in my life. When I was jilted by my first boyfriend, I decided it was her fault. She'd looked at him wrong and driven him away or she hadn't made him welcome enough. When I got poor grades at college, it was her fault. I'd tell myself that if she'd taken time to help me with my homework or hired someone to teach me how to study, I'd know what I was doing. Of course I never asked for help.

"When I graduated and started working, I was a wimp, a victim of every office bully. I blamed her because I'd sworn to myself that I'd never be assertive—except I called it aggressive—like my mother."

They were silent, needing time to think.

Finally Paul said, "It's easy to blame someone else for our failings, isn't it?"

"Yes. I've never had the guts to tell her any of this."

"Things changed in our family when Terrance died."

"You're right, it was as if the sunshine went out of the house. No one smiled anymore or seemed to hear a word I said. It got worse after you left, Paul. I was not quite sixteen. Dad never stopped scowling or looking worried. Mother buried herself in work. If I tried to talk to her, she'd look up from her papers or books and I felt as if I were invisible. When she did listen, I was certain I was disturbing and distracting her, and I felt guilty.

"Remember how Dad stayed at the office later and later, and hardly came home for dinner? They must have been going through their own private hells, but we didn't realize it. To me, it was just rejection. They adored Terrance. They loved you. I was unimportant— and I felt terrifyingly alone a lot of the time."

Paul slid a comforting arm about his sister's shoulders. "I don't think that's true. They loved us both. I think losing Terrance scared them terribly. If they withheld affection, perhaps they were afraid to love too much, afraid to be hurt again.

"Remember how Mother fussed every time we went out on the boat?" he asked. "She worried about us drowning like that little girl from down the street did one summer."

Amanda nodded. "I remember, vaguely."

"My joining the navy really upset her. She'd always been scared she'd lose me to the sea. In a way, she was right."

"You'd think that when you left, I'd become more important to her," Amanda said in a small voice.

"They were probably afraid to love you too much. I've seen something like it in men on my ship. If someone on the crew dies, the other guys turn off all feelings for their close friends. I tend to do that myself. The pain of losing that person is too hard to bear."

"When Dad died, I blamed her," Amanda said. "I thought, Mother's cold—she never loved him. I fumed, thinking that if he'd been married to a woman who was soft and gentle and stayed home with her kids, and didn't drive them both so hard in business, he wouldn't have died that young."

"Funny how memories differ among kids in the same family," Paul said. "I saw them as a team. I thought they loved working and being together. I thought they needed each other. I think Mother's been lost without him."

Amanda racked her memory and came up blank. "How come I never saw them being loving to each other?"

"I sometimes wandered about at night. If they were up, I'd hide, watch and listen."

She pinched his shoulder. "You scoundrel. You didn't?"

His eyes twinkled mischievously. "I sure did."

"And you never told me."

He flexed his muscles. "Real men don't tell. Anyway, one night they were in the living room. Dad was sitting on the couch. Mom had her shoes off, her legs up, and her head in his lap. Dad was stroking her hair. They were talking quietly, and they looked happy. I went back to bed feeling warm and safe. That image of them as a couple stayed with me."

Amanda said, "I wish I'd seen them like that. Why don't I remember any of the good times? There must have been some when I was there."

"There were good times for you. I wish you remembered some of them, too," Paul said.

"You should have seen Mother when she first arrived," Amanda said. "She'd been dancing—maybe she told you? And she was flushed and perhaps overwrought, but underneath, there was something in her eyes: an excitement, and anxiety, too. I've been afraid to talk about the wedding with her. I'm afraid she'll try to take over, run everything, like she did at home. I guess I don't trust her."

"Mother's had some therapy and done a lot of thinking. You might want to open up to her sometime before she leaves. I'm glad I did. It's a heck of a load off my mind and heart."

28

A Little Chat

Her talk with Paul primed Amanda to the possibility of healing the wound between herself and her mother. So, when Claire approached her the next morning as she was picking wildflowers, she was willing to talk.

"Could we sit for a bit under the tree over there?" Claire asked. She carried a blanket. "I saw you from my room, and brought this blanket in case . . ."

Amanda set down her straw basket. "Sure."

They walked to the tree, where Amanda helped her spread the blanket, and they sat with their backs propped against the wide trunk.

"Mornings are my best time," Amanda said. "I'm an early riser. Do you still get up at the break of dawn?"

"Not anymore." Claire rubbed her neck with a kneading motion. "I know it's not the most propitious moment, but I'll be gone when you return from your honeymoon, and I can't leave here without—well, without letting you know that I love you, and that I'm proud of you and happy for you."

"I appreciate that."

"I haven't been much of a mother, and . . ." Claire lifted and lowered her hands in a helpless gesture. What was she doing, trying to make up for a lifetime in a few stolen minutes? "I want you to know how very sorry I am."

"Sorry for what?"

"For not being the mother you needed."

Amanda rammed her hands under her armpits. "The mother I needed? Well, who would she have been? Someone who stayed home like all my friends' mothers? Would you have done that?"

"Probably not. But I could have set aside special time for you. I could have listened better. I know more about listening now."

"Paul said you'd been in therapy." Amanda's eyes challenged her mother. "I've been in therapy for *years*, trying to understand, coming to terms, letting go my expectations of what a mother should be, should have been. You think a few words are going to wipe away a lifetime of feeling unloved?"

"No, I don't. But maybe it can be a start for us, for the future. Because I do love you."

The silence that followed felt awkward to Claire, but she waited for Amanda to respond.

"Paul told me about Terrance. How awful carrying that guilt all these years was."

Claire turned abruptly. "It wasn't Paul's fault. It was mine. I was selfish and self-centered. Amanda, I know I can't turn back the clock. I just want you to know I'm sorry about so many things, and I hope in time you can forgive me."

"My therapist talked a lot about forgiving: forgiving you, forgiving myself." Amanda beat a fist against the blanket. "How does a person do that? Is there some method, a step-by-step approach? If there is, she sure didn't tell me."

"I don't know," Claire said. "I hoped when you knew that I'd do anything to make it up to you, you could forgive me."

Amanda started up. "It's just not that easy. I do appreciate your talking to me. I wish you'd done it sooner, but better late than never, I guess." She shrugged. "I have to go; Tom's waiting for me. We have a wedding to do and a honeymoon to go on."

Claire sat under the poplar, watching the shadows created by the dancing leaves. She wiped her tears with her hand. Should she stay here and wait for Amanda to return from her honeymoon? Or just get on with her life?

No more pity party, as Larry calls it. It's time to make a life for myself.

29

The Wedding and
Its Aftermath

While Claire liked Tom well enough, she felt
this marriage was a dead end for her lovely,
talented daughter. The other evening at dinner, Amanda had boasted that she intended
to immerse herself in the "simple life."

"I'm going to grow as much of our own
food as possible organically. I plan to freeze
and can vegetables and fruit, raise free-range
chickens, and when I have children, give birth
to them at home."

She seemed to consider a picnic by a
river the epitome of excitement. Why was
her daughter doing this? Was it some kind of
rebellion? Was it immaturity? If Phillip were

alive, would Amanda have gone to California, would she ever have met Tom? Well, it was too late now. Better to make the best of things, smile, and never show Amanda her true feelings.

Informal and haphazard, the ceremony began with a woman singing "Simple Gifts." Tom and Amanda arrived late, and when Amanda slid down from the seat of Tom's huge pickup, she landed on her behind on the grass and burst out laughing.

Stifling laughter, Olden helped her to her feet, and the bridal party traipsed across the damp grass between crooked rows of chairs under the blue tent. The bridal arch had been erected the night before and sagged under the weight of dew-dampened, artificial flowers. The so-called minister wore no vestments or other insignia of his office, and belonged, according to Millie, to no bona fide church she'd ever heard of.

Amanda giggled as Olden escorted her down the aisle, and to Claire's annoyance, Olden's lips curled upward and his eyes twinkled. What could he be thinking? She found the whole business ludicrous.

The ceremony was short, with a paucity of

traditional vows. With the pronouncement that Amanda and Tom were man and wife, the couple kissed in a far-too-long embrace, after which the guests straggled back to Larry Harden's farmhouse.

The usual round of toasts followed, gallons of champagne were consumed, the buffet was devoured, and when the cake was cut, everyone cheered. Amanda started upstairs to change into her travel clothes. Halfway up, she stopped and threw her bouquet of white and yellow roses, which was caught by a thin young woman who squealed with pleasure and clasped it to her chest.

As Amanda continued up the stairs, panic struck Claire. Their conversation yesterday hadn't really conveyed what she wanted it to. This was her last chance.

She turned to Millie. "I'm going up and talk to Amanda before she leaves."

"You sure you want to do that? Might not be so good a time, what with Tom lookin' at his watch every two minutes and signalin' Mandy to get a-going."

"What I have to say to my daughter won't take long."

Millie shrugged and turned toward the

kitchen. "Big mistake, whether she's your daughter or not."

Claire followed Millie into the kitchen. "Why is it such a mistake? Why?"

"If you had things to say to her, you had plenty time to do it. But not today." Millie shook her head. "Lord be praised, not today!"

"But there *isn't* any other time. Amanda's going away, and I'm going home!"

"You wake up this morning with your head screwed on wrong? Mandy just got married and is about to go off on her honeymoon. People don't want to talk about bad things in the past at a time like this."

"I talked some to her yesterday; told her I love her and asked her to forgive me."

"Forgiveness don't happen overnight. People got to think about that and pray on it. It takes time."

Claire sank into a chair at the kitchen table. "I know. I know."

"Look, Claire. You're a good person; Mandy's a good person. Given time, it'll be okay. But you can't fix it in a minute. You got to be patient. Now, I got this tray to take in." Millie picked up a tray of pastries and headed into the hall.

Claire checked to see if Millie could see her, then headed upstairs.

When Claire opened the door, Amanda was in the process of kicking off her shoe. It spun across the room and landed by the chair under which the first shoe was wedged. Her wedding gown, yanked over her head and tossed onto the chair, followed.

Claire rescued the dress, folded it neatly and laid it across the back of the chair. "You were a beautiful bride."

Amanda tugged on slacks and tucked in a blouse. She brushed her hair, pulled it back in a bun, and secured it with a tortoiseshell comb. "I thought everything went smoothly."

"And it didn't rain."

"We had the tent just in case." Amanda studied her mother in the mirror. "What's up, Mother?"

"I'd like to talk to you for a few minutes before you leave."

"This is hardly the time. Can't it wait until we get back next week?"

"Amanda, you coming?" Tom called.

"Coming!" But Amanda hesitated.

"You're right, of course. This is hardly the time. Just know that I love you very much, and want you to be happy."

"Thank you. I must go now. You stay well."

"Have a wonderful honeymoon."

"I certainly will." And Amanda was gone.

Suddenly very tired, Claire leaned by the window and watched Olden and Larry carry the bags to Tom's truck. Tom assisted Amanda up into the truck, and moments later the big tires crunched on the unpaved road and they were gone. It was over.

Claire walked slowly to the chair, retrieved Amanda's shoes, and placed them neatly in the closet. She collected the scattered hairpins and laid them on a small silver tray. She clasped the discarded wedding gown to her chest and stroked the soft material. If she had talked to Amanda when she'd first arrived, maybe she would have been invited to go along when Amanda picked up this lovely dress. *Don't spill tears on this dress.* Claire hung it in the closet.

All these weeks, when she was recovering from the flu and her daughter had been available and amiable, she had failed to grasp the moment. Claire sat in the rocking chair and rocked back and forth.

A knock on the door startled her, and Olden entered.

"You okay, Claire?"

Reach out my hand to Olden. That's all it would take; just that one simple gesture, and I will never be alone again.

"I'm fine. I've been putting away Amanda's things."

"Come on down. I'm leaving now; I want to put a couple of hours of driving behind me before dark."

On the porch, Olden hugged Millie, shook hands with Larry, and kissed Claire on both cheeks. "Come home soon, Claire. I'll be waiting," he said softly.

Tell him to wait—that I'll pack and go with him. But she couldn't. It wouldn't be right.

Olden swung his suitcase into his car, and then was gone. When a cab arrived for Paul later, Claire felt that bits and pieces of her were melting away.

Paul hugged her. "I'm so glad we talked, Mother. I love you. You take care of yourself, now."

"You, too. You'll write to me, call?"

He was halfway to the cab. "I will. And you have my address, too." Then he was gone.

Suddenly the woods seemed oppressively close to the house. An owl hooted. Then silence. The lights went out in the kitchen. Her sense of isolation sent a sudden chill through her, and she hastened inside to the kitchen and snapped on the light. Fresh from the dishwasher, dishes were stacked on the counter, and wedding wrapping paper was neatly folded and placed on the kitchen table. The house was empty and still.

Claire heard a motor start, and she watched from a window as Larry drove away with Millie in the passenger seat. Afraid, she walked from door to door and window to window, checking the locks, turning on the lights.

Why didn't they ask me to drive along with them? They knew I would be here alone.

Claire decided to pack and leave first thing in the morning.

30

To Run Away

In the morning, there were the expected assurances by Larry that Claire was more than welcome to stay as long as she wanted to, followed by the proper thanks from Claire.

"There are business things I must attend to, and I'm eager to be on my way, now that the wedding's over," she said.

Claire wrote a note of thanks and slipped fifty dollars into an envelope for Millie. Larry carried her luggage to her car, kissed her on the cheek, and waved farewell as she drove away. With cruise control set at seventy, the speed limit, she soon passed Johnson City in Tennessee, and headed north.

Reaching Long Island on Saturday, Claire pulled into a parking space in a strip mall on Queens Boulevard, had a cup of coffee and a piece of apple pie with cheese in the restaurant there, then she phoned Olden. "You win," she said. "I'm almost home."

Traffic increased as New Yorkers headed to their vacation homes on the island, and when cars cut her off, as they invariably did, Claire cursed beneath her breath. Impatiently tapping the steering wheel, she waited for red lights to go green. It was past four in the afternoon when Claire entered the street where her lovely Tudor home stood. She parked, dropped her hands from the steering wheel, and waited for she knew not what. Nothing happened. No one entered or left the house, and if they had, what would she have said or done? Tell them it had been her home? Say that she regretted selling it? Ask to come inside?

A siren startled her, and she turned to see a policeman who looked familiar striding toward her car. She rolled down the window. "Officer Cramer," she said. "How are you?"

"Mrs. Bennett. What are you doing here? I thought you'd moved away. The people who live here now called. They were concerned about a strange car parked for a long time, with someone they didn't know looking at their house."

"I am sorry. I didn't mean to alarm them. I just got back into town and wanted to see the house, that's all." She started the car. "I'm leaving now. Good to see you."

The policeman saluted and walked back to his car. She could hear the crackle of a voice breaking up on his car radio, and she rolled up the window.

A short while later, Claire turned into the drive of Olden's old colonial house and stopped in front of the three-car garage. She had once asked Sarah why they had three bays in it, since they had two cars.

"It's Olden," she said. "He prefers to use a golf cart to go to the bank. He takes the back roads." She shrugged. "He's concerned about the environment, pollution, that sort of thing. We added the third bay to accommodate his golf cart."

Claire exited her car. Her knees were stiff, as was her back, and she leaned against the hood of the vehicle. Tired and chilled, she recalled Olden saying that cold weather was predicted well into May. The weary trees wore grim brown jackets; the evergreen hedge was gray and dusty. A curled, dry leaf blew against her leg. She picked it up, crushed it in her fist, and crumbled it into tiny pieces before letting it drift to the ground.

A car pulled into the driveway behind her then. Olden raced toward her, his eyes concerned. Whether from discouragement, exhaustion, or resignation, Claire leaned into him and rested her head on his shoulder as they walked slowly into the house.

There she undressed, struggled into pajamas, and collapsed into bed.

Olden had canceled all his appointments at the bank and was reading a book in the den when she awakened the next day and called for him. He climbed the stairs two at a time and knocked at the slightly open door of the guest room. "Claire, how are you? Hungry?"

She appeared ashen, her eyelids heavy, her hair lackluster, and it frightened him. "Can you make it downstairs to the kitchen? Mrs. Greenlee's off for a week, so I'm chief cook. I've got fruit, bagels, smoked salmon, banana pudding, fresh sliced roast beef, and rye bread. You name it, I've got it, or I'll get it."

"Tea, I think, and a slice of roast beef on rye toast sounds good." She smiled.

He handed her a blue terry cloth robe. "Put this on and come downstairs. Can you manage?"

In the kitchen, Claire sank onto the upholstered banquette in the bow window. Her gaze traveled outside to the high brick wall that enclosed a backyard lush with plantings. In a narrow bed, thick clumps of lilies of the valley heralded the coming of spring.

Olden set the cup of tea before her and plunked the bread into the toaster.

"Sarah was a wonderful gardener," Claire said. "I envied her green thumb."

"I've hired a service to keep the place up. An untended garden goes to rack and ruin in less than a season," he replied. "Now, tell me about you. What happened in North Carolina? Something did, or you wouldn't be here, so don't gloss over anything."

"It was Amanda. I decided to talk to her, to set things right with us. I did it the day before the wedding, but tried again while she was changing her clothes after the wedding. Very bad timing."

"What did you say to her?"

"That I love her, that it was a lovely wedding,

that I was happy for her, and sorry for the mother I'd been. At least, that's what I think I said. I was rushing, as was she."

"What did Amanda say?"

"I don't think she believed a word I said. She asked me if I thought I could make things right at such an inconvenient time, or something like that."

"Your intentions were good, I'm sure, but it was rather an inauspicious moment to discuss a matter as serious as this."

"I made a real mess of it, didn't I?"

The toast popped up with a snap and Olden brought it to her, along with the roast beef, mayonnaise, and mustard. "I can't remember what you like on a roast beef sandwich."

He slid into the seat across from her with a cup of coffee. "I don't think you blew it permanently, Claire. In my book, as long as you're alive and in sound mind, there will be opportunities to make things right. Amanda will talk to Tom about this. He's a levelheaded fellow, not given to stirring up trouble."

"You're right. Tom's good at turning down the heat." She smeared mayonnaise on the toast, layered slices of roast beef, and cut the open-face sandwich into neat, manageable pieces. "What am I going to do, Olden?"

"I'd say, do nothing at all. Stay here and rest, walk on the beach, maybe see one or two old friends, maybe Dr. Delanny. If you don't get frantic, act impulsively, and fly away in a huff, you just might find some answers."

"You think so? I've been to Florida and North Carolina and haven't found answers."

"You're home now, where you ought to be. Sometimes we have to stand still and let things work themselves out around us. Let things jell in those inscrutable pathways inside our brains. You can't rush it."

"It *is* a process, isn't it? Like when you're confronted with a life-threatening diagnosis and your mind stops working. You're sure you won't be able to cope with it, but you do."

A picture of Sarah smiling flashed into Claire's mind. She'd been given a diagnosis of stage four cancer and offered little hope. Everything associated with illness and death frightened Claire, and she had visited Sarah only once in several hospitalizations. Phillip had spent time with Olden during Sarah's illness and after her death, while she had merely attended the funeral service. She'd

never known what to do or say when someone had lost a loved one, so she said nothing and stayed away. That was how it had
been for her family when her mother died.
Maybe people hadn't known what to say, especially about a suicide. No, she had not
been there for Sarah—another regret. And
yet Olden cared for her. Why? How could
he?

Olden was saying, "A mind's like a muscle.
It can be overworked and need to rest in
order to function efficiently. Your mind's on
overload right now. Give yourself time, Claire.
Stay here with me; let yourself heal."

"You're so good to me, Olden. A much
better friend than I've ever been to you, or to
anyone." She cupped her head in her hands.
"You're right, though. I'm not thinking clearly.
I can't decide about anything. But I'll listen to
you, for a change. I'll stay here, and thank
you."

31

And Time Goes By

It was three weeks before Claire called Dr. Delanny's office for an appointment.

"You're looking well. It's good to see you. Are you back for a visit, or home to stay?" Mary Delanny asked.

"I'm not sure."

They sat in the familiar armchairs in their accustomed places. Claire waited, expecting additional questions. Then she realized the therapist was waiting for her to choose her opening.

"I'm afraid I've made a mess of my life since I left here," Claire said.

"In what way have you made a mess?"

Claire plunged into a description of her adventures and misadventures in Florida: how young and desirable she had felt with Jason; the youthful exuberance and excitement of that one evening with Andrew; and Fred, who caused her to distrust her judgment.

Dr. Delanny listened, nodded occasionally, and did not interrupt. Now and then, Claire noted curiosity, concern, and even sympathy in her eyes.

"What would you say you've taken away from all this?" the therapist asked when Claire had finished.

Claire looked down at her hands. "That running away solves nothing? That my desperate need for a man to fill my life, to make me feel whole, blinded me to what's important? To my own sense of who I am?"

"I have no answers, Claire. Just questions." Dr. Delanny leaned forward. "You have the answers, and if you choose, we will work together to find them. But for now, our time is up. Where are you staying?"

"With Olden Riverdale, an old friend of Phillip's and mine. I'll see you next week."

Claire strolled along Main Street toward Rowdy Hall, the restaurant where she was meeting her friend Susan. Although the sun was out, the wind drove a cool mist off the Atlantic. She hurried on, eager for the warmth and cozy English pub atmosphere of Rowdy Hall.

Already seated, Susan was looking at the menu.

"Hi, Susan."

Susan jumped up and hugged Claire. "Let me look at you! You're so nice and tan. You live near the water in Florida, don't you?"

"I did, yes, and I walked the beach, but usually in the early morning. The sun can be very hot later in the day. Have you ever been to Florida when it's really hot? It's muggy, stifling. You're only comfortable indoors in air-conditioning."

"Well, Florida agrees with you. You look well."

Claire pulled out the chair across from Susan. "You look well, also," she said, and picked up the menu. "What are you having?"

"Grilled tuna. I'm watching my weight. You've lost weight, haven't you?"

"A few pounds, maybe." Claire studied the menu and debated between a sandwich or a salad, finally choosing Mandarin chicken salad.

"I ordered white wine for me and iced tea for you, like old times," Susan said. "That okay?"

Claire nodded.

"So you're staying with Olden?" Susan asked. "How come?"

"Amanda was married recently in North Carolina. Olden played surrogate father and walked her down the aisle. We've been friends for years." She reached for a roll in the covered basket the waiter had set on the table.

Susan's eyebrows shot up. "Surrogate father, eh? That's all?"

"That's all. Olden's my friend. He's handled my business affairs since Phillip died." "Phillip died" slipped off her tongue without any constriction of her heart. *Hooray!* "What have you been up to while I've been gone?"

"Well." Susan buttered a roll. "If you'd answered my letter or called me, you'd know all about it."

"About what?"

"Chuck and I are being divorced. Didn't Olden tell you?"

"He didn't; I'm sorry. You don't seem unhappy. Are you?"

Susan pouted. "Claire, don't play innocent.

Before you left, I was involved with Alfredo, that gorgeous Italian hunk with the fifty-foot yacht. You were with me when I met him at the Devon Yacht Club." She smiled. "You were there when it started. You just didn't pay attention. Chuck found out, and, well . . ."—she rolled her eyes—"he got all bent out of shape and insisted on a divorce.

"It was quite a struggle, getting what my attorney considered an equitable settlement, but then Chuck found someone he wanted— and then he couldn't wait to get out. I ended up with quite a nice settlement."

"Chuck found someone? Who?" Claire spread her napkin on her lap and reached for her glass of iced tea.

"He plans to marry her soon, the little floozy."

"Who?"

Susan's mouth twisted. "Colonel Parker's daughter, Julia. The redhead, remember? She had come home from college and paraded around the pool at the club in that itsy-bitsy bikini, with her boobs falling out the top and that firm little ass on display."

"She can't be more than twenty-two or -three."

"Right! Chuck's thirty years her senior.

Men have the option of much younger women, but not us gals. I show up with Alfredo, and tongues don't wag—they scamper. Anyway, Chuck and I are both getting what we want, so you could say all's well that ends well." She leaned toward Claire in a conspiratorial manner. "The Denisons are going out of business, so there are great buys on shoes, if you hurry. They lost their yacht and all their cars, except that old clunker of a station wagon. Their youngest boy had to quit college. If they weren't so snobbish, he *could* go to the local community college."

"I am so sorry to hear all this," Claire said, feeling genuinely concerned, especially for the Denisons and their son.

Susan flushed. She appeared to enjoy her self-appointed role as gossip maven.

"Mark Denison gambled, you know. That's how he lost it all. Ellen quit college to marry Mark and raise those four children, so she's got no career to fall back on. I think she'd like to leave him." Susan rolled her eyes again. "What could she ever do: be a waitress, or a sales clerk in some gift shop? From what I hear, he can't afford to support one household, much less two, so she's stuck."

Aren't we all stuck in one way or the other?

Claire thought. *Some of us are in unhappy marriages, have delusions of grandeur, or are haunted by failure, or blindly going around and around in the same old rut.* "It must be so hard for Ellen, for the whole family," she said. "It's terrible to have financial reverses, and to be so dependant on another person for support."

"I couldn't agree with you more," Susan said. "Ellen let Mark do whatever he wanted, and imagine—she never had her own checking account. Can you believe that? He gave her money every week for food, and he scrutinized her one credit card bill and questioned every expenditure."

Their lunches arrived. Susan waited until she'd finished her tuna before offering more news. "Margaret Verey went in for simple gall bladder surgery and developed an infection in the hospital. She nearly died. She's down to half her size, if you can picture that." She lowered her voice. "Rumor has it she's got cancer."

"I'm sorry. I hope it's not." So many seriously sad things had happened to so many of the people she knew, and in such a short time. Had she been here, would she have cared what happened to Margaret Verey?

At her next visit with Dr. Delanny, Claire spoke of Terrance and her recent conversation with Paul. "It's hard to believe that Paul walked around all those years tortured by guilt, especially as I had those same feelings. I stuffed them down because I couldn't bear to face my own life."

"It must have eaten away at the very core of your being."

"It certainly did—more than I knew."

"I'm glad you're able to talk about it now," Dr. Delanny said.

"I felt as guilty as Paul. If I hadn't gone to the beauty parlor that day! It hadn't been necessary. I just wanted to get away from the kids." Tears filled Claire's eyes.

"Cry if you want to. It's okay." She handed Claire a box of tissues.

Claire dabbed at her eyes. "I'm past tears, I think. I really need to get it behind me, and I think I can since I talked to Paul and you now. When he told me, I was so upset at the thought of him carrying such a burden all these years."

"Talking with him was good for you both."

"It was. It definitely was."

They sat in silence, then Claire said, "I was taught to bury my feelings. No one dared complain about anything in our house. We acted as if my mother was fine, and never spoke openly about her illness or its effect on us. I'd like to talk about that now."

"Go ahead."

Claire described the way she and her siblings had referred to their mother as "alive" during her good periods, and "gone" when her mother was hospitalized. "As I grew older, she was 'gone' more and more often. It was hard and confusing. Sometimes I hated her. Sometimes I pitied her, and I always felt guilty for not loving her. It felt unnatural—a daughter not loving her mother."

Mary Delanny said, "I'd like to recommend a book on bipolar disorder written for the layman. It's an historic approach, and discusses old treatments as well as modern therapies and medications. It might help you better understand her illness and the ways in which it can affect everyone in the family." She wrote on her pad and handed the sheet to Claire, who folded it and put it into her handbag.

On her next visit, Claire spoke of Olden and his feelings for her. "I wish I were attracted to him, but I'm not. I can't settle for that."

"Surely you know that passion fades, and

that it's good, solid qualities that matter in a companion: kindness, respect, consideration, and trust," Mary Delanny said.

"It doesn't seem to be enough," Claire replied. "I wish it were. There's not a finer man than Olden Riverdale."

From her office window, Mary Delanny watched Claire cross the street to her car and drive away, then went to her notes and added, "Real breakthrough. Can speak of the painful past." And she jotted down a few details in more technical terms.

Claire stopped at the supermarket on her way back to Olden's and bought veal cutlets. She had the butcher cut a pocket in each cutlet. Tonight she would prepare veal cordon bleu and rice flavored with curry, as she had enjoyed in restaurants in France. She hoped he'd like the dinner. She wanted to reciprocate his kindness, and, well, she enjoyed doing little things for him.

As springtime turned to summer, Claire's days assumed a pattern. During the week she slept late. Some days she met Susan for lunch, and once she lunched with Ellen Denison, who grew teary several times during their meal. She visited Margaret Verey in the hospital and was shocked how wasted the woman looked.

"Who would have thought?" Margaret said, her voice hoarse. Pinioned by fluids dripping into her veins, her arms peppered with black and blue marks, she lay unmoving on the bed. "It's not worth living like this," Margaret whispered and closed her eyes.

Claire agreed, but would not say so. She wondered if Margaret had made arrangements not to be kept alive on life support systems and vowed to see her own lawyer about this.

In June, Margaret died of cancer that had metastasized rapidly. Claire and Olden attended the services and took seats at the rear of the crowded church. It surprised Claire that so many people knew or cared about Margaret Verey. Her astonishment continued when one person after the other rose to eulogize Margaret. Claire listened, abashed. She had played bridge with the women for years and never knew that Margaret had been the mainstay of fund-raising for the Children's Aid Society. She had also volunteered at the Humane Society and worked to have a new, more modern building constructed. Her eleven grandchildren sat in the front row of the church and wept and blew their noses.

For days afterward, Claire thought about Margaret Verey, and wondered how she could have been so self-centered and never asked Margaret about her family or her life. They'd been ferocious rivals at bridge and had never chatted over lunch, never shared simple news or local gossip. There was so much more to each of them than a bridge game, lunch at the club. The more Claire thought about this, the more shallow and myopic she felt, and she took her concerns to Dr. Delanny.

"Knowledge and understanding are powerful," Mary Delanny said. "Now that you see all this, do you understand that you have choices, and can choose to change the things you don't like about yourself?"

Tears welled in Claire's eyes. A fine theory, but how to do it? "I never believed that old adage, what you sow you reap, but that's what it's all about, isn't it? It's like a circle."

"A circle? Perhaps it is."

Claire's eyes narrowed. "But what about people who cheat, crooks who get away with robberies, murderers who outwit the law?

And what about a nice, quiet church-going person who grabs a knife one day and stabs his wife or shoots strangers from a balcony?"

"We don't know how they end up, or where, do we? But most people don't steal or kill anyone. Most of our lives are circumscribed by where we live, by our finances, our family, our values and belief systems, and we're measured and evaluated within that circle."

"It's about more than just material things. It's how we are with people. How we treat them. Are we kind? Do we take the time to talk with someone? Do we listen to them? Do they feel we care?"

"I'm sure Margaret didn't think I cared a hoot about her. And I didn't, then. Yet she was happy to see me when I visited her at the hospital. I wasn't very friendly or forthright with anyone—not even Phillip. If I died tomorrow, the people who came to my funeral service would take up just two pews in church, if that."

"Is that what you think?"

Claire nodded. "I do, and it makes me feel hollow and empty." She leaned forward, her elbows on the arms of the chair. "I don't want that for myself. You know, Dr. Delanny, in all the years I called this place home, I've never felt that it *was* my home or that I fit in here. For me, it was all about the business. I can't recall ever going to a PTA meeting or a ball game at the kids' school. I attended one play that Amanda was in when she was twelve. I found it utterly boring. I guess all parents feel like that, but they go and make a fuss about their kids, and pretend to enjoy themselves. I must have yawned all the way through it, and hardly said a word to Amanda on the way home."

"And did you once tell me you felt contemptuous of other women? Your daughter's friend's mothers, especially?"

"That's right. I did. They attended their kids' ball games with no makeup, in jeans—big, fat women yelling as if they were children. I never could see what all the fuss was about. I considered football and soccer dangerous and never encouraged my boys to participate." She held up her palms. "So here I am today without a trusted woman friend to chat and relax with, much less confide in."

She cupped her chin with one hand. "I had a girlfriend once—Melanie Glinka, in college. She and I were as close as I've ever been to another woman." Claire's eyes grew dreamy and she smiled. "That was nice. We had some good times together." Then her eyes hardened. "But Melanie transferred in our third year, and I felt abandoned again—like with my mother. I was devastated, and I never had another woman friend. It was all about Phillip and our work."

"Did you stay in touch with Melanie?"

Claire shook her head. "No. She called and wrote for a while. But I was hurt and angry, and I never answered her letters."

"Sounds like you bit off your nose to spite your face. You transferred your anger at your mother, and the pain of what you considered her rejection of you, to Melanie."

"Yes. Even now, it's hard for me to trust that any female—even my daughter—would really be there for me. I can't let myself care too much, for fear of being hurt."

"Sooner or later, unless we die young, we'll all lose someone we love deeply," the therapist said. "Some people rush out and try to fill the space in their hearts as quickly as possible, while others never love again, for fear of loss."

"That's why I never let the kids have pets: I didn't want them to be hurt. So many dogs in our area were killed by cars."

"We can change. *You* can change," the therapist said. "I suggest that you look back at your adult life and see where women could have supported you, had you let them be a part of your life: when Terrance died, when Phillip died, and I'm sure there were other times. A woman friend can provide solace, companionship, and an understanding one rarely gets from a man. As much as they may love us, they think differently than we do."

Mary Delanny smiled. "Small steps, Claire. Change isn't easy, but it's certainly possible if you're earnest about it and take it slowly. Sometimes one tries too hard, too fast. That rarely works, so it's easy to say "this isn't working" and just give it up.

"A couple of simple rules might help. In any given situation, ask yourself: How would I like this person to treat me? What would I want him or her to say to me, or to do? And second, don't act immediately. Think a minute or two, and never tell people what to do. People hate advice, unless they ask for it. So just listen to people. Nothing attracts people like a good listener."

On her way out, Claire thought about the intensity with which Zora had listened, how the questions she had asked made Claire feel special and certain that Zora genuinely cared about her. She had really liked Zora—but then, of course, the woman had vanished. So what was the point?

One day soon after, Claire helped stock shelves at the library. A whole new staff had replaced those she had worked with. She did all that was asked of her, and spoke little. She listened to what the librarians said and what they complained about: a lack of funds for books and videos, the need for computers for the public. She smiled at their excitement about an upcoming fund-raising festival, a simple event compared to fund-raisers she had coordinated, and was pleased when they asked her to man the punch bowl.

One day each week she drove with Susan to Sag Harbor, Amagansett, or Shelter Island, where they lunched and browsed the shops. Some days she stayed at home, read, and prepared a simple meal for herself and Olden. Sometimes he cooked, and at least twice a week they ate out, and there was her weekly visit to Dr. Delanny, whom she now liked and trusted. And so May and part of June drifted by, and Claire dreamed less, worried less, and smiled a lot more. And she listened—not just to people, but to birds, and the winds and sea, even to the traffic humming along on the highway.

On a Wednesday evening, as the fading light burnished the leaves along the back wall of the yard, Claire and Olden sat in the kitchen having dinner.

"The Rotary's throwing a beach picnic this Saturday evening," Olden said. "There'll be a bonfire. If it's a clear night and we walk a ways from the fire, we'll be able to see the stars. Would you like to go?"

Of course she wanted to go! The streets were deliberately dark at night here, so that one could see the sky and the stars. On the beach, they would be even more glorious.

"The food's being catered, so it's not the usual hot dogs and hamburgers. Should be nice," Olden continued.

"I'd like to go. Is it something you'd like to do?"

He looked at her with a puzzled expression. "Why, yes. I would, but if you don't want to go, I'd never go and leave you here alone."

He's so thoughtful and kind. In all these weeks, he's asked me no questions, made no sexual advances to me. He accepts

me for who I am, good and ill, and his patience is infinite.

"Let's do it!" she said.

"Terrific." His voice was eager, as happy as a schoolboy who had anticipated a "no" and gotten a "yes" from a girl he'd been wanting to ask out for a very long time.

"I love the night sky on our shoreline," she said. "It would be nice to be there with you." She reached over and squeezed his arm, and saw his eyes light up. *Careful, Claire. Don't do anything that will hurt this good man.*

"I'll get us comfortable folding chairs. You know just about everyone who'll be there," Olden said.

Claire considered what she would wear. *Something long and flowing? Goodness, no. Pants and high socks to tuck the pants into, and a long-sleeved shirt to stave off those tiny, stinging creatures that erupted from the sand when you disturbed their lairs.*

They walked between the dunes down to the beach, and heard the sounds of laughter mingled with the sounds of the sea and the voices of people talking. Stars splattered the sky, and the Milky Way rode like a white steed across the darkness. Olden opened their chairs and set them on the sand among the widening circle of people. Claire moved among them chatting with this one, hugging that one, responding to their "Where have you been, Claire?" with "Traveling, but I'm back now." Finally, she sat in the chair next to Olden.

"Ready to eat?" he asked.

The buffet was amazing: crab legs and shrimp, barbecued ribs, salads of all kinds. Tom and Agatha Richardson, the vice president of Olden's bank and his wife, filled their platters and pulled their chairs close to Olden's and Claire's.

Agatha was a social worker and had always, if Claire remembered correctly, worked at the Help Center for battered women and children.

"How do you like being back?" Agatha asked.

"It's home," Claire replied. "And Olden's been so kind."

"He's the best," Agatha said. "I know he must be delighted to have you here. He's been lonely in that big house since Francine and the boys left."

She's itching to ask me if I plan to stay on,

or what's up with Olden and me. "If I stay in the area," Claire said, "I'll probably buy a condo."

They talked then about the way the whole area was growing, about how taxes soared every year, and Tom suggested that if she planned to buy, this was the time to do it.

People circulated, and the Richardsons eventually strolled off down the beach.

Olden asked, "Would you like to take a walk, Claire? It's a lovely night."

She nodded, and he helped her to her feet. They ambled off, hand in hand.

"Are you serious about buying a condo, Claire?" he asked.

"Not really; I felt that Agatha was prying. It was easier to tell her that, rather than explain why I'm staying with you, or what's between us. You know how gossipy people can be."

"Agatha's not that kind of person," Olden said. "Confidentiality is important in her work, and I've never heard her gossip about anyone. I think she's genuinely interested."

"In you, then," Claire said. "She hardly knows me. Why would she care about me?"

"Have you always been this suspicious of people, Claire?" His voice was in no way condemning or critical, only concerned. But his question startled her.

"I am, aren't I? It's amazing how we go along behaving in certain ways, without ever realizing what we're doing. We don't even recognize our behaviors as habitual and automatic. I guess I am very suspicious. And you're right, of course, I don't know Agatha."

"You'd like her."

"I probably would," Claire admitted. "I wish things were clearer to me—that I knew what I want to do, and to be. Shall I stay here, or make my peace with Amanda and live in North Carolina? Were you serious when you said maybe you'd retire there, Olden? Did you like that area?"

She could see his face clearly in the light of the bonfire. He looked speculative, taking her question seriously.

"I liked it there, and I liked Larry. Fishing was enjoyable. I don't know when I'll retire, or where I'll want to live. I certainly won't move away from here to a new place alone."

"If I stay here, I'll need to buy or rent a place. I can't live with you forever, Olden."

"You can live with me as long as you want to." He slipped his arm about her, and she relaxed and went with the moment. She was getting quite used to Olden, to having coffee with him in the morning and anticipating his coming home in the afternoon. At night, it was comforting to know she was not in a house alone. He would be there if she needed him, if she became ill—and she would be there for him, as well.

32

The Ups and Downs of Life

"Claire, Larry Harden here. I'm afraid I have some sad news."

Claire's heart skipped a beat. Paul? No, they wouldn't contact Larry if anything . . . She sank into the closest kitchen chair. "What is it, Larry?"

The tears in his voice were unmistakable. "It's Mandy."

Claire went cold. "What's wrong? Is she ill? An accident?"

"She lost the baby."

"What baby? I didn't know she was pregnant."

"She was a month pregnant when they got married, and she miscarried two nights ago at four months. Two more months and the baby would have been viable, the doctor said. I wish he hadn't said that. It just made it harder for her."

"Two nights ago?" That was the night of the beach picnic.

"Yes." Larry sniffed and blew his nose. "I'm sorry. It brings back what Olivia and I went through when we lost our baby. People might think, well, she was just a few months pregnant, but for the woman it happens to, the loss is devastating."

"Yes, I imagine it is. And you're right: people will gloss over it and say stupid things like, 'You'll get pregnant again,' or 'At least it happened before you carried to term.' Where's Amanda now?"

"Here. She started to miscarry at home, so we called 911 and they rushed her to the hospital in Asheville. It seems the fetus didn't attach properly to the wall of the uterus."

He cleared his throat. "She asked me to phone you. Mandy's very depressed, and I think the depression itself terrifies her. She'd like you to come."

"Me? You're sure she wants me to come, Larry? We had a rather upsetting conversation before I left. Are you sure?"

"I doubt if your daughter's life has ever been touched so deeply by loss. She was very young when her brother was killed, and while losing her father was desolating, losing this baby has absolutely devastated her."

Or the accumulated losses have added up to such enormity that she simply cannot cope anymore.

"Look, I know things haven't been great between you, but maybe this is the time to make it right. She needs you now, and she wants you. Will you come, Claire?"

"Yes, of course!" Claire's mind grappled with the mundane: cancel her appointment with Dr. Delanny, cancel lunch with Susan, let the library know she would be leaving. "I'll call you back as soon as I make arrangements."

For a few minutes after hanging up the phone, Claire stared out of the kitchen window. Amanda needed her. That in itself was a shock. What would she say to her daughter? What could she do? She could listen. What if Amanda had expectations of her that she couldn't meet? Well, she'd meet them as best she could.

Olden listened calmly. "Of course you must go. Dear little Amanda—I'm so sorry. Shall I make plane reservations for you, or do you prefer to drive? And would you like me to go with you? What can I do to help, Claire? Just tell me."

"I can't think straight at this moment. Can we just talk now and decide how and when later?"

Olden's cell phone rang. "Marilyn. Tell Mr. Granger I'll be with him in a few minutes. No, tell him I'll call him back soon. No, I won't be coming in. Something's come up."

Olden took Claire's shoulders and turned her to face him. "It's going to be all right. You'll be fine, and so will Amanda. Go call Dr. Delanny. Do whatever you need to do. I'll make this call from my office here."

Claire picked up her car keys and left the house, relieved not to be dealing with this alone. She drove to Dr. Delanny's office, hoping against hope that someone had canceled, but this was not to be and she left a note for

the doctor with the secretary explaining everything.

What must it be like to miscarry? How did
that differ from carrying to term and then losing a baby, or having your infant die of SIDS,
or your son killed when he was only seven
years old? Loss was loss, at whatever age and
stage of life. She would remember that, and
not fall back on clichés with her daughter.

But Claire worried, remembering the anger in her daughter's eyes during their last
encounter, and the old sense of inadequacy
as a mother swept over her. Would she be
able to meet her daughter's needs?

Millie answered her call. "How are you,
Mrs. Bennett? Yes, Mandy's here."

"How is she?"

"She's had a bad time of it. She cries too
much and eats too little."

"Is Tom there?"

"No, only me and Mandy are in the house.
I'll go upstairs and have her pick up the
phone. She never answers it."

It seemed an eternity before Amanda's
fragile voice came on the phone.

"Mother, will you come?" She began to
cry. "I need you."

Pain stabbed Claire's heart. "I'm so sorry,

Amanda. And it's okay to cry. Do you want me to call you back in a little while?"

Sniffles. "No. I'll be okay in a minute." Silence, then, "Did Dad call you, Mother? I asked him to call you."

The "Dad" momentarily confused Claire. "Yes, Larry called me." *Careful, Claire. Go slow. Let her tell you what she wants.*

"Will you come, Mother? I was so rude to you that day. I'm so sorry. I was nervous, and I'd had too much champagne."

"Forget about that—it's *you* I'm concerned about. Of course I'm coming. Olden and I are deciding if we'll fly or drive. Do you mind if he comes?"

"Of course not—Uncle Olden's been so good to me. He can go fishing with Dad. I know this is a terrible imposition."

"Stop right there. This is no imposition," Claire said.

"Come soon, then."

Claire hesitated a moment. "I love you, my darling, and I'm so very sorry."

"Me, too, Mom. Me, too."

By noon, Claire and Olden had packed and joined the flow of traffic on the highway west. They crossed the Triborough Bridge and headed south through New Jersey. Claire leaned her head back, closed her eyes, and dozed. When she awoke the sun was setting, coloring the sky a shimmering copper. She stretched. "I'm sorry I fell asleep."

He turned his head and smiled at her. "You needed to sleep, and it tells me you trust my driving."

"I trust you in every way, Olden."

His face turned pink, and he cleared his throat. "Are you hungry?"

"Starving."

"We'll get off at the next exit and find a place to eat."

"That sounds good."

When they exited, the sign to food and gas pointed to the right, and they traveled several miles past open country planted with corn. The small town they arrived at had one gas station and a general store with a family-style restaurant.

"Not what I had in mind," Olden said. "Want to go back to the highway and drive on a bit?"

"No, this will do. We're hungry, and you've been driving for hours. We need to stop."

They shared the small restaurant, with its aluminum-legged, Formica-topped tables, with two old farmers in overalls whose wide-brimmed hats had left white bands on their sunburned foreheads. The farmers nodded to them as they entered, and a young girl brought them menus.

"The catfish is caught fresh. It's real good tonight," one of the farmers said.

Claire kept food simple when she traveled, avoiding anything spicy, exotic, or unfamiliar to her palate. She ordered a club sandwich and iced tea. Olden ordered the fish, which pleased the old men.

One of the farmers sauntered over to a jukebox and plugged in a quarter, and Johnny Cash's booming voice sang "Ring of Fire." Claire had heard the song, but never actually listened to the words. She was embarrassed by their intensity, for the song spoke of a passion so sexual and all consuming that it frightened her to even imagine being caught up in its deep feelings.

"Cash was my first introduction to country music," Olden said.

"I like his voice," Claire said. "It's deep and clear, with no electronics needed to enhance it."

"You folks headin' south?" the older of the two farmers asked.

"Yes, to North Carolina," Olden said.

"Just heard on the radio that there's been a wreck, twenty or so cars involved, down the highway about twelve miles."

"A truck spilled logs all over the highway—banged-up cars, smashed windshields, a big mess," the other man said.

"That sounds just terrible," Olden said. "Any shortcuts you want to recommend?"

The waitress set their food before them. "They even had a helicopter carryin' off people. Four or five of 'em got hurt real bad."

"Oh, how awful. I'm so sorry." Claire said. Her initial annoyance at the delay gave way to concern and pity for the victims.

One of the farmers scratched his head and focused his attention on his companion. "Well, lemme see now. I reckon they could take the old Pine Road north a ways, then turn on back by the old mill. What do you think, Eb?"

Eb shook his head. "I dunno. I heard the rain took out that bridge up by old man Sandrin's apple orchard. Not sure they got it built back up yet."

"Where's the next town where we can find a nice motel?" Olden asked.

Claire noted the tiredness in his eyes, the slump of his shoulders. Accident or not, they needed to stop.

"Crandon the next town of any size; it's about seven miles," the first man said. "Nice couple of motels there."

"Thank you," Olden said.

Johnny Cash's song ended. Eb and his companion paid their checks and departed, tipping their hats as they passed their table. "Have a safe journey, now," one of them said.

Claire and Olden took adjoining rooms at a motel, and later sat in Claire's room and watched the eleven o'clock news.

"The highway's open again, but use caution," the newscaster said.

They talked a while of their spouses, and about the pleasant times they had spent together as a foursome.

"Remember when Phillip miscalculated and we got stuck on a sandbar and had to have the Coast Guard come and pull the boat to deeper water?" Olden asked.

"Yes, Phillip was furious with himself. He prided himself on being a top-notch sailor."

"And he was, Claire. One of the best. Must have had his mind on other things that day."

He had, Claire thought. She and Phillip had fought the night before and again that morning about his lack of interest in sex, and she had yelled that he was driving her to find sex outside their marriage. He had retorted that she'd best not find it anywhere near East Hampton, and that he would not tolerate being humiliated and the butt of gossip. Of course, she had recanted and wept, and he had held her—which did nothing to assuage her frustration. No, Phillip's mind had not been on sailing.

Olden spoke of his daughter Francine's divorce, and how it had hurt him. "I really liked Sam, and I could see how it devastated the boys to have their father gone. I attributed their wildness when they stayed with me to acting out. They missed Sam terribly. It's hard to explain to kids that their parents don't love each other anymore, but still love them, even though one of the parents isn't around. I wish I could have changed things between Francine and Sam, but one can only live one's own life."

"Do you like Francine's new husband? He seems like a nice man, and he's kind to the boys."

"The boys do seem to like him, and they see their father more often, now that they live in Connecticut."

"Are you sorry they don't live closer to you?"

"Not really. It's best not to know too much about the day-to-day life of your children. And those boys did wear me out. Five hours' drive away is perfect."

When he rose to leave her room, he said, "Claire, I want you to know that whatever you decide—to come back with me, or stay with Amanda—having you in my life these past weeks has been a gift from God and a blessing. You're a pleasure to have around. I almost said 'wake up to,' but that wouldn't be correct." He grinned, and for a moment he quite appealed to her.

"And for me, you and your wonderful home have been a haven. You've been so good to me, so caring." *Loving, too.* "I'll always be grateful for your kindness."

"Do you think you might stay in North Carolina permanently?"

"I have no plans. I'm not finished with my work with Dr. Delanny. We've done some good work lately; I see some things differently. I haven't even decided if I'm going down to Boca Raton when the apartment closes next month, or if I'll have a mover ship my stuff or store it. There's also the furniture I took with me originally, which is stored there. All those things used to be so important to me, but no longer. And there's a very good market for fine antiques in Boca."

"Well, at least I know you're not moving back to Florida. And whatever you decide, my proposal from Boca Raton still stands. Not looking for a commitment; just reminding you."

"Thank you, Olden. Good night."

"Good night." Olden closed the door between their rooms.

The Shenandoah Valley, lovely in summer green, fell behind them as they proceeded toward North Carolina.

"We must come back here someday," Olden said.

"I'd travel with you anytime." Claire had never felt this relaxed traveling with Phillip. Their sexual incompatibility had created tensions that surfaced in every five-star hotel room and colored whatever the day or evening brought with a ubiquitous anxiety.

Perhaps, as Dr. Delanny had said in a recent session, Claire had invested so much energy in sexual frustration that she had neglected other parts of herself.

"You might want to explore the things Claire enjoys, and do them," the therapist had suggested.

As a girl she wanted to paint, and she had loved the theater. She'd considered majoring in set design in college. Just before Larry's call Claire had been about to enroll in a watercolor class, and she had looked into volunteering at the little local theater. Life could and did change in the blink of an eye.

Her mind drifted to Amanda. Her daughter hadn't mentioned being pregnant, but then, why would she? They'd hardly ever talked. Claire closed her eyes. How could she possibly help her daughter? A support group of women who had also miscarried might be more helpful.

"Just listen and let her do the talking," Dr. Delanny had said when she had called just before they left. "Don't tell your daughter what to do, and especially not how she ought to feel."

I'm not that stupid, Claire had wanted to say. But she might have been that stupid a few months ago.

Claire closed her eyes and dozed until Olden said, "We're in Roanoke." He pulled the car under a motel marquee. "We'll stay here tonight and be in Weaverville tomorrow afternoon. You might want to call and let them know."

33

Thank You for Coming

"Thank you for coming, Claire." Tom helped her from the car. He looked distraught, with dark circles ringing his eyes. "I'm frightened for Mandy. She hardly eats—we count the spoonfuls. I have a friend whose wife had a miscarriage, and she didn't take it this hard." They moved up the porch steps and into the house. Tom lowered his voice. "It's as if she feels she's responsible, as if she killed the baby through some kind of neglect. She wasn't neglectful. She took good care of herself, exercised and ate well.

"I feel so helpless and frustrated. Nothing I do or say gets through to her. I want to be there for her, to comfort her, and she won't let me. When I go into her room, she turns away. What have I done or haven't done? I rack my brain, and I don't know. I feel utterly useless." He pressed Claire's hand. "Thank you for coming."

Amanda's hair had lost its lovely sheen. Her eyes were dull and red from crying and her arms, when she lifted them to greet her mother, were thin. The lost, hopeless look in Amanda's eyes tore at Claire's heart, and she struggled not to cry.

"Mama," Amanda said.

"I'm here, my darling."

"I was afraid you wouldn't get here in time."

Claire gathered her daughter in her arms. "I'm here," she said, and wondered what Amanda meant. God forbid she should lose her daughter.

Amanda closed her eyes, and lay still and quiet for so long that Claire felt panic rising within her. She took a deep breath and focused on Amanda's breathing, the way her daughter's chest rose and fell rhythmically.

Amanda gave a small sigh. "I'm going to go to sleep now that you're here, Mama."

"I'll be right here when you wake up."

"Good," Amanda said softly. "Thank you for coming."

Millie stuck her head in the door and waved two fingers. She smiled and then her lips moved. "Thank you for coming." She closed the door.

If one more person thanked her she would scream, Claire thought. This wasn't something you were thanked for. It's what you did for your child because you loved her.

34

Mama, Mom, Mother

After a couple of hours, Olden appeared in the doorway of Amanda's room with a cup of coffee laced with cream. "I thought you'd need a refresher. How is she?"

Claire beckoned him close and whispered, "Sleeping. I promised I'd be here when she wakes up."

"I put your suitcases in the guest room across the hall. Millie's gone out shopping for dinner. Tom says she's pretty much been with Amanda day and night, and the larder's bare. His dad went into Weaverville to fill a prescription the doctor called in for Amanda."

Amanda stirred.

Claire's finger touched her lips, and she motioned Olden away. "Later," she whispered.

He nodded and tiptoed from the room.

"Mama?" The voice was soft and needy as a child's.

"I'm here, Amanda."

Amanda turned over, and by her steady breathing, Claire saw that she was again asleep. After a time, Claire stepped into the hall and found Olden in his room reading. She asked him to move the rocking chair from the window close to the bed. The chair she'd been sitting on was straight-backed, and after a while it was uncomfortable and hurt her back.

When Olden left, Claire settled into the rocker. The soothing motion took her back to those early weeks after her children's births, when she had rocked Paul and Amanda. Nanny had rocked Terrance. Dear little Terrance, so needy of her, so clinging to her. If she had spent more time with him, given him the attention and love he craved, he would not have been clingy, not irritated her so much.

How often she had pushed him away, too busy to bother. *Terrance, my dear son, please forgive me.*

Claire forced her mind to the early days with Paul and Amanda.

She had taken pleasure in Paul until he was about two and his growing vocabulary had been reduced to a determined "no." When Amanda began to walk and get into his things, Paul threw tantrums, at which point she'd hired a nanny for them and spent more time at the office.Those were the years when the business exploded and the money began to roll in, the years she had plied her children with material things to assuage her guilt for her increasingly long absences.

If she could only relive her life, she would do it so differently.

"Mama?"

"Yes, my darling girl?"

Amanda had turned over and was facing her. "You're rocking a pillow?"

"I was remembering how I rocked you when you were a baby."

"You rocked me?"

"Yes, and Paul, too."

"And Terrance?"

"I was too busy at work by then. His nanny rocked him."

"I rocked him, sometimes. She let me."

"Terrance must have liked that very much."

Amanda smiled. "He did." She closed her eyes. After a while she said, "Can you ask Millie to bring me up some chicken soup?"

"Millie's shopping for food. I'll get it for you."

"No, don't leave me. I'll wait till she gets back."

"I can ask Olden to get it."

"Olden's so kind. Are you going to marry him?"

"I don't know."

Olden found a can of chicken soup on a shelf, heated it, and brought it to Claire, who slowly fed her daughter. When Amanda shook her head at the next spoonful, Claire persisted and Amanda accepted it. Finally she lay back.

"That was good. Thank you. Will you brush my hair for me, Mama?"

"Certainly." Claire found the brush on the dresser, and with Olden's help propped four pillows behind Amanda. "Turn your head, darling. I'll do one side and then the other."

Amanda next asked to have her face and arms washed, and then to have her night-gown changed. Olden left the room and returned when Claire called him to help Amanda to the rocker, which he moved back near the window.

"Will you open the shades for me, please, Uncle Olden?"

Light spilled into the room, brightening every corner. Claire selected crisp blue and white sheets and soft white pillowcases from the hall closet and changed Amanda's bedding.

"I feel stronger already," Amanda said.

"Well enough to let us help you downstairs, perhaps sit out on the porch a while?" Olden asked.

Amanda studied Olden. "You're the nicest man I've ever known, and I've known you all my life. I think you ought to marry my mother and be my real stepfather."

He smiled. "I'd be happy to oblige, and thank you for asking, sweetheart. You're very special to me."

"I remember when I was little and you let me dive off your shoulders at the beach. You had hairy shoulders. I dug my toes into them and pushed off. What I really wanted to do was grab a handful of hair and yank."

Olden laughed. "I'm glad you didn't. What's missing from my head ended up on my shoulders, I guess."

Claire saw how easy they were with each other, unburdened by father/daughter stresses or strains, not trying to please, no excuses necessary.

Millie returned with a car full of groceries, and Olden helped Millie carry them into the house.

Then Millie, plainspoken as ever, came upstairs to join them. "Thank God you came, Claire. Our girl looks much better already. I knew you could help her get a grip on life, bring her around."

"It'll be all right, Millie," Claire said. "You know it takes time."

"I've seen what it does when it never ends," Millie replied.

They helped Amanda downstairs and out onto the porch.

"It feels so good to be outside," Amanda said as she gently rocked. "Thank you for coming, Mama."

"It's the other way around. Thank you for wanting me to come," Claire said.

"I'm so tired," Amanda said. "I think I over-did it coming downstairs. Do you think we might go back up? I'm not up to Larry or even Tom right now. They'll swoop down on me like . . . I don't mean to be unkind—it's just that they're so solemn and so worried about me. They want me to smile when I want to cry. It's burdensome."

Claire nodded, then she and Olden helped Amanda back into bed, where she pulled the fresh, new sheets about her shoulders. "The sheets feel so good. Thank you for changing my bed."

Amanda ate half of the food Millie carried up to her that evening.

"Best meal she's eaten in days," Larry said when he and Tom visited with her after dinner. Tom hovered about his wife, patted her covers, took her hand in his, and stroked it until Amanda gently withdrew it. He offered to fluff her pillows, and chatted about inconsequential things, uncertain what to say, afraid of too much honesty.

It's a scary time for poor Tom, Claire thought, *and Larry's lost in his remembered pain.*

Later—when Amanda slept, curled on her side like a little girl; after Tom, sighing heavily, kissed his mother-in-law good night and trudged to his home in the barn; after Larry wearily shambled off to bed—Claire and Olden sat on the front porch. It had been a long day.

To the left, yellow light lit the front door of Tom and Amanda's home. Like miniature meteor showers, fireflies zinged through the darkness. A rooster in Millie's chicken house crowed, dispelling the belief that they crowed only at daybreak.

"It's going to be all right, Claire," Olden said.

"Yes—I know in my heart that it is. It's just painful to watch. She loves you as if you were her father, Olden. And she needs you now as much as she needs me. I'm so glad you came."

"You, Amanda, Paul, Francine, and the boys—you're all my family."

Deeply touched, Claire nodded. What could she say? That she had come to depend on Olden, to value and trust him? That he brought calm and reason into her life? She couldn't say those things, for each implied more than she could give him at the moment. In comfortable silence, they rocked in unison.

Amanda grew brighter and stronger with each passing day. One day at breakfast, she asked her mother to take her for a ride. "There's a river, a very lovely place over in

Yancey County. I'd like to show it to you. We could take folding chairs and sit on the grass alongside the water."

"You up to going so far? That Burnsville area is a good hour's drive away," Millie said. "Can you manage such a long trip?"

"I feel better, stronger," Amanda said. "You're such a worrywart, Millie."

Millie placed her hands on her hips. "It's just so hot. Hotter this year than I remember." She sighed. "Well, if you must go, I'm gonna pack you a thermos of iced tea and make some sandwiches. Time like this, you need good, wholesome food. And take a pillow, in case you need to sleep on the way back."

"So many mother hens fussing over me," Amanda said and smiled.

Olden placed two folding chairs in the trunk of the car, along with Millie's picnic basket. With the directions printed in large type for easy reference, Claire slipped behind the wheel and they were off.

The day was glorious. The sky was blue, and the white clouds that towered above the mountains looked like wigs worn by grandees at the court of Louis XIV. Amanda took pleasure in the shifting shades of green on the hillsides, and exclaimed at the way sunlight came from behind a cloud and flooded the valleys.

"I love the mountains. Do you like it here, Mom?"

"I do like it. It's lovely country."

"You're footloose and fancy-free, as they say. Why not move here? I don't mean with Larry, but in your own place, maybe closer to Asheville."

"I'd have to think about that. It's a major change, a huge decision." Claire considered the prospect, another move, starting over, finding a doctor, and the myriad other details involved in the process of adjusting to a new environment. Pleased as she was that Amanda had asked, it seemed somehow overwhelming. "I don't know what I want to do, or where or even when," Claire said.

"Think about it. What are you doing with yourself back home?"

"I am seeing a therapist. I don't think I'm quite finished, and I planned to get involved— to volunteer at the theater."

"There's a really good playhouse in Mars Hill, not far from here." They drove for a time in silence. Then Amanda said, "Paul told me you were seeing a therapist. Maybe I should go home with you and see her."

"If you want to. I'm sure Mary Delanny would be happy to see you. And you'd be more than welcome at Olden's. We have plenty of room." She looked away, unwilling to discuss the implications of that "we."

But Amanda's thoughts were centered on herself. "They think I'm overly upset about losing the baby. Tom called me hysterical one day. But it's not just the miscarriage. It wasn't my first."

Claire went cold. She could feel her neck tighten. "Not your first?"

Amanda hugged her own shoulders. "I have to get this off my chest, but I need you to promise you won't tell anyone."

"You have my word." Preparing to listen, Claire slowed the car to fifty-five and set cruise control. Whatever Amanda revealed, she was determined to accept it without judging or comment. "I'm listening."

Amanda sighed heavily. Her voice was flat. "Four years ago, before I met Tom, I lived with a guy named Jerry in California. He was an artist—creative, irresponsible, a wild man. I was crazy about him, even though in my gut I knew he wasn't dependable and that responsibility frightened him. I became pregnant. I told him one evening when we went to bed, and the next morning he was gone: paints, brushes, his guitar and clothes— everything gone. I never heard from him again. By then, I was close to three months pregnant. I panicked, but before I had to make any drastic decision, I miscarried, like with this baby." She turned stricken eyes to her mother. "Maybe I won't ever be able to carry a baby to term." She broke into sobs. When she could speak coherently, Amanda said, "That's why it's been so hard on me, losing this baby."

A second miscarriage! The impact of her daughter's words hit her full in the stomach. "I'm so sorry, so very sorry. And no, I don't think it means you'll never have a baby. You need to discuss this with a doctor, a specialist in this kind of thing. I'm sure there's some medication, or bed rest—something."

"I haven't been able to think clearly, or tell Tom about that other time. It's weighing on me. I feel so guilty, keeping a secret from him."

"Why have you kept it a secret? Tom strikes me as a reasonable and sensitive man."

"I was ashamed. Tom means the world to me. I didn't want to bring my past into our lives in such a negative, sad way."

Careful what you say. Just listen.

"Losing this baby brought it all back, the terrible sadness and regret."

"There are stages to grieving, my therapist tells me, and it's possible to get stuck in any of those stages, like depression or anger. I wallowed in denial for a very long time after your father died."

"I've heard that, too. But you know what it's like when you're the one stuck there: you can't see it." Tears spilled from Amanda's eyes and ran down her cheeks. She dug a handkerchief from the glove compartment and wiped her face.

"Tom loves you, Amanda," Claire said. "He's worried sick about you."

"You think I ought to tell him?"

"That's a decision only you can make. Do what feels right in your heart."

"You don't think I'm a bad person, do you?" Amanda asked.

Claire wanted to stop the car and take her daughter into her arms, but she kept on driving. "You, a bad person? Why, heavens no. You're a fine human being, whom I love very much."

"You're not ashamed of me?"

"Not at all, my darling girl. I only wish that

things had been different, that I could have been there for you during that terrible time."

Amanda's voice dropped to a whisper. "I'll tell Tom. Thanks for letting me talk about this." She smiled, and Claire's heart grew lighter. "Look, Mom, that's where we turn right. See the sign? 'Pensacola Ten Miles.'"

Claire turned and they started along a twisting two-lane road through pleasant countryside, past narrow bridges that led to houses on the other side of the river.

They soon arrived at a grassy hillside that sloped down to a wide river, so shallow that they could have waded across the ankle-deep water. On the opposite bank, clumps of tall trees barred from view the gently rising fields across the way. Claire carried the folding chairs down the hillside and opened them under a tree close by the river. Returning to the car, she slipped her arm through Amanda's, and they made their way carefully down the slope.

Amanda pointed to a large, dry boulder in midstream. "Look at that brown snake," she said. "It's almost completely camouflaged by the boulder. If it hadn't moved just now, I'd never have noticed it. It must be out for an afternoon sunning."

The snake, completely indifferent to their presence, had uncoiled its full length across the rock to bake in the warmth of the sunshine.

"It gives me the shivers," Claire said.

"It's a water moccasin, probably," Amanda said.

"Are they dangerous?"

"Very. Poisonous."

Smooth stones beneath the water formed unusual patterns: a roadway, a circle; others had been washed atop one another pyramid fashion. Where the river lay placid, trees spilled impressionistic reflections on its surface. Claire wished that she had brought along her new digital camera.

The quiet beauty of the place soothed them, and they chatted about Tom's new office in Weaverville and the job he'd recently bid on for an environmentally friendly apartment complex.

"What does that mean, 'environmentally friendly'?" Claire asked.

"Solar panels on the roof, better insulation, special shading on windows facing south—things like that."

"Those sound like worthwhile features," Claire said.

"They are, and Tom's in the forefront of this movement."

Amanda asked about her mother's time in Boca Raton, and Claire told her about her seventh-floor apartment, the bridge that rose to let one boat go through while many cars waited to cross, and the parks she had found so peaceful and refreshing.

Afterward, Amanda stood and walked the few steps to the bank. "Come see the bottom, Mama. The patterns of the rocks are beautiful."

Claire joined her at the water's edge. The earth there was soggy, less solid than it was higher up on the bank. For a long moment they stood side by side and neither spoke. As much for a sense of balance as for affection, Claire put her arm about her daughter's shoulders. To her great pleasure, she felt Amanda's arm slip around her waist.

"Are you all right, Mom?"

Claire nodded.

"Okay, then," Amanda said. "Let's go sit down."

The odor of damp soil and grass, crushed beneath their shoes, followed them back to the folding chairs. A cool breeze caressed their faces. On the surface of the water the reflections of trees rippled, then re-formed when the river quieted.

Amanda's arms dangled over the edge of the chair; her fingers played in the grass. "What a great day this is."

Confession is good for the troubled mind and heart. Heal my daughter, dear Lord. Be happy again, my child. Be free of fear.

"There's one more thing I want to say, Mama. Tom's reaction when I lost the baby was withdrawal. His own grieving process, I imagine. I didn't feel his sympathy. That was probably related to everything he'd heard over the years about his mother's losing a child, and her cancer and death. When I went into a tailspin, Tom must have figured he'd soon be losing his wife. And my depression sent me reeling, thinking that I was headed in my grandmother's direction and would end up in a mental hospital. A great combination we were—both of us scared and unable to tell one another why."

Claire said, "As we get older, we worry about our ancestors' illnesses and how they died. I expressed this to my internist recently, and he said something that comforted me."

Amanda crossed her arms and turned toward her mother. "What did he say?"

"He said not to make those comparisons. If our parents and grandparents had had the benefit of the medical advances that we have today, their lives and deaths could have been very different, and they'd have lived longer."

"That *is* a comforting thought."

"I used to worry that I, or you, or Paul might inherit my mother's manic depression, which is now called bipolar disorder. Every time I felt down for more than a day or two, I imagined it was the start of severe depression. It never was. The only treatment available to my mother, poor thing, was electric shock therapy, which must have been horrible. Today there are medications that keep a bipolar person even-keeled. Your depression seems normal after going through what you did. It just takes time to recover from any loss, especially such a loss."

Am I preaching too much? I don't want to preach, but Amanda seems to want some response from me.

"It does, doesn't it? It took me a year to recover after the first miscarriage. I remember sitting on the trolley going to and from work, staring at nothing. Sometimes I'd miss my stop and be late for work. Eventually they fired me. And I remember, after Dad died, how I wandered around in a daze for a long time. I cried at the slightest thing, especially movies with father-daughter relationships. But this is worse—much worse than anything I can remember."

"It's the ultimate grief, losing a child," Claire said. "After Terrance died, I thought I'd never wake up again without that stab of pain to my heart."

Amanda nodded. "If we could have talked, it would have helped, don't you think?"

"Yes, it would have helped a great deal. I'm sorry about so much in the past—but we only have the future." She patted her daughter's shoulder. "So, let's share that future, shall we?" Claire extended her hands to Amanda, who took them and held them for a moment. Then they rose, folded the chairs, and started back up the bank.

"I'd like that, Mom," Amanda said. "I like the idea of looking forward, not backward. I think I can handle things now. You've been a huge help to me—you knew all the right things to say."

Claire's heart swelled with happiness and pride.

Three days later, Amanda moved home with Tom. Larry, his mind freed from worry, purchased a new ancient truck and began to gut its engine. Millie sang again in the kitchen, and Olden and Claire, after promising to return soon, started back to Long Island.

At home, a letter awaited from a new buyer who wanted all the inventory and the contacts, and Claire agreed to the sale.

35

The Retreat

The bell rang, its peals rising over the thick stone walls of the cloistered garden, the rich vibrant sound sweeping across the open lawn. In years past, this bell had once called monks to prayer. Now it summoned her and the others to dinner.

Claire entered the walled garden and walked swiftly across paths bordered by neat fall flowers. Slipping open the heavy wooden door, she stepped into the silent, wood-paneled dining room. People looked up and smiled. Returning their smiles, she took a seat between two women whose very presence warmed and welcomed her.

The food, still strange to her palate, was at least interesting. The smell of fresh-baked bread seeped from the kitchen each time the swinging doors opened, and with the fresh butter and cheese made at St. Dunstan's, Claire never felt hungry. The water pitcher traveled the length of the table, and she smiled as she accepted it from the woman beside her. Claire felt calm and at peace.

She had brought a journal, and every day sat on a bench in the garden and expanded her lengthening reflections. She wrote about Phillip with appreciation and pity. Poor man, how he must have dreaded bedtime, with her relentless badgering about sex. Before they married, she had known that his sex drive was less than hers. Her experiences with men at college had made that clear.

Because other men had found her desirable and former lovers considered her excellent and innovative in bed, she'd believed that she could awaken Phillip's latent sexuality. To her deep frustration it had not happened that way, and over time her frustration increased, then anger at Phillip developed, and hurt that he failed to respond to her. These feelings seethed below the surface and found their outlet in work. It was the reason she disliked women who manifested affection for their men in public, who spoke in whispers with shy smiles, or proudly, about their sex lives, or who merely looked knowing when others spoke of sex. Claire took on the persona of a sexually satisfied wife who was too refined and private to indulge in such talk.

Over time, in therapy, she had come to understand the many ways in which she had punished Phillip: she'd pushed that gentle, noncompetitive man to compete in sailing and in business, pressured him to assume roles and make decisions he did not feel comfortable with. The boomerang effect was that as he gained confidence and grew in his roles as businessman and sailor, her confidence slipped away, and having no support system of her own, she had come to depend heavily on him. His early death stunned her. With no one to talk to and no real friends, she believed that replacing Phillip was her only recourse. Refusing to evaluate her life or make the necessary changes, she had fled to Florida and humiliation. She had been a stubborn, foolish woman!

But there had been glorious moments in Florida, too, and as Dr. Delanny had pointed out, there was no reason to deny or abnegate

the exotic and exciting evening she had
shared with Andrew, or the fact that Jason,
honest from day one, had affirmed her femi-
ninity and sexuality, and had reintroduced
her to the joys of sensuality.

One night, after she and Olden returned
from North Carolina, she'd walked on the
dunes alone. The sea grasses had shim-
mered in the moonlight. As she looked back,
she felt nothing she had done, no one she
had met in this last year, had been substan-
tial. Everything had slipped through her fingers except Olden—reliable, dependable
Olden, with whom she still shared a house,
with whom she would spend Thanksgiving
with Amanda and Paul, and Christmas with
Francine's family.

It had been Claire's idea to return to St. Dunstan's. Mary Delanny threw up her hands in
astonishment, but her eyes revealed how
pleased she was. "You're sure now?" she'd
asked. "It's going to be as silent as it was a
year ago."

"I know that, and yes, I want to do this.
I've been living with Olden for over six
months now. I'm enrolled in a watercolor

class, and I'm volunteering at the local theater and love it."

"You're planning to stay with Olden,
then?"

"That's one of the reasons I'm going back
to St. Dunstan's retreat center. I need to be
alone and think this through. You're going to
laugh when I tell you this, but I'm not sure I
want to marry again. Olden's not pressuring
me to. And surprisingly, sex with him is easy
and satisfying. It's funny, how long I resisted
that kind of contact with him, but then it happened so naturally. We were sitting on the
couch watching TV, and he put his arm
around my shoulder, and I moved closer, sort
of snuggled against him. The next thing I
knew, we were making love on the rug in
front of the fireplace. It was romantic and
spontaneous. It's not fireworks with Olden,
but it's pleasant and satisfying." She had giggled nervously.

"Fireworks are short-lived: remember that.
Pleasant and satisfying may be the best it
gets," Mary Delanny had replied.

Claire now stared down at the blank page.
There were two issues she had come here to

resolve. Her future work and Olden. Work was easier to contemplate. She was already comfortable financially, and with the business's buyer, an antiques dealer from upstate New York, ready to sign the papers, she would be set for life.

Letting a thing just happen, allowing it to unfold, was not something that Claire had been comfortable with before. She'd had to plan everything step by step, moment by moment, and maintain control of situations. She was learning to let go. It was enough that she enjoyed her art and the theater, and she could continue those here. If she and Olden moved to North Carolina, as Amanda suggested in every phone conversation, she could do those same things there.

Claire wrote Olden's name across the top of her page. It was his grandfather's name, an old Norse name. She drew a line down the center of the page and listed the positives on one side. He was kind, gentle, loving, considerate, thoughtful, trustworthy, reliable, and he made no demands on her. Best of all, he accepted her as she was. Claire added "good in bed," and "he wants me more than I want him." What a relief that was, after the years of begging Phillip. It was an impressive list.

On the negative side she wrote that Olden was balding and that he disliked going out at night, preferring to stay at home and watch a movie or read.

Claire bit the end of her pencil. Tears filled her eyes. *I admire him. I respect him. But do I love him? Would I be settling? Is that so terrible? I could do much worse. But that wouldn't be fair to him.*

And so it went, back and forth, and the silent days passed.

Claire returned home without having reached a decision about Olden. She paid special attention to her reaction when he opened the front door, delighted to see her, and took her bags. She was glad to see him, hugged him, and did not feel the need to break from his hug until he was ready to release her. It was good to be home. It was good to see him.

What was love, anyway? Was what she had always called love actually lust and physical attraction? Or was love gentler, milder, the result of adjusting to differences, commitment, and acceptance, of coming to a safe and comfortable place with the other? With Olden, it was as if she had skipped over the lusty days and had been comfortably married to him for twenty years.

Claire's final session with Mary Delanny was a tearful one. "You've helped me so much." She wiped her eyes with a tissue. "You helped me grow up. I was stuck in the past, and ignorant of what life was really all about."

"You helped yourself, Claire. You did the hard work, but I thank you for your kind words."

"I'll thank you forever—especially as I know there were times in the beginning when you were ready to stop seeing me as a client."

Mary smiled. "It's been a hard road, but you've come a long way, Claire Bennett."

"Amanda's pregnant again. I'm worried it's too soon, but she tells me her doctor gave the okay and is watching her closely. Olden and I are going to 'test the waters' in Asheville. We'll go down for Thanksgiving when Paul comes, and I want to be there when the baby's born next spring. Olden says then he'll decide if that's where he'd like to retire."

"Sometimes we come to our destiny by a long, hard route," Dr. Delanny said. She rose from her chair. "I'm going to miss you, Claire. I wish you well."

"Could we ... Could we perhaps have lunch together when I come back, after the baby is born? Since we're no longer client/therapist?"

"I'd like that. Give me a call, Claire." They shook hands warmly.

And with a light heart and a light step, Claire walked out into the sunshine.

Discussion Questions

1. When Claire is widowed, she is frantic to find a man. Without a man, she feels like half a person. Yet when Olden makes his feelings known, she rejects him. She wants more glamour and excitement than he offers.
   a. Are her goals realistic?
   b. Would you have chosen the path she did, flying off to someplace new, plunging into affairs?
   c. What would you have done?

2. Paul's secret tortured him for most of his life and alienated him from his family. It

drove most of his life decisions. Should he have told his parents about his guilt at his brother's death? Would you have?

3. Did you like Claire? If not, did you grow to like her or empathize with her? When did your feelings about her change?

4. Identify and discuss the point at which she begins to change.

5. How did you react to the final chapter?

Turn the page for a sneak preview of

JOAN MEDLICOTT'S

next book,
coming in 2008
from
Pocket Books

Across the road, the lights in Max's down-stairs rooms switched off. *Strange,* Amelia thought. She went inside, placed her teacup in the kitchen sink, then climbed the stairs to their bedrooms and knocked on Hannah's bedroom door. "You awake, Hannah?"

"Come in, Amelia."

Hannah sat on the edge of her bed, one foot shoved into her bedroom slipper, the other wiggling under the bed in search of the other slipper. Amelia bent and retrieved it for her.

"Ever notice how shoes, especially slip-pers, are never where you put them when you go to bed? I think they walk about while we sleep," Hannah said.

"Slippers can't walk." Amelia realized, then, that Hannah was being facetious. "There's a strange man and a very pregnant woman at Max's. I was on the porch when a taxi deposited them at his front steps. The man opened the front door and walked right in."

Hannah hastened to the window, which overlooked Cove Road. "I don't see anything or anyone, and there's no light in Max's bedroom."

"They've shut off the downstairs lights, so they must have gone upstairs."

Hannah fumbled with the buttons on her pajama top. "I'll go right over."

"I'll go with you," Amelia said.

At the front door, Amelia handed Hannah a mug of black coffee without sugar and they started across Cove Road. Hannah's key opened the front door, and she flipped on the foyer light. There sat three large suitcases.

Max's heavy footsteps sounded on the stairs. Seeing Hannah, he smiled. "I was just about to phone you. Guess who's here?"

"Who?"

"My son, Zachary, and his wife, Sarina,

have come home from India, and she's about to have a baby."

Hannah stepped back, uncertain that she had heard him correctly, but there he stood, beaming and happy. "Zachary, here? But, I thought . . . ?"

"I know. He said he hated Covington and would never come back, but you know how unpredictable life is." Max shrugged. Taking Hannah's arm, he urged her toward the kitchen. Amelia followed, and when they reached the kitchen, Max sank into a chair and ran his fingers through his uncombed hair. "Sometimes things don't work out as planned. They've been through hell, from what they've been telling me."

"What's happened to them?" Hannah slid into the chair across from Max. Amelia leaned against the wall and waited for his reply.

"You know that her people are Hindus. Well, it seems there was an issue about a mosque being built on what was considered a Hindu holy site, which triggered hostilities on both sides. The mayor, a Hindu, was ambushed and killed, which led to the looting and burning of a prominent Muslim business-man's home. After that, it degenerated into a free for all.

"Sarina's brother-in-law, the accountant, was shot in the leg on the way to his office. They think it was a random shooting, but it's crazy over there, Zachary says, and everyone suddenly has a gun. Sarina's entire family and all their servants have fled to their home in the south. Just as well, for after they left, one of their stores was torched. Sarina's baby is due next month, and they felt they'd be safer here until the turmoil gets straightened out. If it ever does."

"It sounds like Kashmir, reenacted on a smaller scale in India," Hannah said, and Max nodded.

"How frightening to live in a world like that," Amelia said. "People shooting other people, burning property."

"After 9/11 and the twin towers going down, I wonder if we're any safer, or if safety is just an illusion." Hannah looked up at Amelia.

"I think of India as a peaceful country, and Hindus as tolerant of all religions," Amelia said.

"This Muslim/Hindu hatred has taken root in many parts of India," Max said. "No one knows where it will lead. Zachary did the right thing. Sarina will have the baby here." Satisfaction showed in his eyes.

Hannah knew that Zachary had been hard-headed and adamant in expressing his dislike of Covington. He had rejected both his father and his father's business, and had hurt Max deeply. Max had buried the hurt but despaired of ever seeing any future grandchildren. Had Max told Zachary that she and Max were married? And if he had, what had been his son's reaction? Hannah did not trust or like Zachary, and she was certain that if his reaction had been positive, it was not sincere. An uneasy feeling settled over her. Their pleasant lives were about to be cast into confusion.

Hannah looked at Max. "Have you told Zachary that we're married?"

Max shook his head. "There's been no time. Sarina was exhausted, as you might imagine with traveling this late in her pregnancy. She collapsed when we got her upstairs. The fright and the stress of it all, leaving her family and home, the trip; it was too much for her. We got her into bed, and Zachary took her up some chicken soup that Anna left in the fridge. If she relaxes and falls asleep, he'll be down, I imagine."

Max reached across the table and laid his large hands over Hannah's. "You're trembling.

Now, don't you worry, sweetheart. We'll tell him about us as soon as he comes down. How can their being here affect us? We'll go on with our lives as we have been."

"Do you really think so?" Hannah asked.

"I'm sure of it. Zachary's never liked cows, the dairy business, or Covington. They'll stay until the baby comes, then in a few months they'll move on to a city."

"Don't be too sure of that. Things change." There was a knot in Hannah's stomach and her head was beginning to hurt.

Through her open windows, Grace heard the slam of a car door. She had been up most of the night worrying about her health. This particular bout of insomnia started weeks ago when her internist had advised her to see a kidney specialist.

"Your blood work indicates there may be a slight problem with your kidneys. Nothing serious, but we need to check it out," he had said in a voice that Grace considered much too casual for the information it imparted.

The nephrologist had been young, pleasant, and patient. He had taken a thorough history and drawn a sketch of kidneys and arteries on a notepad. He explained that high blood pressure, compounded by diabetes, could, over time, adversely affect one's kidneys. "I'm going to have my nurse set you up for a sonogram to see if there's a blockage in the arteries that go to your kidneys."

Grace's mind snapped shut. Blockages sounded ominous. "And if there's a blockage?"

"If there's a restriction of blood flow to your kidneys, we'll go in and clean out the arteries. It's a routine procedure these days," he replied and smiled, but his smile had not reassured her. Grace remembered Bob's heart attack several years earlier and his angioplasty, a surgical procedure to clean the plaque from an artery to his heart. The prospect of a probe snaking through her arteries terrified her, although Bob had made light of it, saying that he felt absolutely nothing. When the young doctor suggested a possible "procedure" to clean out her arteries, Grace felt weak and had had to clutch the cold metal arms of her chair for support. The nurse had walked her from the office to her car.

Later, when she told him, Bob said, "Now don't you go worrying yourself silly while you wait to have that sonogram."

"How can I not worry? I'm scared out of my mind."

The more she learned about diabetes, how serious and dangerous it was, how it could affect one's eyes, feet, everything in her body, the more upset she became. These days, even after seeing the nurse dietician at the hospital, she hardly knew what to eat or how to cook, and found it increasingly hard to get a grip on a whole new way of thinking about food. And exercise! The doctor said that was very important. She walked some, but the length of Cove Road was hardly what he meant, and when she had signed on at a gym, all those tight-bodied young women leading other tight-bodied young women in aerobics classes made her want to never return, and she had not.

"It's going to be all right." Bob ran his hand across her arm in a gesture he intended to be soothing but that had annoyed Grace.

The sonogram had been painless, so when her doctor said that the test revealed no arterial blockages, Grace relaxed—until she heard his next words.

"But what we found is that your kidneys are functioning at forty-four percent of capacity."

The doctor had perched on the edge of the examination table. A chart of kidneys, bright with veins and arteries, hung like a photograph on the pale gray wall behind him. The seriousness of his words bounced off of Grace's consciousness. Had Bob not accompanied her to his office, she would have denied the truth, as she was wont to do.

"Why are my kidneys functioning at only forty-four percent?" she had asked.

"We all lose kidney function as we age. If you were twenty-seven years old, I'd be concerned, but since you're seventy-two, I'm not worried, so long as we keep that function at forty-four percent. Your new blood pressure medication will help protect your kidneys."

But at night, lying in bed, Grace wondered what else was silently deteriorating deep within her body. She prayed, and tried unsuccessfully to meditate and visualize herself whole and perfect, and wondered if her efforts were too little too late.

Then Amelia's and Hannah's hurried footsteps went down the hall, and the closing of the front door roused her from self-pity and from her bed. Grace grabbed a robe and hastened downstairs, hoping to catch them, but too late. Through their kitchen window, she watched her friends enter Max's house. For a moment she considered following them.

But she needed breakfast and her medication. If she waited too long to eat, her blood sugar dropped, resulting in a weak, slightly nauseous feeling. Gone were the days of well-sugared morning tea and coffeecake. Instead she piled a thin wheat cracker with two slices of Swiss cheese and poured a small glass of skim milk. She carried the snack into the downstairs guest bedroom, settled into the glider rocker, and flipped the television on to the house and garden channel. Whenever she was alone and the room not occupied by a guest, she breakfasted in this lovely room with its large windows and view of the shady hillside behind the house. Somehow, it helped compensate for the less than satisfying change in her diet.

The room faced north, which was good, for glare bothered her eyes. It always had, as far back as she could remember, as far back as her thirteenth birthday, after which she started to wear glasses. Grace had recently visited an ophthalmologist, who checked her yearly for retinopathy, another possible side effect of diabetes. To her great relief, he had assured her that her eyes were fine. There was no change in her prescription, but he had suggested darker lenses, which she had gotten.

Whatever's keeping Amelia over there? she wondered. *And why is Amelia intruding on Hannah and Max's Saturday?* Then Grace's attention went to *Design on a Dime,* a makeover show that never ceased to amaze her—what could be done with so little money—and she didn't hear Amelia until her friend entered the room.

"Grace. Didn't you hear me call you?"

"No. I didn't. Look at that room." Grace pointed at the television. "They're showing the before and after pictures. Marvelous what they've done, don't you think?"

"I have really big news for you. Guess who's come home?"

Grace clicked off the set. "Who?"

Amelia's eyebrows arched. "Zachary and his very, very pregnant wife, Sarina, that's who. They arrived about an hour ago. I was sitting out on the porch having a cup of tea, enjoying this glorious spring morning. They came by taxi with lots of luggage. But until we went over there, I hadn't a clue who they were."

"Didn't Zachary declare Covington anathema?"

"Sure he did, until the Muslims and Hindus over in India started shooting at each other and burning homes."

Grace's hands covered her mouth and her gasp, then fell to her lap. "That happened where they were living?"

Amelia nodded. Her face was flushed, and she literally quivered with excitement. Rarely did she have the opportunity to be "in the know" and to break exciting news to her housemates. She told Zachary's story to a wide-eyed Grace.

"I can hardly believe this."

"Every word of it's true," Amelia said, thinking that if Hannah had imparted this information, Grace would have believed *her* right off the bat.

"How will this affect Hannah and Max, do you think?"

Amelia shrugged. "*Mon ami,* you know men. They really aren't aware of the undercurrents of people's feelings beneath their noses. He says nothing is going to change." She leaned forward. "Hannah thinks that it's all going to change, and I'm sure she's right."

"It can't change the fact that they're married."

"But it can affect their lifestyle, can't it?" Amelia said.

Grace nodded. It was hard to imagine Zachary here and his wife about to have a baby. "He never sent a cable, didn't let his father know they were coming?"

"When did he ever let his father know anything about his life, except after the fact?"

"It's all been going so well for Hannah. I wonder what's going to happen." Grace's words were more comment than question.

Amelia raised an eyebrow. "Your guess is as good as mine. Well, I have to run. Mike and I are taking Miriam and Sadie to the Toe River over near Celo. Mike has a job there, and Miriam's bringing a picnic lunch for us."

The house was suddenly too quiet, and Grace, needing to keep busy, trudged up the stairs to her room and began rearranging her closet. She removed turtleneck shirts, sweat pants, and sweaters, then folded and stored them in the drawers from which she had removed her summer shirts and skirts. She considered getting out the ironing board, but decided instead to hang the summer clothes in the closet, hoping that the wrinkles would smooth themselves.

After that, she decided to read for a while.

When Hannah finally got home, she found Grace asleep on the living room couch, *The Long Summer* open across her stomach. Hannah leaned over, picked up and closed the book, and patted Grace gently on the shoulder.

"Grace, wake up. I need to talk to you."

Startled, Grace opened her eyes. Being awakened precipitously always caused her heart to thump in her chest. "What time is it?"

"Almost noon."

"I was reading while I waited for you. I must have dozed off. What's happening at Max's?"

Hannah sank into a nearby chair. "It's been a heck of a morning."

"Amelia said Zachary and his wife are back."

"They certainly are, and Max is so delighted at the prospect of having a grandchild born here, he can't think straight. He says nothing will change for us, but he's wrong. For starters, I'm home and it's a Saturday."

"How long are they going to stay? What does Zachary say?"

"It's not clear. Nothing's clear. When we told him that we're married Zachary looked as if he'd been kicked in the stomach, but he got a grip on himself, shook his dad's hand, kissed me on the cheek, and asked if he should call me Mom. I put that to rest fast. I told him to call me Hannah."

"Sarina, if I remember, is sort of formal. She'll find it hard to call you by your first name."

"She was wiped out and asleep upstairs, so I never saw her. Max asked Zachary what he plans to do, but Zachary hasn't a clue. He appears to be in shock from the whole experience. I assume Amelia told you what happened in India?"

Grace nodded.

"I suggested that this wasn't the time to talk about long range plans." Hannah paused and looked out of the wide, low window.

Grace drew her legs up under her. "You're almost as stunned as Zachary, aren't you, Hannah?"

"You've got that right. Things were going so smoothly for Max and me, so easy and happy. I wonder if it was just a reprieve in life, allowing us to rest and prepare for this next difficult challenge."

"Maybe so." *Hannah's not given to introspection,* Grace thought. Zachary's return has really put a crimp in her life. "Surely they're not going to stay here? Why would Zachary suddenly want to stay in Covington when he hates the dairy business?"

"I sometimes think that Max has held on to the dairy in the hope that Zachary would have a change of heart and return. Why would a man of seventy-seven continue to operate a dairy, with all the problems with milking machines, the health of cows, delivery trucks, and on and on? Without Jose, he couldn't do it."

"After the baby comes, Zachary will probably leave with his wife and child," Grace replied.

"I'd hate to see Max get his hopes up again and get hurt."

"It's out of your hands, don't you think?"

Hannah's knee bounced up and down, up and down. Grace rarely saw her this agitated. "I just don't know what to do."

"Let Zachary and his wife settle down, get over the exhaustion they must feel, and gather their wits about them. Then, see what happens," Grace said.

"Can't do much else, can I?"

Grace leaned over and placed a hand on

Hannah's knee. "You can be gentle with Max and give him time. He loves you very much. It'll all work out, Hannah, you'll see."

"I wonder."

"Nothing's going to change with you and Max. Not the way you two love each other."

"Thanks, Grace. I needed to hear that. I hoped you'd be home and we could talk."